I'm Still Here

J.D. Ashdown

The Conrad Press

I'm Still Here
Published by The Conrad Press in the United Kingdom
2025
Tel: +44(0)1227 472 874
www.theconradpress.com
info@theconradpress.com
ISBN 978-1-917673-06-8
Copyright ©J.D. Ashdown 2025
All rights reserved.
Typesetting and Cover Design by: Levellers
The Conrad Press logo was designed by Maria Priestley.
Printed and bound in Great Britain by Clays Ltd, Elcograf
S.p.A.

Chapter 1

No soul had ever entered the Tavern realm twice before. Diego was the first and he felt privileged to have been selected. He smiled subtly at the infinite whiteness as if he was immersed inside a giant cloud. Specks of blazing amber twinkling around him everywhere like stars. Their faint energies beating like baby heartbeats in his ears. How he managed to get here again he didn't know, because unlike the other realms, the Tavern had no entry points. It was a place designed only for the souls who were travelling from Earth to the afterlife. A journey of which he had done himself over five hundred years ago. What he did know however, was that he had a job to do.

He strolled across the realm on its fizzing split-rail fences. A magical pathway which appeared beneath every angel's feet when roaming through the skies of Earth and the realms beyond it. The fences rippled with the colourful energy of whichever realm they found themselves in and here they shone like glistening pumpkins, matching the Tavern's strange amber specks.

It didn't take long for the realm to sense Diego's presence and soon the little lights surrounding him began to cluster together to create the illusion he was walking down a narrowing corridor. The white began to disappear and realising he was reaching his destination, he readjusted his black suit and tightened his sunny yellow tie. A twinkling amber doorway quickly revealed itself at the bottom of the light tunnel and he didn't hesitate to step through.

Immediately, he felt a welcoming warmth as if he'd stepped out of the cold and in front of a crackling log fire. The room itself appeared more like a small stage set. Its walls and contents completely aglow in the bold amber energy and as he approached the bar ahead, he spotted the word *'Tavern'* etched in the counter. 'Finally, I'm here,' Diego said, taking a seat on the single barstool available.

He tapped his thumbs together as he waiting to be served and he soon caught his reflection in the twinkling mirror background in front of him. He sat up straight to show off his height and admired his smart appearance, stroking his smooth bald head and clean-shaven face. Despite his actual age, he didn't look a day over forty. This was because every soul who enters the Tavern can choose which age they want to permanently remain as before moving on. A lot of them decide to stay as they were when they passed, but some liked to look youthful again or even how they would have looked liked if they'd lived longer. For Diego, this was how he looked when he was at his peak. When he was living his best mortal life during a time of great fortune. Even with a few shrivelling wrinkles around his mouth from the scorching sun, he knew this was his best look. Although, as his hand fell onto his neck he creased his nose up at the sight of an ugly scar and quickly pulled his collar up to hide it. 'Where are they?' he grumbled, slapping his hand on the counter and right on queue, a small plump lady appeared through the background. She was wearing a bright orange tuxedo and had a wide smile on her tanned face.

'Hello,' she said. Her curly ginger afro bouncing as she nodded at the drink in her hand. 'For you.'

'I don't think so,' Diego replied, unfazed at her sudden appearance. 'This is my second time here. I believe I was summoned for something?'

'Summoned?' The lady tilted her head.

'Yes. I don't know who by, I only heard a voice and then a fence appeared. I believe I am here to get someone?'

'Ah, yes. It is about time,' the lady said, rattling an amber beaded bracelet on her left wrist. 'I'll move you on. There's something odd about this one. I can't read them like I can the others. They haven't made their decision yet and they really should have left by now.'

'I understand. I'm sure I will sort it.'

'Hmm, I'll leave this here. Just in case.' The lady tapped on the glass containing his drink. 'Good luck,' she said before disappearing back through the background.

The Tavern fell quiet once again and Diego welcomed it. Especially now with the enticing scent of the raw-fruity beverage near him. All the racket and disorder back in the G.A.F was becoming more intolerable by the day and this felt like a well-needed break. He closed his eyes and inhaled the soothing warm air, pretending he was soaking in the sun on an isolated island beach. The waves washing his feet. He pictured himself pulling the cork out of a bottle of rum as he heard the sound of a sudden pop and imagined gulping down the coarse grog. It was a moment of true bliss, right up until he heard a horrible dry cough next to him.

He snapped his head to stare at the culprit, frowning in disgust at the round man who was now hunched over the bar beside him. He was wearing a suit too, but it wasn't one like his. It wasn't one of the G.A.F's. His creased white shirt was untucked from his navy trousers and he had no tie or jacket. It was this dead beat appearance which made Diego certain he was the one he'd been sent for and he wanted to get work quickly. So, he swivelled on the stool, crossed his legs and straightened his jacket before going to introduce himself, but before he could say anything the man began sniffing and coughing endlessly. Each noise made Diego's body shudder. To the point where he had to close his eyes and clench his fists to stop himself from lashing out as he thought the man was doing it on purpose. Eventually, the noises stopped and Diego went to try again, only to be interrupted this time by the sound of the man slurping his pint of ale and that was the last straw. Diego slammed his palm on the counter with a mighty thump, making the man jump.

'Where did you come from?' The man frowned.

Diego ignored him however, and just stared into his tired face. He could tell he'd been here a long time just by looking at him, let alone the strength of the citrus ale flowing off his breath. 'Now you're being quiet and I have your attention,' he said, pulling his cuffs down. 'My name is Diego and I have been sent here to force you into a decision.'

'A decision?'

'Yes. You have been in here for too long, so what is it to be? The G.A.F?' He pointed to a lonely twinkling yellow fence to the far right of the bar. 'Or Yutopia?' This time pointing at a purple one to his left. Both of them glowing brightly within the amber glow. 'So? Which is it to be?'

The man didn't respond and turned back to his drink.

'Don't ignore me!' Diego raised his voice. 'You need to go!'

'Why?'

'Because... you must. It is the rule.'

'Rule? I have no idea what you're talking about. I have no idea about anything. Just, let me drink in peace, yeah.' The man cuddled his drink, taking another slurp.

Diego pinched the top of his nose and sighed. 'You must choose a fence and leave. You can't stay here for eternity.' He raised his eyebrows with anticipation as the man's mouth began to move, but rather than answering him, a loud belch echoed off his lips.

'Right,' Diego said annoyed. 'In that case I'll choose for you based on your life, so, tell me about yourself, what's your name?'

'Stephen?'

'Stephen...' Diego probed, but he was met by silence once again. 'You do have a last name?'

Stephen shrugged, staring dumbstruck at his drink. 'I can only just remember my first name.'

'Fine.' Diego rubbed his jaw. 'You don't have to tell me, but I will warn you it wont effect the outcome.'

'I'm not being difficult. I actually don't know.'

'Ridiculous. How can you not know your own name?'

'I don't know... I just don't.' Stephen drank some more.

Diego tapped his fingers on the counter and shook his head. 'You're not making this easy! Come on, give me something, anything.'

'Like what?'

'Do you know when you were born?'

'Nope.'

'Where you were born?'

'Nope.'

'Why you were born?'

'What?'

Diego sniggered. 'Come on. There must be something you can tell me?'

'I...' Stephen sighed. 'Nope. You're going to have to help me out.'

'Me? Help you with what?'

'Well, I obviously have no idea what's going on here so I'm assuming you do? I mean, look at you. Dressed as smart as that you must be some sort of authority figure or something.'

I wish, Diego thought as he reached for his own drink. It was a little common for newcomers to suffer with denial, but never this bad. How does he not know his own

7

name? Stephen looked like he was in his late forties yet he acted senile. 'You genuinely don't know anything?' Diego asked again.

'Nope, not a clue.'

Both of them took a drink at the same time. Stephen gulping down his ale as if he hadn't had a drink in years, whereas Diego only had a slight taster.

'Stephen... Do you know where you are right now?' Diego asked, putting his glass down.

'A bar?'

'Yes, obviously, but do you know which bar?'

'Nope. A weird one? The lighting is a bit funky and honestly, I don't even remember walking in. I just... stumbled here.'

'Stumbled here,' Diego puffed, scratching his forehead. *Surely he knows?* But the longer he watched Stephen's behaviour the less certain he was. 'Stephen... you realise you are dead?'

Stephen stopped mid-drink to stare at him. 'What?'

'You are dead, Stephen. That is why you are here, in the Tavern realm, and now you must choose whether to go to Yutopia, your own personal Heaven, or come with me to the G.A.F. The choice is yours, but you must make it now.'

'I... I'm dead? What? How?' Stephen scowled, his head jittering from side to side. 'No, this can't be right. What happened to me?'

Diego grew more agitated with the questions as he believed Stephen was putting on an act. 'Seriously? Are you messing with me?'

'Messing with you?' Stephen spat, hitting his glass down onto the bar. 'You appear out of nowhere, tell me I'm dead and you think I'm messing with you?'

Diego found Stephen's aggressive behaviour intriguing. In the hundreds of years he'd been doing his job, he'd never witnessed this from a newcomer before.

8

Even those who suffered from dementia still knew they had passed, but it was as if Stephen had no memory whatsoever. 'What is the last thing you remember, Stephen?' Diego asked, sipping more of his drink.

'Darkness. Just darkness,' Stephen replied, running his thumbs over the rim of his glass. 'Before this place anyway.'

'Darkness? Most people see light before they get here.'

'There was no light,' Stephen's voice went croaky. 'It was nighttime out there. No moon. No stars. Sparks maybe, but I just assumed it was lightning or something from behind the clouds.' Stephen took another long slow slurp.

As interesting as his story sounded, Diego didn't care. Everyone had a sob story and he had grown tired of hearing them. Right now he just wanted to fulfil his task so that he could get back to his normal duties.

'Why is it,' Stephen began to ask. 'No matter how much I drink, the glass always stays full? I must be drunk. Asleep. You're not really here.' Stephen finally turned to face Diego with raised eyebrows.

'Don't be stupid! You can't get drunk in the Tavern. It's just a placebo effect on your weak mind.'

'Then, how do you explain the never-ending ale?'

'It is your final drink!' Diego snapped. 'It's to help consolidate you on your transition after death. If you had half a brain you'd understand that. It will disappear when you do.'

Stephen turned back to stare into his frothy amber ale. 'I don't want to disappear. I am quite happy here.'

'You can't stay here!' Diego growled through gritted teeth. 'You need to go. I need to go.'

'Go where?'

'To the G.A.F!' Diego exasperated, wiping his face. 'The Guardian Angel Force.'

'Guardian Angel? Ha! Yeah, good one!'

Diego scrunched his face up and snatched the glass out of Stephen's hand before he could take another sip and threw it out into the void beyond the Tavern's glow. 'Your last drink has lasted long enough. Do you think I am joking? Look around! Does this look Earthly to you? You are dead and this is your reality now.'

Diego straightened his jacket as he calmed down and rolled his eyes when he thought Stephen was about to cry. Despite the original pride of being chosen for this, he was now beginning to wish someone else had been sent. Why was he chosen anyway? He didn't have time to think on it however, as Stephen quickly spoke again, 'fine, maybe I am in denial or whatever, but I've been sat here for...'

'Far too long,' Diego stated, sipping more of his drink.

'Whatever, and I have no idea who I am or what happened to me. I was hoping, if I kept drinking, something would come back to me. It has to.'

Diego looked up to the opaque apricot air above. Perhaps he was being too harsh on Stephen. He was clearly lost, but his mind was obviously weak and it infuriated him. It was bad enough having to deal with the weak minds in the G.A.F, mortals and angels alike. He could sense this was going to be hard work, but nevertheless, he knew what the right thing to do was. He took another mouthful of his homely cachaça before sliding off the stool and slapped his hand on Stephen's shoulder. 'Come with me,' he ordered. 'I have made my decision.'

'What?'

'If you do not know who you are, then, your Yutopia will be useless because you wont have any ideas or memories to recreate there. You will come with me to the G.A.F. Perhaps the experience will help you.'

Stephen leaned back as if examining him. 'You want to help me?'

'I want to do my job and get you out of here. So, if that means helping you, then so be it. The information you have given me is sparse, if not useless, however, I believe we can find something. Just like on Earth, we all have a path and I will help you find yours.'

'Alright. Deal.' Stephen held out a chubby hand as if expecting him to shake it, but Diego didn't even humour him. Instead he quickly turned away and straightened his tie as he headed over to the luminous yellow fence. Its energy humming like a mild machine. 'If you are coming with me some rules need to be set,' he called over his shoulder.

'Like what?' Stephen replied now following him.

'Do exactly as I say! Do not dawdle, argue or venture off. I will not have you wasting my time or getting the attention of the Idlers, understand?'

'Umm, sure. Yes.' Stephen nodded fast, scratching his thin brown hair.

'Good, now, on you get.'

'What is it?' Stephen asked, cautiously creeping closer to the fence.

'What does it look like?' Diego scowled.

'But why is it glowing?' Stephen reached out a hesitant hand.

'It is the entrance to the G.A.F,' Diego said, stopping in front of it. 'It is a gateway. Wherever there is a boundary, there is a fence. You go over the fence, you go over the boundary.'

'But there's nothing behind it.'

'You are not going to see it until you go over!'

Stephen took a step backwards. 'I-I don't know. This is a bit surreal to me.'

'I don't care. Stop being foolish. I was sent to get you out of the Tavern and that is what I will do. Now come on!'

'What? Why do I have to go first?'

11

'Because I said so!'

Stephen shook his head. 'No, sorry, this doesn't feel right. Can't I stay?'

'No.'

'Why not? I'm not doing any harm here.'

'It is the rules,' Diego said, trying to control his temper. He could see the uncertainty in Stephen's eyes, but he didn't care, it shouldn't have taken this long. Besides, he knew full well that if Stephen didn't go over then an Idler would likely send him somewhere he really wouldn't want to go.

He waited for Stephen to move, but he just seemed to stand there like a dim-witted child. 'Come on!'

'Okay!' Stephen shouted back rubbing his right arm. 'Calm down.'

Diego watched as Stephen trudged over to the fence and heaved himself up on to the top rail. He made it look so awkward as he kept getting his legs tangled up while trying to balance his weight and not fall off, but eventually he sat down facing Diego. His chubby cheeks flustered from the workout.

'What now?'

Diego remained silent as he knew what was about to happen. The fence's energy suddenly illuminated brighter and completely engulfed Stephen like an awakening star.

'What's going on?' Stephen squealed uncomfortable.

'Be quiet. It'll be over in a second,' Diego replied.

The light quickly returned to normal and Stephen re-appeared, pale with fright.

'Nice to see you finally look the part.' Diego smirked, walking up to him and putting a hand on the rail. 'It's the suit of the G.A.F. Anyone who joins gets one.'

'Oh, cool...' Stephen investigated his new look. 'So, what now?'

'Now... we go over.'

Before Stephen could ask another question, Diego shoved his free hand into Stephen's chest and chuckled as he watched him disappear into the void behind. The sight made him reflect on his first experience with the realms fences. Still not believing he was even given the choice to walk along them in the first place, but grateful nonetheless. He remembered its warm holy energy fill up his otherwise empty body. How it sparked a new lease of life inside of him, making him want to be good, to do good. That's how he used to always feel when walking on the G.A.Fs fences. All warm and fuzzy inside, but over the last few decades it hasn't felt the same. It was as if he'd grown numb to the magic.

After a few more seconds, Diego gripped the rail tightly and effortlessly jumped over. Still feeling a little inkling of energy wash over him as he did, like stepping into a pocket of sunlight. He crossed the Tavern's boundary and landed on a bright lemon carpet. A carpet so soft it was like walking on cotton wool; fragranced in an appropriate citrus punch which hit him like an energy shot when inhaled. He gazed around at the familiar oak bookcases which spread out as far as the eye could see in a never-ending grid formation. All of them towering up higher than redwoods into the pale cream sky. Fences flashed into view everywhere, at all different heights, as other guardian angels came back and forth to fetch the relevant books and files they needed for their tasks. It truly was a remarkable sight, but he then rolled his eyes as he saw Stephen laying on the floor next to him like a seasick sailor. 'Get up,' he ordered, not wanting to help him. *Honestly, what is with this fool.*

Eventually Stephen found his feet. 'Wh- What is this place?' he slurred, still swaying slightly.

'This is the library. The hub of the Guardian Angel Force. This, is the G.A.F.'

Chapter 2

The bus rocked David's body from side to side. A cold draft tickling his cheek from a crack in the window where he rested his head to watch the gloomy English countryside fly past him. Field after field appearing like a washed-out watercolour despite the bright midday sun hanging in the sky and it was the same atmosphere on the bus. There was a gloomy blue vibe lingering over everyone's heads and he was sensing a lot of it was coming from the driver. Every now and again he'd peer towards the rearview mirror and see her looking deflated in her seat and, although her eyes were fixated on the road, she was clearly lost inside her own thoughts and driving on autopilot. It was a theme he'd grown used to now, sensing this sort of sadness. For a long time he had convinced himself it was a gift. To identify the signs and attempt to make a difference, but ever since it came at his expense he's found it more of a chore and now he only does it out of a misguided feeling of morale obligation.

After a few more minutes the bus entered the town centre and came to a squeaking halt. Its doors swooshed open and the queue of passengers started to shuffle down. David meanwhile, waited patiently for the end of the line before heaving his tired body off the old burgundy seats, doing his best not to inhale the cloud of dust which followed. Everyone ahead of him moved in silence. One by one exiting the bus before they started talking as if it was an unwritten rule. None of them paying any attention to the driver who was still staring vacantly through the windscreen. The strange blue aura becoming more visible the closer he got and as he reached the front he tapped on the coin tray to get her attention. 'Thank you,' he said.

The driver broke out of her trance and stared back at him as if she'd never heard the words before. 'You're welcome...'

'I hope your day gets better.'

'Thank you,' the driver replied, her face brightening up a little. 'I'm sure everything will be alright.'

'I'm sure it will too,' David concluded tapping on the coin tray again before stepping off the bus.

The doors slid shut behind him and he watched the driver wave at him as she pulled away. He waved back briefly to acknowledge her just as a sharp stabbing pain dug away at his ankle. 'Where did you come from?' He frowned curiously at the small dog attached to his trouser leg, growling playfully. He got down on his haunches and stroked the dog's solid body of short white fur. Its tiny teeth now nibbling away at his hand and making him laugh.

'Patch!' a frantic voice called out. 'Patch!'

He looked down the pavement to see the owner running over to them. A broken lead in his hand. 'I'm guessing that must be you,' David laughed, noticing the patch of brown fur around the dog's right eye.

'S-sorry!' the man panted, finally catching up. 'His collar just broke and I-I haven't got much control over him yet.'

'It's okay, no harm done,' David said, continuing to make a fuss of the puppy.

'I don't know how I'm going to get him home at this rate,' the man added. 'He's too energetic to carry. He keeps squirming around and trying to jump out. I don't even know how this thing broke. Piece of cheap tat.'

David could see the genuine worry on the man's face. His cheeks flustered with embarrassment. 'How far away are you?' he asked.

'Only ten or fifteen minutes that way.' The man pointed North through the town.

'Is that an extendable lead?'

'Uh, yeah. Yes.' The man held it out, 'but without a collar...'

'May I?'

'Umm, sure.'

The man passed David the grey lead and he slowly pulled the smooth material out of the holder and hooked it around the puppy's neck before clipping it back on itself to make a noose.

'Will that not hurt him?' the man asked.

'I mean, its not ideal,' David answered, getting to his feet. 'But, it'll do the trick until you get home.'

'Yes, I suppose. Okay, thank you. I wouldn't have thought of that. Thank you.'

'No worries. Have a good day...'

The pair of them went their separate ways and David crossed the road, zipping his coat up closer to his chin as the cold wind crashed against him. He jumped onto the pavement and headed towards the café on the far corner, hearing the joyful shouts of some kids playing football on the large square island of grass to his left. The limited sunlight shining on the happy group of teenagers, who were deliriously chasing the ball around in the wind without a care. At first the sight made him chuckle, but all of a sudden the ball looped up into the air and bounced into the shadowy road towards him. A young kid still chasing after it.

Alert to the situation, David held out a stern hand and yelled, like a concerned teacher, but they ignored him.

'There's nothing coming!' the kid shouted back retrieving the ball.

'How do you know? You never looked! You need to be more careful.'

'Get lost.'

The kid picked up the ball and ran back to his friends. A brief flash of red hovering over the kid's head as he blinked angrily at them. *Silly kid,* David thought as he continued towards the café. The bell jangling above the berry red door as he stepped inside. The sweet smell of pastries quickly filling his nostrils and making his stomach grumble. He closed the door behind him and rubbed his hands together, looking around at everyone clasping their hot drinks in front of them while nattering away over wooden tables. He clomped over to the counter and squinted at the large chalkboard above with the menu on although, the café was too dark to read it. It was as if the sun was now only emitting bright shades of grey through the windows, but a few seconds later things got a lot brighter, triggering the sensation of butterflies in his stomach as he saw Laura's beaming smile from behind the counter.

'Hello again, David,' she said as cheerful as always.

'Good morning,' David replied, looking into her happy hazel eyes.

'Morning?' Laura giggled, looking at the clock behind her. 'Bit late for that isn't it?'

'So it is.' He ruffled his thick black hair.

'It's okay. You must struggle to tell the difference with the amount of hours you do. When did you last have a day off?'

'It was... no, umm... you know I can't remember,' he chuckled.

'Thought as much. How are you anyway? Other than tired?'

'Ah, you know me. I'm al-'

'Always alright,' Laura tutted, tucking some stray hairs behind her little ears. 'The usual, yeah?'

'Yes please,' he yawned, leaning on the counter as she got to work. 'How about you, Laura? How are you today?' he asked as she operated the coffee machine. Her brunette ponytail bouncing in a green scrunchy as she moved around.

'I'm good, thank you,' she called over the sound of the grinding coffee beans. 'Just another day.'

'And the acting? How's that going?'

'Umm, yeah its going okay I suppose. I've got another audition this Saturday.'

'Oh, that's cool! What's it for?'

'Some show up in the city. I don't think I'm going to go to it, though.'

'What? Why not?'

'I'm just getting tired of all the rejections, you know,' she said sadly. 'I'm not sure I can take another one. It makes me think maybe I'm not cut out for it.'

David frowned at Laura's unusual negativity. She's told him numerous stories about different auditions she's been to, but she never got down about them. They always seemed to drive her to do better. 'What makes you say you're not cut out for it?' he asked.

Laura finished stirring the blend and pushed a cup of coffee towards him with a sigh. 'It's just, I know so many who have been successful through special contacts or luck, but then, someone like me is always having to work extra hard and jump through these extra hoops. Just because I'm not the tallest gal or the best looking... etc. I've discovered it's more of a 'if your face fits' kind of thing rather than a talent thing and mine never seems to fit so, I don't know,' she sighed again, brushing her hands on her apron. 'Sometimes it just feels like something bigger is challenging me, you know?'

'Hmm.' David nodded slowly while raising his eyebrows. 'Maybe there is... who knows?' He shrugged, making her laugh. 'What I would say is, think how great it would feel when you do finally get there. You must be doing quite well to keep getting offered the auditions?'

'I suppose,' Laura replied. 'They are more of an open invitation, though.'

'I see, well, even so, hard work always pays off and I doubt many work harder than you. I've even seen you rehearse back there in the storage room.'

'Wait, what?' Laura's eyes widened. 'You haven't!'

David smiled as he watched her cheeks reddening.

'Well, that's embarrassing.'

'No it's not... look, you enjoy acting, right?'

'Yeah, I love it!'

'Then, why would you quit? Stick at it. You'll get there one day. Maybe this one will be the break through you deserve and you'll never know unless you try.'

'I suppose. We'll have to wait and see.'

David reached into his back pocket to get his wallet and pulled out his card to tap the card reader.

'So, what about you?'

'What about me?' David asked, putting his card away. 'I can't act if that's what you're asking,' he joked as he collected his coffee from the counter.

'No.' Laura rolled her eyes. 'Is there anything new with you?'

'No. Nothing really,' David said, looking out to the shady world outside. 'Same old same old.'

'And your mum?'

A cold shiver slid across David's shoulders. 'She's good.' He smiled weakly back at Laura. 'We're good. Look, umm, I'd better head off to work.'

'Oh, okay.' Laura backed away from the counter. He could tell he'd made her feel awkward and he knew she was only being caring, but it wasn't a topic he wanted to discuss.

'Sorry Laura, I'll catch you later. Good luck with your next audition. I want to know how it goes.'

'Of course. I'll see you soon.'

'Will do, bye.' He hastily left the café. The wind whistling past his ears the moment he stepped outside. He rubbed his eyes harshly as he walked down the street, taking a sip of coffee to test its heat. He could still hear the kids yelling on the other side of the road, getting in the way of others passing by as they kicked the football about. One of them nearly knocking an old man over. *Something will happen at some point if they aren't careful,* he thought.

He took another sip of coffee when all of a sudden, his arm fell numb. It was as if his circulation had been completely shut off and a sharp tingling sensation stung his fingertips. Time slowed down. His coffee fell out of his hand as he watched the football roll out into the road. The same bus he'd caught into town earlier was hurtling towards it on its reverse route. A slow piercing bark shot through his ears along with screeching tyres. A petrified kid standing less than a metre away from the bus's navy blue bonnet. The coffee hit the pavement and splashed up David's trouser leg as if a signal for time to return to normal and all the sounds suddenly hit him at once. He could hear Patch barking madly on the pavement adjacent to him with his owner holding him back. The female bus driver tending to the frightened kid in the road while all his friends and other strangers watched in shock, but thankfully, no one was hurt.

David slumped down on the nearby bench to catch his breath. 'That could have been so much worse,' he mumbled, rubbing his forehead. He began to shake his trouser leg to dry it off when he heard a voice.

'You're right, it could have been worse.'

David looked up to see a boy sitting beside him. He was wearing a pair of denim jeans and a navy shirt with a white diamond tie which oddly matched eyes. Although the boy looked to be a similar age to him, he had the presence of someone much older.

'Sorry, I didn't see you there,' David said.

'That's okay, most people don't.'

'Oh, right.' David frowned, getting a strange vibe.

'It's strange isn't it,' the boy continued, flattening his blonde hair.

'What is?'

'Well, just think... what would have happened if that dog wasn't under control? Or If that driver wasn't paying attention? This could have ended up much worse.'

David stared at the scene in front of him slightly baffled. 'Yes... it could have.'

'Weird how these things play out isn't it. How something so silly and insignificant, like a 'thank you', can actually have a big influence on things.'

'What are you saying?' David asked, but the boy was already disappearing down the alley behind him, leaving him alone with the thought. *It is strange.*

Chapter 3

David was now nearing the end of his shift and the strange boy's words were still playing on his mind. It was nice to think his words and actions earlier had benefitted everyone and to make that kind of universal impact was truly something. It made him wonder how many other situations he might have unknowingly helped. After all, he did try to make a difference.

Right now he was restocking the wine section of a supermarket, putting the daily delivery onto the shelves and breaking down the empty boxes. He went to grab the next box to put out when he heard some bottles clang together from the other side of the fixture behind him. *Strange, I'm sure I was the only one round here,* he thought. The noise didn't come back however, and so he carried on as normal, hearing the belts of laughter roar across the store as the night team entered the building. A sign that his shift was now over and his next one was starting. He rubbed his eyes harshly at the thought of working in the pub after this. It was only for a couple of hours, but it all helped to make ends meet. He wasn't even technically employed there, but he liked to help out and listen to the drunks tell him their stories. Both the deliriously happy and the depressed. It made him feel useful when giving out advice and besides, he was paid cash in hand for his efforts. He'd stay there longer if he could, but he needed to catch the last bus home or he'd end up coming back to the store for the night shift and he didn't want to do that again.

David tore open the dusty box and placed a bottle on the shelf when he heard a loud smash. *What's going on?* He left the box where it was and walked round the corner to investigate. As he went round, he immediately saw shards of broken glass swimming in what smelt like a sweet brandy. 'Great, guess I'll have to tidy this up.' He went to pick up a piece of glass when he suddenly spotted someone sitting in the mess. The sight making him jump back to his feet. They were dressed in all black, looking like a shadow beneath the dim reddish store lights. Deep down, he knew he should go and get his manager, but there was something bothering him. A fiery crackling vibrated in his ears as if it was radiating off their body. His hands twitched by his sides while he stared at the dark figure and watched them take a swig from a bottle in their hand.

'Ar-Are you alright?' David finally asked. 'Are you hurt?'

The person's head slowly turned towards him, but their face remained hidden. 'Never better,' a female voice slurred.

'Is there anything I can help you with?'

The woman chuckled. 'You, want to help me?'

'Well, if I can...'

'Yeah, right,' they scoffed. 'Shouldn't you be asking me to leave or something?'

'Perhaps...' David slowly approached them. Doing his best to avoid the spillage. 'But I'm a better listener than I am a security guard.'

The woman chuckled again more sincerely and David could finally see her tired rugged face. Dirty blonde hair covered up her left eye which had mascara smearing down her cheek. 'I appreciate the gesture, but I'm a bit too far gone. Leave it.'

'Why are you too far gone?'

'Let's just say a bad day led to a bad week, which led to a bad month and... well, it just goes on and on... for eternity.'

'So you've had few dark days...'

'Dark days? Yeah. There's been no light in my world for a long time.'

'Well, you won't find any light down there either,' David continued to speak innocently, pointing at the bottle.

'Think that's the point isn't it?' the woman laughed, taking a few more gulps. 'I'm bored of looking for the light. The positives. The good. It's never there. It's just a load of false hope. Everyone can go do one for all I care.'

David began to get more unsettled the longer the woman spoke. She had a sense of unpredictability he didn't quite trust, but at the same time, he could see she was hurting. 'Do you want to talk about it?'

'Talk about it? Talk about what?'

'Whatever it is that has caused you to sit here and drink like this.'

The woman fell quiet and went to drink some more, but stopped. She lowered the bottle and stared at David. 'You really want to know?'

David shrugged. 'Wouldn't have asked if I didn't.'

'Alright. I'll tell ya. I-'

'Oi!' the manager's voice boomed across the store as he stomped into view. 'What are you doing? We're closed. Get out.'

'It's okay.' David tried to defend the woman, but his manager showed no interest.

'It's not okay! I don't want a drunk in my store. Look at the mess she's caused! C'mon get out!' David could only watch as his manager dragged the woman to her feet. 'Come on, out!'

'Alright! Alright! I'm gone.' The woman held out her arms, leaving the bottle on the floor. 'Thanks anyway, mate.' She saluted David. 'Appreciate the effort.'

David watched her stumble down the aisle and once she'd exited the building he turned to confront his manager. 'Why did you do that? She wasn't dangerous, she needed help.'

'Well, I helped her find the exit!'

A horrible heat rose up in David's arms like a boiling kettle, causing his skin to itch.

'Anyway, isn't it time you went home, David?' his manager spoke again. 'You've already been here longer than you should have, again.'

'Well I...'

'No, you know what, I'm sending you home. Better yet, take a week off. Take two. You have the hours available and we both know you need the rest. You haven't been yourself.'

'I'm fine.'

'No you're not. Go home and have a break. Sort yourself out. Come back to work when you're ready.'

His manager quickly scurried off before he could argue his case. *A rest, hey. That's the last thing I need.* But he knew there was nothing else he could do about it tonight. There was no point arguing and so he went to gather his things and left the store. The cold air immediately struck him like an arctic blast as he entered the car park, causing goosebumps to awaken on his arms and make his hairs go static against the sleeves of his coat. The swaying lampposts creaked eerily in the wind. Their dim lights barely bright enough to light up the moths flapping around them. The moon however, unlike the daytime sun, was bright enough to light up the whole world, beaming down like a giant white beacon in the cloudless sky. A faint blue glow around it, like an iris, which filtered out onto the speckled black canvas.

He slowly made his way to the pub, but soon changed his mind and headed back to the bus stop instead with his hands firmly planted in his pockets. He replayed the incident in his head and kept an eye out for the woman incase she was still around, but she seemed to be long gone now. His body shuddered as he passed the bench from earlier and he couldn't help but picture what had happened here again too, but this time, it wasn't a pleasant thought.

Why does it only seem to be me? he thought. *Anyone could have checked in on the bus driver. Anyone could have helped the man and his dog and anyone could have spoken to those kids, possibly even have done a better job than I did. Yet I rarely see anyone else helping these days. They are all too fixated in their own little worlds that they don't think to look outside of them. Just like my manager. Would it have been so wrong to have helped that woman? All she wanted to do was talk, but instead she was chucked out into the night and God knows where she is now.*

The more he thought about it, the angrier he got. He pushed his fists down as if he was trying to punch a hole in his coat pocket. His arms straining from the tension as he thought about all the neglect that exists in the world. The amount of sadness. He saw it everyday, everywhere and it drove him insane. His rampant thoughts began to overpower his mind and he knew he needed an outlet. Something to take his mind off it all and so once he checked no one was around, he took out his right hand and struck the wooden bus shelter. A strong pulsation immediately throbbed in his hand and he slowly cradled it against his chest, breathing through his nose to endure the pain better. He slumped down onto the seat and closed his eyes, opening and closing his fist to make sure he hadn't done too much damage. 'Stupid thing to do, stupid... but at least it worked.'

After a minute or so, the pain in his hand had calmed down and he took a quick glance at his watch. 'It's only an hour or so... I can do it,' he sighed. He picked himself back up and headed to the pub after all.

26

Chapter 4

As Diego leant on a bookcase, he watched Stephen walk around the library cluelessly. They'd been trying to locate his file ever since they arrived and so far they were having very little luck. Stephen's mind was so scrambled that even the library's resources weren't helping him and Diego didn't understand why. Part of him wondered if Stephen was faking it, but there was something about him. Something off with his very nature.

The sound of laughter blurted out from his left and he snapped his head across to see a group of angels standing around talking. 'They are not here to socialise, they are here to do a job!' His blood boiled. 'This place really has gone down hill.' He scowled around at the masses of angels who were just plodding along or having a friendly chat to their colleagues. It was as if they had forgotten that they were actually here to work.

What happened to this place. Why do we allow all these weak minds to even have the choice of coming here? It's obvious they're not cut out for the role. No wonder the system is so broken. One day they'll get caught out and I hope I'll be around to see it. 'Speaking of weak minds,' he said to himself, turning his attention back to Stephen, tapping his foot on the ground. Stephen was still roaming about like a lost tourist and then, to Diego's disgust, he suddenly started waving his arm about stupidly as if he was trying to swat a fly. 'Any luck?' Diego barked. 'You look ridiculous!'

'Thanks!' Stephen shouted back, slapping his hand against his thigh in annoyance. 'And no! I don't understand what I'm doing.'

'What don't you understand? You are trying to locate your life file not buried treasure.' Diego rubbed his forehead. 'You should have an impulse in your energy to help you locate the file, like a heartbeat. Once you have your file it should bring your memories back.'

'That's the only reason why I've persevered with this, but its been ages! Surely I should have something by now?'

'Yes, you should,' Diego sighed, turning away. 'Come on, try again.'

'Do I have to? I mean, of course I want my memories back, but this is just embarrassing. Is there not anything else I could be learning? Like, what do I do here as a guardian angel? Or a G.A as you put it? What's my job?'

'Nothing at the moment.'

'Why nothing?'

'Because the purpose of a G.A is to help those still on Earth with their fate,' Diego spoke fast. 'You are currently a G.A who doesn't know what his own fate was, therefore you cannot help anyone else with theirs.'

'Okay... So how would you help them? A G.A who was ready?'

'Influence.'

'Influence?'

'Yes, if the person's mind allows us to.'

'If the person's mind... What? You aren't being very clear.'

Diego rubbed his eyes harshly and pushed off the bookcase with a loud sigh. 'Okay,' he began, walking over to Stephen. 'So, the important thing to know is that fate is not a rule or a bind. Everyone has the free will to do what they please, including controlling their own fate. They set their own path, what they want, and it is our job to help guide them there to achieve it through influence. However, if their mind is too strong, stubborn, or weak, stupid, then they will ignore our influences and have to fend for themselves. Thus living a harder life and will more likely succumb to failure, struggles or become a criminal.'

'Wow.' Stephen double-blinked. 'That's...'

'The job of a G.A. And it could be yours, eventually, possibly... unlikely.'

'So, what if...'

Diego quickly held out a firm hand to cover Stephen's face. His attention drawn to a G.A walking past the aisle. His face hotted up at the very sight of her and he quickly followed. *What is she up to now?*

After turning a few corners, the G.A approached a bookcase and used her fence to teleport up and grab a file from the fiftieth shelf before coming back down. As expected the file had a grey cover, not yellow, meaning it was inactive.

'Uh-Hmm,' Diego cleared his throat, strolling towards her. 'Hello, Grace, what have you got there?'

'A file,' Grace replied brashly, trying to walk away.

'I see it's not yellow. You're not trying to help another lost soul are you?'

'You know damn right I am Diego. Someone has to. Now if you would excuse me...'

Diego lashed out to grab her arm. 'I don't know how you've been getting away with this for so long, but let me warn you. The Idlers have become more active recently, so watch out.'

'Is that a helpful warning or a threat?'

'Can't it be both?' He sniggered.

Grace pried her arm free from his grip and he watched her disappear over a yellow fence without another word. The content in her eyes saying it all. He savoured the confrontation until Stephen suddenly bumbled back into view. 'What was all that about?' he asked.

'Nothing. Just another troublesome G.A who should have been clipped a long time a go.'

'You don't get along with many people do you?'

'Why do you say that?' Diego glared at him.

'Well, since we've arrived here you've done nothing but moan about other angels like a grumpy old man and out of the hundreds we've come across, not one has even said so much as a 'hello' to you. What is it you have against them?'

'It is not them per-say,' Diego replied sternly, wanting to make his attitude clear. 'There are rules here and I believe those rules should be followed.'

'Why?'

'Remember where you are!' Diego stepped closer to Stephen. 'This is not a school. This is not a game. This is not a land. It is fate and nature we are dealing with, breaking rules and cutting corners here can have severe consequences.' Diego barged past Stephen to walk away, but Stephen was quick to call out.

'Even if it's for the greater good?'

'There is no such thing,' Diego shouted turning back. *When will everyone understand.* 'Every angel here wants to do the good thing. Not the right thing!' He slowly lunged towards Stephen with every emphasising sentence. 'We are supposed to be impartial watchers who can help influence when necessary, but somehow the G.A.F has become a mass of do-gooders wanting to give everyone everything. They try to save lives that shouldn't be saved. Give fortune to those undeserving. Help those who are helpless. There must be a balance.' Diego hit a fist into his palm. His body shaking from the aggressive tension. 'For someone to gain, someone has to lose. Why would we want that responsibility? We should leave that for fate and stay within our means. Stick to the rules.'

'What's the point in having rules if there is no one here to enforce them?'

The library's light suddenly dimmed where they stood as if a shadow had been cast upon them from the cream-coloured sky. 'Oh, there is.' Diego sneered, knowing what was coming. He bolted upright and straightened his suit

30

when a crimson fence burst into life ahead of him as if it had been conjured by lightning.

'Diego, what's happening?' Stephen asked, but Diego ignored him. Too distracted by the wonderful energy he was witnessing. If only he had that power he'd be able to turn the G.A.F into what it should be. Do the job these Idlers were clearly failing at. Suddenly, someone leapt over the sizzling fence. A ghostly crimson aura buzzing around her dark thin body, with a black ponytail wafting behind her and Diego got straight to business. 'You just missed her? She's taken a lost soul's file from...'

'Diego,' the lady said creepily, folding her arms. 'State your business.'

'Me? I was tasked with getting this useless soul out of the Tavern,' he replied, pointing at Stephen. 'It's Grace you should be after.'

'This soul cannot be here. It doesn't belong.'

Diego took a deep breath. 'What do you mean?'

'Its print isn't one the G.A.F recognises.' She strode forwards, pulling out a crimson blade from nowhere and pointed it at Stephen.

'Woah, he hasn't broken any rules!' Diego argued. 'If you are going to clip anyone it should be Grace! Or every other angel here for that matter because they don't belong here either!' Diego's heart raced. He didn't realise just how riled up he'd gotten until that outburst. He held his breath as the Idler rested her blade on his tie. Its energy crackling like fire.

'Very well, Diego. But when they do break a rule, you go too!' She quickly retreated her blade and jumped back over the crimson fence before Diego could reply and the light slowly returned to the library.

'What was that?' Stephen blurted out.

'That was an Idler,' Diego replied, brushing the creases out of his suit.

'An Idler?'

'Yes,' Diego's voice drifted as he lifted his tie up to inspect the new shade of red it had become, before returning to its original yellow. *Strange.*

'What... what were they going to do?'

'They were going to banish you to Idle.'

'Idle?'

'It is where all the other idiots and sinners are sent to. The only way of escaping is through the gates of Hagitol. That's if you ever reach it of course, before your mind crumbles from your soulless body.' Diego smiled as if enjoying the sight of Stephen struggling there. 'Clipping troublesome G.As to Idle is what the Idlers should be doing, but for one reason or another they are not fulfilling their purpose like they used to. It's like they are otherwise occupied... and yet they came for you?' Diego turned back to face the flustered Stephen.

'Okay.' Stephen gulped. 'I get it now. Don't break the rules.'

'Glad you finally understand.'

A yellow fence now appeared ahead of them and Diego gestured to Stephen with a wave of the arm to go over it.

'What's that for?'

'I'm tired of this place. You clearly haven't got the strength to find your file so you can join me on my duties. I will determine if you are up to the task of being a G.A and if not, I will send you to Yutopia regardless of your blank mind because I can't risk an Idler coming back and clipping me too. I won't allow it.'

'I see. Very well.' Stephen wandered over to the fence. 'Yutopia sounds better than Idle.'

Diego watched him closely as he approached the rails and then Stephen said something he found interesting. 'You know, as scary as that Idler was, I would still say you are scarier.'

Diego simply smiled out the corner of his mouth and as Stephen disappeared over the fence, he stroked his tie from top to bottom.

Chapter 5

The night was quiet. The light bleating of sheep in a nearby field was the only thing David could hear as he walked down the lane towards his house, cradling his aching hand in his pocket. Thankfully, his shift at the pub flew by and now he just wanted to go to sleep. He took a deep breath as he approached his driveway. Only one thought in his head now as he began to count his footsteps on the scrunching stones... *ten, eleven, twelve.* He stopped. A chill blew across his shoulders as he turned to the vacant area on the right. Half hoping to see a small black car with a red towel on its dashboard and scuff marks by the rear wheel arch where they always had trouble parking, but as expected, it was still gone.

Without dwelling on it too much, he headed over to the front door. He struggled to get the keys in the keyhole with his left hand, but eventually the door swung open and he was instantly greeted by a fast wagging tail.

'Hello, Bud,' he said, crouching down to make a fuss. 'Have you been a good boy?' He ruffled his collie's soft fur of black, white and tan. 'Where's Mum?' Right on queue a light snoring came from the living room. 'I see.' He smiled.

He got up to close the door behind him and picked up the letters from the door mat. Doing his best to ignore the bold red words written on the envelopes as he hung his keys up and slipped out of his black shoes. With the letters still in hand he entered the living room. The sweet cinnamon fragrance from a candle on the coffee table wafting up his nose and there, on the sofa, he saw his mum fast asleep in the light of the tv. Her tired face scrunched up as if she was judging her dreams.

'Seems about right,' David whispered walking over to her. He reached for the fluffy purple blanket on top of the sofa and carefully pulled it over her. 'You're okay, Mum,' he whispered. 'We're okay.'

He fetched the tv remote from the table and turned everything off, blowing the candle out before exiting the room. He left the door slightly ajar in case Buddy wanted to go back in and as he went to turn the hallway light off his hand hovered over the switch. Something caught his eye beneath the coat rail. A dusty brown briefcase. *So weird he didn't take it with him. Probably just something else he didn't want anymore.*

He sighed heavily as he switched the light off and gently rustled Bud's head, who was now curled up in his bed. 'Goodnight, Bud,' he said.

When he got upstairs, he immediately entered his room and slapped the letters down onto his desk along with the others and sat down on a little wooden chair. The soothing smell of vanilla now tickling his nose from the air freshener on the shelf above. He tapped the keyboard in front of him to wake up his laptop and set the alarm on his phone for five am while he waited. Once the bright white screen came on however, he tossed his phone onto the bed. Now concentrating on the spreadsheet and the red digits that stood out to him.

He rubbed his tired eyes and rustled his hair before beginning to go through the letters. One by one he ripped open the envelopes and entered the new digits on the screen. He was no accountant, but he knew how to handle money. Even if it did take four part-time jobs between his mum and him to make ends meet.

He punched the last few numbers in and even though the reading didn't look great, he knew significant progress was being made. It had taken seven years to get to this point and he was comfortable knowing that they were staying afloat. He nodded in satisfaction before closing the spreadsheet down and was instantly caught in a trance, forgetting that his desktop picture was still of him and

35

Jess, his ex-girlfriend. He found himself lost in her hazel eyes as if she was literally there in front of him. Her soft arms around his neck. The sight caused him to glance down at the drawer by his left knee and every inkling inside of him was saying 'don't do it' but he couldn't help himself. He pulled open the drawer and plucked out a blue letter which had been previously tucked inside an old birthday card. He admired it fondly before carefully unfolding it and making sure he didn't tear the worn out creases. His eyes skimmed across the pages, knowing the words written off by heart, but it still felt good to read the actual thing. To hold the evidence in his hand.

'Dear David.
How can I possibly begin to describe my love for you. You have stood by me through the messiest culminations of my life. Been through things with me that I wouldn't even wish upon the worst fictional villain. You've held me when I've cried. Lifted me up when I've been low and laughed with me when I've been high. You've brought colour back to my monochromatic world and although I will never be able to repay you, I will try to with kisses everyday lol. Happy 22nd Birthday! I look forward to celebrating many more with you. My Guardian Angel.
Lots of love, forever, Your Jess xxx'

Having lost himself in the letter, David's body suddenly jolted as he heard a knock on the doorframe. His mum then entered half-asleep in his dad's dressing gown.

'Jesus! Mum, you made me jump,' he said, dropping the letter back into the drawer and closing it. 'You okay?'

'I'm fine,' she answered softly. 'Are you?'

'Yeah, I'm okay. I've just been updating our finances.'

'I see,' his mum yawned. 'How was your day?'

'Yeah, umm, it was okay. A bit tough.'

'Tough? In what way? Do you want to talk about it?'

'No, your tired and its nothing important.' David smiled weakly.

'Are you sure?'

'Yeah, I'm sure.'

His mum sighed.

'That was a big sigh,' he teased.

'Hmm.'

David frowned at his despondent mum. 'What is it? Something the matter?'

'No, I suppose not.' His mum looked around the room. 'I just worry about you, that's all.'

'Yes Mum, I know.' He rolled his eyes. 'You keep telling me that and I keep telling you not to.'

'Well, that would be easier to do if you weren't so secretive all the time. I never know what's going on with you anymore. We live in the same house and yet this is the first time I've seen you in days.'

'Unfortunately that's what happens when you work the hours we do,' David joked, subtly closing the lid of his laptop.

'It's not right, David. You are only twenty five! You should be out having a life of your own. Not working yourself to the bone for my sake. You can't be okay with this?'

'I'm always okay.' He shrugged.

'David. I am your mother. I know that isn't true.'

David rubbed his shoulder as he stared at the wall. Not wanting to meet his mum's gaze. 'Does it even matter?'

'Of course it matters!' His mum stepped further into his room. 'You put your heart and soul into everything and everyone around you, but you forget about yourself. I don't even know what goes on in that head of yours most of the time.' His mum pointed at him as she took a seat on his bed. 'You never speak. About anything. You've never said a word about Jess and I know that must have hurt you. You've never even spoken about your dad and that was years ago! You just keep it all locked away.'

'So?' *That's the best place for it.*

'It's not healthy, David. You need to let it out once in a while. Do something outside of this rut your in.'

David scratched the back of his head agitatedly. What did she expect him to do? Just up and disappear and leave her to fend for herself? No way was he going to do that to her. He needs to help. Has to help.

'You need to talk about these things, David,' his mum continued. 'You will feel better for it.'

'Will I?' Why was she so adamant on him talking? What would it solve? Would talking about his Dad make him come home? Was talking about Jess going to make her come back? No, it wont. So there's no point. 'Look, I appreciate you caring Mum, but there's no need. Honestly, I'm fine.'

'You're not fine.' Another small sigh escaped from his mum's mouth. 'I don't understand you. You used to talk to your dad.'

'Dad's gone!' David shouted, the word triggering him to shoot to his feet. 'He walked out that door and didn't come back. Who knows why, but maybe he got tired of listening to me? Maybe he grew tired of you. Of us.'

'You don't know he left us like that,' his mum teared up.

'Of course we do. He never came home that night because he thought he found something better. Same as Jess did to me. End of. Part of me wishes he has died, though, at least we could cash in on his life insurance rather than have to be put through all of this!' David swiped the letters onto the floor.

'You don't mean that,' his mum said calmly.

Didn't he? His mind was so rampant at the moment he didn't know what he was feeling. His ribs were vibrating with every thumping heartbeat, but seeing the tears in his mum's eyes wasn't a sight he wanted to see and he quickly sat down on the bed to comfort her. Doing his best to calm down. 'Sorry,' he whispered. 'You're right. I didn't mean it. Any of it.'

'Your father is gone David, yes. We can't change that, but you are still here. You are my priority.' She squeezed his hand tightly. 'No one should have to deal with things alone and despite your beliefs, neither should you. You need to let someone in every now and again otherwise your mind will consume you and you'll never escape the dark place you've found yourself in.'

The tension in David's body slowly began to ease. Why was he being so difficult? It wasn't her fault. He knew she was only trying to help, but for some reason he couldn't accept it. Not from her. It was like he has this mental block when it came to her. As if there was something telling him not to burden her with his problems.

'And for the record,' his mum continued. 'I'm not gone either. I'm still here. I'm always here and I want to listen.'

'I know, Mum. I know.'

'If you don't want to talk about things, then fine, but please find another way to deal with your frustrations and look after yourself.' She pointed at his bruised hand, making him retreat it away from her. 'Otherwise, those demons in your head, they will get the better of you and you'll inevitably do something reckless. You're like your dad in that way.' She smiled weakly. 'It's great you want to look out for everyone, help them or do whatever it is you do. These days it's a rare attribute to have and I know your dad would be proud, but you can't be everyone's guardian. You must learn to look after yourself too.'

David continued to sit in silence and just absorb her words. He understood everything she was saying, but they had no effect on him for he didn't believe them. It was as though he'd accepted this was what his life was about.

Being there when needed. Especially for his mum, but then she said something he wasn't expecting.

'Sometimes I think you want to be miserable. That you don't believe you can be happy or worse, you don't want to be.'

That hit home. His body fell heavy and flustered as if he'd been caught red-handed doing something wrong because a part of him did think that, but how can you tell your own mum that? How can you tell her you don't believe you matter? The answer is you can't. Those words would be more crushing to her than when his dad left and he couldn't do that to her.

'Everything happens for a reason,' his mum concluded. 'That's what your dad would say.'

'Yes, he would,' David said getting up.

'Where are you going?'

'I just, need a bit of air,' he replied flatly.

'Okay, but don't be too long, its very late and dark out.'

'Okay.'

He headed downstairs, grabbing his coat on the way to the kitchen and as he put on his walking boots he could hear Buddy's paws pitter-patter on the tiled floor. 'Hey Bud, you need to stay here and look after Mum. I won't be too long, just need a bit of time to sort myself out.'

Buddy barked and whimpered as he left the house and closed the door. There was only one place in his mind to go.

Chapter 6

It took approximately half an hour for David to get to the reservoir. Normally, he would go to the shoreline when he wanted time to think, but as it was located in the middle of a woodland he didn't think it would be a good idea to go there this time of night. Instead, he stayed beneath the moonlight and trekked up the neighbouring hill which overlooked it and perched himself on the fence looking down at the water. Even at night the view here was spectacular. The full moon shone down on the keyhole shaped reservoir to make the the water look like a pool of shimmering silver. Although, David wasn't in the right frame of mind to enjoy it tonight. He was too preoccupied with what was going on inside his head. So much so, he didn't notice the light rain begin to fall.

Why is this world so difficult? He sighed, tucking his hands under his armpits for warmth. *It never used to be this way. The more years that go by, the harder it seems to get. It's not just me either. So many people seem to struggle now. Even just trying to belong here is hard work. I know I can handle it, no one needs to waste their time or efforts on me, but it doesn't make it right, or fair.*

David looked up at the large moon as if he was communicating with it directly. *My life hasn't been easy, but neither has a lot of peoples. Some of whom I know first hand and helping them gave me a purpose, but now without them, without Jess. Without Dad. I just feel useless. Thank goodness for mum I suppose. Even if it is tough at least we have each other and I have a purpose. Someone to be there for.* He tightened his arms around his wet shivering body and ever so slightly leaned forward. *Although, I have always wondered if I were to...* He gazed down the cliff edge. The wind grooming his back as if inviting him over. *Is there a place where I can be of*

41

use? Help more? And if it doesn't exist, at least all this would be over.

He slowly edged closer and closer. His backside now sliding off the rail as if his body was being drawn forward and he didn't fight it. His brain going blank with all sense and logic. He now felt as if he was hovering over the edge in midair and something finally snapped. The fear of falling triggered a strong reflex and he quickly gripped the slimy fence rail, straining his biceps as he locked his arms in place.

'Idiot! Idiot! What am I doing!? Nothing is worth that,' he panted as he swung his legs back over the fence. 'Time to go home I think. Time to go.'

A wave of guilt washed over him as he pictured his mum home alone, knowing she would probably still be awake waiting for him. Perhaps it was time to open up to her about everything. Let her know how he's really been feeling. What harm can come from it? It was now obvious he needed some sort of help, but he was just so used to bottling it all up, he didn't know where to start. 'I've got to try.'

He was about to jump off the fence when a horrible snap sound split his stomach in two. The fence jolted backwards and the sudden motion caused David's hands to slip. He flung his arms out furiously to try and grab hold of something as he toppled over. His adrenaline pumping like an electrical surge through his cold body as he dug his nails into the soft soil, but he couldn't get a good enough grip to stop himself. Little clumps of dirt and rock followed him as he helplessly fell over the cliff edge and headed straight for the reservoir's rocky shore.

SMACK!

A gasp of air left David's lungs as his chest collided with something solid. His hands instinctively grabbing hold of whatever it was he landed on. His feet kicking wildly beneath him. At first he thought he'd crashed onto a branch, but once he got a foothold he realised whatever it was, it was bright yellow.

What? Maintaining his grip, he cautiously investigated further and it soon became clear he was on a glowing fence, hovering ten metres or so above the ground. Not only was it glowing, but there was something else. It was as if it was emitting some sort of energy.

'Umm. Hello?'

David gulped and slowly turned his head to see someone sitting on it, a girl. A beautiful yellow aura shining over her like the glow of the fence. She looked a little older than him and appeared quite small. Her straight blonde hair swung just below her shoulders. Although, it was neither that nor the fact she was wearing a black suit and yellow tie that caught his attention. Her eyes. Her spectacular eyes sparkled at him like holy treasure in sunlight and he couldn't turn away.

'Can I help you?' the girl quizzed.

David struggled to reply and continued to gawk at her.

'Did someone send you?' she asked sternly, raising her fists. 'Because...'

'N-no,' David finally spluttered, clearing his throat. 'No, I... fell.'

'Fell?' The girl smirked lowering her hands. 'What, off your fence?'

'Umm, yeah?' David frowned, peering up the cliff face.

The girl chuckled. 'You beginners really are funny sometimes.'

'Beginners?'

'Oh, come now.' The girl smiled. 'You can't tell me you've been in the G.A.F long? If you have, then, this is pretty embarrassing for you.'

'T-the what?'

'The G.A.F. Guardian Angel Force?' She raised her eyebrows. 'Who is your mentor?'

43

'My mentor? I-I don't have a mentor. I don't know what you're talking about. You're an angel?'

'Oh, my. You really are new.' A sad expression spread across her face. 'I'm sorry, but I can't help you.'

'Why not?'

'It's difficult to explain, but you are better off finding someone else.'

'Well, umm, are they likely to come by any time soon?'

'No... you'd better head back to the library.'

He continued to stare at her. His arms beginning to ache from holding on to the rail. 'I'm sorry, you're going to have to help me a little. The library?'

The girl sighed. 'Just get yourself back on the fence and then go over it with the library in mind and you'll get there.'

David double-blinked. 'O-Okay.' *Perhaps I should humour her.*

He puffed out his cheeks and slowly tried to lift his trembling leg onto the fence, doing his best not to look down. He managed to get one leg over and straddle the top rail, tensing his legs around it to try and keep his balance, but he could sense the girl watching him and it wasn't helping.

'Why are you acting so scared?' the girl asked.

'Well, I'm not overly sure what's happening here and that is still a very long way down.'

'So? It doesn't really matter if you fall does it.'

'Oh, I beg to differ.'

'You'll be fine. If you fall on the ground you'll only get brought back here. It's about as painful as a static shock. You can't die twice you know.'

David froze. A strange feeling filtered through him as if his soul was leaving his body.

'Oh, I've seen that face before,' the girl whispered. 'Are you okay?'

'I...' He bit his tongue.

He peered back up at the cliff and then at the fence he was clinging on to. He hadn't, had he? The sudden realisation of what happened hit him like bad news at a doctors office and the fear of falling was now irrelevant. He sprang up onto the fence to sit on it normally. His arms shaking as he squeezed his hands together, breathing deeply through his nose to try and cope with the surging emotions. *No, no, no. I can't have... I... I'm such an idiot.* 'I need to get back! I need to get back to my mum! I'm all she has.'

'You can't go back,' the girl said softly.

'But I must! I have to. I can't leave her. Not after...' he trailed off. 'There must be someone who can help? Something I can do? I'd do anything! I just...' David put his head in his hands. His raging mind soon began to calm however, as a strange warmth appeared on his lower back and spread through him like central heating. He exhaled through his mouth and as his body relaxed, he saw the girl had moved closer. An inquisitive look on her face as if she was examining him. 'What is it? Why are you looking at me like that?'

'You mean it, don't you?' she said. 'You really would do anything.'

'Well, yes. Yes I would.'

Rather than replying, the girl raised a hand and waved it around his face.

'What are you doing?'

'Your energy,' she finally said, lowering her hand. 'It's strong.'

'What does that mean? Can I go back?' he said excitedly.

'There may be a way,' the girl said, still examining him. 'But, I can't make any promises.'

'If it's a chance I'll take it!' David bolted upright.

'Thought you would. I've heard many people say those same words and that's all they has ever been. Words. But you seem different somehow... what is your name?'

'David.'

'Well, David. There's something about you I can't quite put my finger on, but I'm willing to find out what it is. If you help me with my tasks, then I will help you try and get back. You have my word.'

David frowned. A second ago she wasn't wanting to help, but now she was willing if he helped her first? 'Help you with what exactly?'

'My guardian duties.'

'Guardian?' His mind flicked back to what his mum had said to him earlier. 'I've got some experience with that,' he tried to joke.

'Yes, I'm sensing that.'

David frowned at her again, uncomfortable with the way she was assessing him.

'Come on. Let's get going.'

'Now?'

'Yes, well, the sooner the better right? I can't stay here much longer anyway,' the girl said looking around.

'Okay, I suppose, but where to exactly... Heaven?' he hesitated to say the word.

'No,' she giggled, a bright broad smile spreading across her face. 'The library. It's the hub of the G.A.F.'

David just stared at her blankly.

'Come on, you'll see when we get there. I'm Grace by the way.'

'Grace? That's a fitting name.'

'Hmm.' Grace's cheeks glowed. 'Okay, ready?' she asked, putting her hands on his shoulders and gripping them tightly.

'Ready for...?'

Before David could make another sound, Grace effortlessly cartwheeled across him, making him spin round a hundred and eighty degrees to face the cliff rather the woodland. 'What was that about...' His jaw hit the ground.

The cliff was gone. The moon was no longer hanging in the sky. Of a matter of fact, everything changed. The fence he was on had disappeared and he was now standing on a bright lemon carpet surrounded by bookcases. The distilled silence of the reservoir had also disappeared as he watched hundreds of, who he assumed were angels, rushing about and chatting to each other like important business people. All of them wearing the same suit as Grace. Their fences popping up everywhere as they came and went from this magical place.

'This... is the library,' Grace said disturbed.

'What is it?' David asked, watching her nervously scan the area.

'I can't be here. I shouldn't be here.'

Grace quickly swivelled round and buried her head in David's shoulder, making him gulp. Her hair lightly tickling his chin. He slowly moved his hands around her, unsure whether it was appropriate or not, but it felt like she needed the comfort. His eyes widened as he noticed the black jacket sleeves over his arms. 'Are... are you okay?'

'Sorry, we need to go.'

A fence quickly appeared beside them and he took one last glance at the place before he followed Grace and stepped over the rails. Again the environment completely transformed and now he was sitting high above the ground watching the sun set over a clear bay. Its brightness painting the sky in light strokes of yellow, orange and pink as it began its descent.

So many questions sat on the tip of his tongue now, but he somehow remained speechless. He patted his body in shock at the suit he was now wearing, fidgeting with the yellow tie dangling from his neck until he heard a flock of seagulls squawking overhead through the pastel clouds.

'Sorry about that.' He heard Grace say as she paced up and down next to him, biting her nails. 'I should have known better than to go there again so soon. I wasn't thinking straight.'

'It's okay,' David replied looking up at her. 'I'm more worried about you. You got so anxious. Why is it you can't be there?'

'It's difficult to explain, but don't worry. We can start from here. As you're new I'll teach you first and we can go from there.' Grace sat down beside him.

'Okay...' She was clearly holding something back, but she had an aura of innocence about her that enabled him put his doubts to one side. After all, she was an angel helping him, how could he not trust her?

'So, what n-' David suddenly dodged out the way of a rogue gull and grabbed hold of Grace's arm, who was now giggling at him.

'Sorry, I shouldn't laugh.' Grace tucked her hair behind her ear. 'We've all been there.'

'Could it not see me? I mean, I thought nature had a sixth sense for... this sort of thing?'

'No, no living thing can see us. They may sense us. Similar to a sixth sense I suppose, but that's why we can't get too close to people. It could drive them crazy,' she joked, twirling her finger around her ear.

David laughed at her imitation, but soon realised he was still holding on to her arm and quickly let go. As he did, he looked down for the first time and his throat dried up. 'So... where are we?' he asked, trying to distract himself.

'This is New York.'

'New York?' David said baffled, gazing around the city. *This is insane!* 'What are we doing here?'

'For her.' Grace gestured to the large glass building in front of them.

David looked through the closest window and saw a young girl fast asleep in a hospital bed. She was hooked up to a machine with wires hanging around her face and chest.

'Who is she?'

'I don't know.'

'You don't know? Then, why are we here?'

'Our job as a G.A, guardian angel, is to help influence those still alive as best as we can to give them a better chance of a successful life, so... what is it? You're looking at me funny?'

'No, not at all,' David replied, feeling like he was daydreaming. 'I was thinking about something like this earlier and it's weird hearing you talk about it now.'

'Oh, I see. Umm, well yeah, usually when helping someone we would have to abide by that person's life file, which you'd find in the library, but I go about things a little differently. I don't always agree with the files.'

'How come?' He could see the uncertainty in Grace's eyes as if she was debating on telling him or not, but eventually she opened up.

'The best way to explain it is... well, influencing fate is like holding out a helping hand. It is always there, but those whose minds are too strong will neither accept nor want it, whereas those whose minds are too weak will try and reach out, but never grasp it. Both are declared as lost souls and therefore forbidden to be helped, but that's where I come in.' Grace fell quiet. 'Everyone deserves a chance in this life and no one deserves to be given up on. No one. No matter what the rules say.'

'It doesn't seem right...' David scowled.

'What doesn't?'

'Well, how can you have rules about helping people? When do you decide if they're a lost cause?'

49

'What would you do, then? If you sought to help someone and they failed to accept it, what would you do?'

'Nothing, I suppose,' David answered immediately. 'But my hand would always be available to them whether they use it or not, like having someone's number saved in your phone. It's a symbol as much as an action. Something to say 'I'm here for you, if you need me'. Sometimes that's all people need. The moment you take that away... the problem will only get worse, surely?'

Grace nodded with an impressed look on her face. 'Hmm, I knew there was something special about you. That's exactly what I believe and it's why I'm willing to break the rules. No one is ever gone, and we're the proof. We're still here. So I vow to help as many lost and forgotten souls as I can. Whether they'd be mortals or G.A's.'

David now looked at Grace in awe. It was so refreshing to find someone who shared the same values as him. Although, listening to her speak did make him wonder. Did he have a weak mind? The talk about how a helping hand is held out to someone only to be ignored. It sounded very much like him.

'Anyway, those who break the rules face banishment...'

'Hence why you're not comfortable in the library?' David added, understanding the situation.

'Yeah, and why I have been solo for so long, but!' her voice perked up. 'It won't stop me and that's why were here.'

'Okay,' David said, clearing his throat. 'What are we doing then?'

'That little girl in there. She's been given up on. Someone so young and yet, her file has been shelved, but I know she's not totally gone. There's still some fight left in her. I can feel it.'

'So, what are you going to do?'

'Help.'

50

All of a sudden, the monitor in the room started flashing and the lights flicked on as a group of nurses rushed in to attend to the little girl. All of them acting quickly in a synchronised routine as they all knew their roles to play. David was so caught up in watching the drama, he'd only just noticed Grace walking towards the window. Fences appearing beneath her feet with every glowing step until she was within touching distance of the window. She then held out a hand and he saw a baby ball of light appear hovering over her palm, like a droplet of sunlight. She lightly blew on it and the light drifted through the window into the room and lightly fell onto the girl's head before trickling down her neck towards her heart.

A long exhale left David's mouth as a few moments later all the nurses left the room and turned the lights off behind them. The monitor now beeping normally.

'Did you just?' David started to ask as Grace walked back to him. 'You just brought her back to life.'

'No I didn't,' Grace said quietly. 'We can't resurrect people. I just helped give her the energy needed to fight a bit harder. She's strong. She has the mind-power. Just, not the power.'

'That was amazing...'

'We need to go.'

'What? So soon?'

'Every time I act outside the rules I leave a mark. A mark... they can track.'

David didn't know what to say. It suddenly felt as though he was in a game of cat and mouse with an unknown threat. There must be more to Grace than she was letting on still.

'Will... you still come with me?'

She could obviously sense the doubt in his mind, but as he looked into her glowing tropical eyes, he couldn't help but trust her. Especially after witnessing her magic.

There was something about her that made him want to stay and besides, where else would he go? He didn't understand what was happening and as far as he was aware, she was his only hope of getting home. Also, as daft as it seemed, he liked the idea she could read him. Ironically, she made him feel alive. Although he'd only spent what must have been a few minutes with her, it felt like they had a connection, like she understood him, and he finally felt like he was somewhere where he could be of proper use. Somewhere he belonged. As long as she kept her end of the deal, he could see this being a wondrous adventure.

'Where are we going now, then?' he asked excitedly.

Chapter 7

The sound of revving engines and honking horns filled the air as Diego sat high above the city. His eagle eyes watching the swarmed street below from his fence, Stephen still with him, but they had hardly spoken two words to each other since arriving. As curious as he was about Stephen's situation, it was proving a lot more problematic than he hoped and he needed a break from it. Therefore he thought he'd test Stephen's capabilities as a G.A instead. There had already been a couple of moments where he'd been able to influence people and he hoped Stephen was paying attention, which he did appear to be doing. Every time he glanced over he could see Stephen was closely studying the ground as if he was taking it all in. Either that, or he was mind was so blank he didn't know what he was looking at.

With the day being quiet, Diego leaned back on his fence and stretched his back, pretending to soak in the rays of the bright sun reflecting off the tall glass buildings. He remembered how once upon a time this place was just a humble town with only a few local businesses dotted either side of a dusty mud track. Its transformation from then to now really illustrated the progress of humanity. However, despite the modernisation with the old rustic mountains overlooking the city from the West coast and the original dirty desert surrounding it, it did make it look out of place, like two eras of history merged into one. Even the people were different now. They no longer had the strong, hard-working nature he was so familiar with seeing. Instead, he spent his time scowling down at them trudging through the streets like brainless zombies. Their limbs dangling from their sweaty bodies while they stared at the steaming pavement. Some looking like they were going to faint at any minute beneath the midday sun.

Luckily for Diego, the only heat he could feel was the warm currents of energy circulating in his body and of those below him.

'There!' Stephen suddenly shouted.

Diego leaned forward to look where Stephen was pointing. A young girl in a red dress, no older than five, was running down the path on her own. Her pigtails bouncing in thin red ribbons as she chased after a red balloon. Her little arms reaching up high to try and grab it.

'Okay,' Diego replied. 'This one's all yours, see what you can do. Remember, focus on their energy and when you sense a gap in their train of thought, that's your window to try and influence them.'

'Like a subconscious.'

'Exactly.' Diego nodded once.

'How will I know when it's time? I can't hear what she's thinking.'

'Were not mind readers, Stephen! It's about energy. Now focus. You'll sense when it's time.'

'Okay.' Stephen puffed out his cheeks. 'Okay.'

'This is quite a low level one anyway, so no harm will come from it.'

He watched as Stephen walked away on his fences and he quickly followed, wanting to keep tabs on the girl himself because despite what he said, he knew children could be difficult to influence. Their windows of opportunity come and go much quicker than adults because they are yet to understand the consequence of any decision, so therefore, they tend to make their minds up fast. That is why a lot of children learn life the hard way. At such a young age they can never see the larger picture of their actions and so can quickly become chaotic, reckless and in the future, even criminal.

'I can't sense anything,' Stephen called out.

Diego ignored him however, as he too couldn't sense a break in the child's energy cycle. Her mind was set on getting this balloon no matter what. He turned his attention to the sleepwalking bodies around her, focussing on their energies instead to see if they could be influenced to get the balloon for her, but they, too, were oblivious. All of them ignoring the child as if she wasn't even there and not giving her a second thought.

'This is ridiculous!' Diego muttered under his breath.

The balloon continued floating over everyone's heads, dancing playfully in the air as if it was luring the girl along.

'Is there something else we could do, Diego?' Stephen asked. 'I'm getting a bad feeling about this.'

Again, Diego ignored him, still following close behind with his fence only a few metres above the ground. The girl was getting closer to road now and he, too, feared the worst. He pivoted on his fence to teleport to the other side of the path and stand above the road. He began scanning the cars zooming past beneath him, but influencing drivers was just as difficult because the majority of them acted on autopilot, thinking about something other than the actual world around them. *Life was a so much easier when it was horse and cart!* he thought.

'Diego?' Stephen panicked.

Diego's heart pounded as the girl approached the curb. She Stretched her arms up high, leaning on her tip-toes to try and grab the balloon which was slowly falling towards the ground. His insides went cold despite the energy beneath his feet as the girl tumbled into the road. A shiny silver SUV hurtling towards her.

Bang!

There was a screech of tyres as the vehicle came to a sudden stop and the driver fell out of the car in panic. They weren't the only one either as the noise seemed to ring out across the whole city and break everyone out of their trances. A sizzling surge of energy raced through Diego's body as could sense everyone's eagerness to now help. Multiple people running towards the road or getting out their phones to call someone. *It's a bit late now!* But despite his anger, Diego got to work. He acted as if they were talking to him directly and influenced the decision making of everyone he could. Even Stephen was acting accordingly as they motivated everyone to do something helpful. One man in particular decided to take off his pink and white chequered shirt and place it under the girl's head. Many others, however, those who couldn't be influenced, continued on their own path and only watched with interest as they passed by. Some even deciding to stop to just take a picture or video on their phones.

Diego clenched his jaw tightly as he watched the outcome of their actions like a movie scene. He'd done everything he could. Now he had to leave things be and allow the scene to play out as intended. Stephen appeared beside him with a look of trauma on his pale face. 'I... I don't understand.'

'She couldn't be influenced,' Diego said bluntly.

'But, she... we did that.'

'We did not!' Diego snapped. 'They did!' He pointed down at the people below. 'Our only job here is to guard people as best we can through influence. Anything else is forbidden and against the rules. They are the one's who failed her by being so selfish and stupid.'

'Sophia! Sophia!' A mortal lady cried out running down the road.

'Her more so,' Diego said, watching the slim lady rush towards the little girl. A large beige handbag squashed under her arm as she tried to run in heels. Her long black hair swinging across her shoulders as she cried out the girl's name. 'Oh, Sophia!' She fell to her knees by the girls side, taking off her sunglasses to cry into her hands.

'Let's go,' Diego said, watching the red balloon drift off into the atmosphere. He grabbed Stephen's arm and tugged him over his fence. The pair of them now standing over a small rocky island in the middle of nowhere. Ferns and tall wild grass swaying beneath them. Diego headed straight for the edge and sat on his fence to gaze out at the calm blue horizon. His arms folded as he zoned out from the rest of the world and ignored the shrieking gulls overhead scavenging for food.

This island was like his own private space within the G.A.F. He accidentally landed here one day after venturing away from his home town of São Paulo, over two thousand miles away, and since then, he had never met another G.A here. He was always alone, until now.

He screwed his nose up as Stephen slowly strolled into view just off the island and sat down ahead of him over the sea. At first he remained quiet, but it didn't last long.

'Sorry...' Stephen spoke hesitantly. 'I can't let this go. What happened back there. We could have avoided it, couldn't we?'

Diego glared back at him, hoping his expression was enough of an answer.

'She was only a kid... surely we could have done something different to help her. That accident was so, needless.'

'It is not down to us.' Diego stared back over the ocean with gritted teeth. *How many times do I have to say it!* 'Our job is simple. There were over fifty people down there who could have made an impact. All they had to do was stop the girl, or her balloon, but they didn't even bat an eyelid. Didn't even think about it.'

'That's why we intervene though, right? To guard and protect them?'

'No!' Diego yelled. 'Fate is fate. What happens happens. It is not our job to intervene with their lives. We watch over them to try and keep them on the most fortuitous path for them. If they were not all so self-absorbed or depressed they might actually make use of their lives without us even having to influence them at all.'

'Surely if there's more people feeling like that there's more reason to intervene?' Stephen challenged him.

'It shouldn't be that way! Everyone's minds are so much weaker now. The world has evolved in such a way with these advanced sciences, technology, politics and social media that it has made them vain, lazy and pathetic and the other G.As don't help. They intervene too much, with their 'do-good' attitude, manipulating environments, sharing energy, all the while they are just feeding these inadequates a false sense of hope and accomplishment. It sickens me. Don't be like them!' Diego paused to catch his breath. 'Once upon a time we used to guide exceptional people to greatness... to glory, now, now we guide idiots to insignificance and I'm getting tired of it.'

'What's the harm in it, though?' Stephen replied. 'Say we, I don't know, somehow popped the balloon and the girl stopped following it and returned to her mum. What would happen?'

'Probably nothing,' Diego grumbled. 'The Idlers haven't done their jobs properly in ages.'

'Then... why didn't we do it?'

'It's breaking the rules! We do not and should not break the rules! How many times do I have to say it! It's forbidden! It was forbidden when I needed help so why should it be any different for them!'

Silence fell on the island. He shouldn't have said that. He knew it wasn't a valid reason, but its true, during his lifetime the rules were in place and he suffered the consequences, so why should it be any different for people now?

Still staring over the ocean, Diego shook his head. *It doesn't matter anyway. Its clear he hasn't got the right*

mindset for this. He doesn't understand. No one does!
Diego shot back up to his feet. 'Come with me.'

'Where are going now?'

'Back to the library. I don't think you are cut out for this. I can tell you're a rule breaker and I refuse to be clipped because of it as well. We'll try to find your file once more, but after that you're going to Yutopia.'

'But I-'

'Don't argue! My decision is made.'

They both swivelled over their fences into the library and Diego instantly made his way over to another bookcase. 'Put your hand back on it,' he said, pointing at the hand-print in the wood that should trigger Stephen's impulse to his file, but Stephen was less than interested. Diego watched with a bite of his tongue as Stephen dragged his feet over and held out a lethargic hand, but there was something wrong. The library was quiet. Dim. No other G.A in sight.

Diego pressed a forceful hand against Stephen's chest to stop him from continuing.

'What now?' Stephen sighed.

'Be quiet!' he hushed, putting a stern finger in front of Stephen's lips, 'stay here!' He crept around the side of the bookcase. A faint buzzing vibrating in his ears and he followed the sound into the increasing darkness.

Suddenly, a flash of crimson speared up across the bookcase to his right, causing him to freeze. There was light murmuring coming from the opposite side and he crept closer. He poked his head round the corner as a thunderous smack vibrated among the shelves, making the files shake in their slots above him. As expected, it was the Idlers. All four of them. Their bodies emitting the powerful crimson aura and in the middle of them, was a G.A. Their helpless body kneeling tiredly on the carpet.

The current Idlers looked like two sets of twins consisting of one male and one female. The women's ponytails matching the colour of the men's beards, one blonde and one black, and they shared the same plain facial features. Although, the blonde-haired twins had more of an athletic figure, whereas the black-haired twins looked more like stone cold bodyguards with a square jaw.

Diego couldn't get a clear look from where he was standing, but the G.A looked like an old man. He could see light seeping out of cuts on his face and float up like smoke from a snuffed out fire.

'What's happening?' Stephen whispered, appearing by his side.

'What are you doing here?

'I wanted to...'

'Ssh! Shut up! And get back!' he ordered. 'Unless you want to be clipped!'

He shunted Stephen back behind the bookcase and continued to watch as the blonde-female Idler stepped closer to the G.A. Her right hand glowing brighter as a long crimson blade appeared in her grasp after a swift flick of the wrist.

'Finally, after all this time, we got you again!' she said, pressing the blade against the G.A's neck. 'Tell us what happened! Why didn't it work?'

'It will,' the G.A gasped. 'Once their essence-'

The black-male Idler cracked a punch across the side of the G.A's face, nearly knocking them flat on the floor.

'There was no essence!' The blonde-female Idler screamed. 'They had no power! Now the Idler involved is gone and the supposed M.G is among us!'

'T-then I don't know,' the G.A spoke calmly. 'You must have done something wrong. I did my bit. Now, leave me be.'

'Oh, no Linus, we're not through with you yet. We will get answers. Bring him to Limbo,' the Idler commanded. 'Let's get out of sight.'

A crackling crimson fence suddenly appeared and Diego watched the black-haired Idlers each hook one of Linus's arms under theirs and drag him over it. The blonde Idlers following close behind and the moment they all disappeared, the library's light returned to normal.

'What were they talking about?' Stephen asked.

'I don't know,' Diego mumbled.

'Who was that guy?'

'I don't know!'

'What's an M.G?'

Diego shot round and pinned Stephen against the shelves. 'Shut up!' he thundered. 'You are fast becoming the most intolerable and annoying G.A I have ever encountered and if you do not get your act together I will personally ensure you are sent to the tortures of Idle! Understand?'

'But I-'

'Enough!'

'No!' Stephen broke free, wheezing slightly. 'Stop treating me like an idiot! I've got no memory! Not no feelings! How would you feel in my position? I'm wandering around a fantasy land with no idea how I got here, where I came from or who I am... a child could have died under our supervision, which you don't seem to care about... so why don't you cut me some slack!'

Diego stared flabbergasted at Stephen's outburst.

'Look, I'm relying on you to help me and when I see, that!' Stephen pointed to the space where the Idlers had been. 'It scares me. It's not normal. None of this is.'

'I could not care less if it scares you!' Diego snarled. 'I told you, you are not cut out for this role. Therefore, all these irritating questions you are asking me are irrelevant.' Diego created a fence to his right. 'Follow me.'

'Where to?'

'You can get to Yutopia from here.'

'No.' Stephen stood firm.

'Excuse me?' The fence disintegrated as Diego marched up to Stephen. 'No? You don't get a say!'

'Why don't I? My thoughts count too!'

'Trust me, they don't, and besides I am helping you. If you stay here and mess up, which you will do, the Idlers will not be so kind.'

'I think I'll take my chances.'

The energy within Diego was hitting boiling point. Who did Stephen think he was talking to him like this.

'I don't understand you,' Stephen ranted. 'You say I'm not cut out for this and yet you're the one who seems reluctant to help anyone! From where I stand you're the one not cut out for it.'

Like a predatory instinct, Diego lashed out and struck Stephen, thumping him in the face so strongly it knocked him down onto the carpet. His eyes and body burned as if he was standing in a furnace. Sweat pouring from his head. Then, the library fell into darkness once again. 'Seriously?' Diego laughed hysterically, throwing out his arms. 'Ridiculous!'

The blonde female Idler came back into view. A stern look on her face. 'Diego,' she spoke. 'I said one chance and yet this soul is still here and has yet to make progress.'

'Oh, just clip him! I don't care. You'd be doing me a favour.'

'And you.' The Idler glared at him.

'Me? What have I done?'

'You have disobeyed a direct order and now you have harmed another G.A.'

'You can't be serious? G.As break the rules every day in the open and yet you threaten to clip me for this! This is pathetic! Do you Idlers even know what you're doing anymore?'

'Watch your tone, Diego,' the Idler replied summoning her blade.

'Or what? You'll clip me? If you clipped everyone who broke the rules, I'd be the only one left! It should be your kind being clipped for failing to keep the G.A.F in order! You're the useless ones!'

The burning in Diego's body flared up like gasoline on fire. The library got even darker as black smoke poured off his steaming shoulders. His vision going blurry as if particles of ash were settling on his pupils. All of a sudden, a loud ping pierced through the library as he heard the blade swinging towards him in a crimson aura, but like a flash, he snatched it out of the Idler's hand. Now holding the blade himself, he could feel a strong power surge through his arm. His tie turning red once more.

'The crimson aura,' the Idler said.

'I...!' Diego sneered as he looked at his new threatening appearance. His sight in a strange infra-red. 'I am one of you.'

The Idler quickly slapped her hands against her legs like a soldier reporting for duty.

'What are you doing?' Diego quizzed.

'You are who Amb. Ermêl was talking about.'

'Who?'

'Amb. Ermêl. Our master. They spoke of this day. You are to come with me.'

A crimson fence suddenly appeared between them and Diego gawked at the zapping energy. Was this really happening? Did he really just absorb Idle's power? Who was Amb. Ermêl? He glanced at his menacing reflection in the blade's steel and swished it around playfully, flicking his wrist continuously to watch it appear and disappear at his will. *Amazing!*

'D-Diego?'

Diego jolted his head back at Stephen who looked like a scared child cowering on the floor. 'What about him?' Diego asked, pointing the blade at Stephen.

'It is up to you.'

'Hmm.' Diego strolled over to Stephen and glared down at him. 'I'll give you one more chance, Stephen. Stay or go, it is up to you, but if you mess up, if you do anything to annoy me, I will come back and I will be the one to clip you.'

Diego quickly turned away from Stephen's sad, clueless eyes and didn't hesitate to the follow the Idler over the fence. The library vanished from sight and he found himself standing on a metallic platform. A giant crimson vortex whirling in front of him. The room itself was huge and dimly lit from a single bowl of stormy energy hanging in the centre

'Diego,' a voice hissed through the vortex.

'Hello?' he replied boldly. 'Where am I?'

'This is Limbo. A chamber between Idle and the G.A.F. The place where Idlers are born.'

'And who are you?'

'I am Amb. Ermêl and I have been awaiting your arrival.'

'Why? What do you want with me?' Diego asked.

'You are not like the other G.As, are you Diego? Some would say you don't help. Don't belong. Don't care. Well, we both know there is a bit of truth to that isn't there. Have you ever wondered how you got into the G.A.F? How someone with a past like yours entered the Tavern in the first place?'

Diego squirmed on the spot. 'You obviously had something to do with it?'

A sinister chuckle bounced around the room. 'Yes, I did. Even with my restraints I still have some influence. You were my little project.'

'Project?'

'Yes. An experiment. You see, the Idlers are simple souls from Idle who are like programmed robots. They are incapable of harnessing any other power or even thinking for themselves. It was all part of the agreement. You however, a soul from Idle who I managed to slip into the G.A.F from the very beginning, these restrictions do not apply to you. You are free to act at your will. My will.'

Diego lifted up his tie and stroked the silky material, feeling the energy running through it sting his fingertips. 'I always knew I was destined for more.'

'That you are and your task starts now.'

'Yes!' Diego rubbed his hands together and summoned his crimson blade back. 'I have been wanting to do this for such a long time. To clip these useless...'

'No!' Amb. Ermêl screamed. 'The G.A.F must stay balanced. It is the M.G you must focus on.'

'M.G? I heard the Idlers speak of this.'

'Yes. Being pure Idle they are numb to the M.G's energy and wouldn't know it if they were standing in front of them. However, they know...' A sudden bolt of crimson shot out of the bowl like lightning and zapped a figure further along the platform, revealing the G.A the Idlers had taken from the library. 'The M.G is the key to fixing everything. To correct mistakes and put the G.A.F back on course for resurrection.'

Diego could feel his eyes widening with excitement. 'Where will I find them?'

'They are somewhere in the G.A.F. The same angel you retrieved from the Tavern.'

'...Stephen? You can't be serious, the angel's an idiot! And I was literally just with him! Wait... was it you who sent me to him?'

'Yes, I could not have him creating suspicion.'

'Suspicion?'

'For my plans to work, discretion is required. Now focus on the task, Diego. The Idlers are now at your disposal. Use them. Find the M.G and bring them here.'

Chapter 8

Snow continued to fall over the quiet pine forest and yet David wasn't cold. In fact, he didn't feel anything. He was quite comfortable sitting in a small clearing of the white wilderness. The glow of his fence glimmering on the rippling stream beneath him. Grace had disappeared a while ago in search for someone, giving him some time to take a much needed break from this bizarre adventure. This peaceful scenery made his spot by the reservoir seem tedious in comparison and he knew Bud would like it too. The very thought of Bud made him wonder how much time he'd lost. What must his mum be thinking? He winced at the idea of her waiting for him. Scared of falling asleep in case that was when he'd walk through the door. *I really ought to check on her.* He tapped on his knees. *Even if it was from high up on these fences, I need to know she's okay, Bud too, but I can't just leave Grace. I'll speak to her when she comes back,* he thought. As strange as it seemed, he was enjoying himself here, feeling like a lost kid in Neverland. He shouldn't be, though, right? How could he be so okay with this? How could he be so... emotionless? He was dead and it didn't seem to bother him. The only thing that bothered him was the fact his mum was now alone.

'Everything alright?' Grace asked, appearing into view again.

'Yep. I'm always alright. I was just thinking, whether we could go and check on my mum? Just so I can see she's okay.'

'Umm, we can do, but you'll have to make it quick.'

'Quick? Why?'

'It's against the rules to see anyone of kin while serving in the G.A.F. It's to stop us from influencing those personal to us.' Grace air quoted.

'That's a bit unfair isn't it?'

Grace shrugged. 'Its not the worse rule up here. You can see them as much as you want from Yutopia because you don't have the ability to influence there.'

'Yutopia?'

'Yeah, it is the alternative to this place, providing you die good obviously. It's like a dreamworld where you can spend an eternity living however you want, but it's a one way ticket.'

'That sounds... well, it sounds pretty cool to be honest. Have you not thought about going? How long have you been here?'

Grace sighed, 'a very long time.'

'What happened?' he asked softly. 'If you don't mind me asking of course.'

Grace stared at him, biting her lip, but she quickly shook her head. 'I don't talk about it.'

'Okay.' David nodded. 'I understand.'

'It's not you, don't worry. I just, don't like talking about it. My life wasn't the fairy tale it could have been and if it wasn't for a friend of mine, well, it would have been much worse,' Grace spoke quietly, her aura dimming. 'They are the reason why I'm the way I am. Why I do what I do. They never gave up on me and without them, I don't know where I would of ended up.'

A sense of sadness wafted off her as she finished talking and David was about to ask another question, but quickly stopped himself. It wasn't right to pry and it was obviously a sensitive topic for her.

'Anyway, on a different note what was your final drink?' Grace asked, wiping away a rogue tear.

'My last drink? That's a bit random. Umm, a cup of coffee I think.'

'Coffee?' Grace laughed. 'Okay. I've not heard that before. Most people go for something alcoholic in the Tavern. I myself had orange juice and lemonade, though, you know, something summery,' she spoke poshly. 'After all, summer is the best season.'

'Yeah, sure.' David nodded to humour her. 'Did you find the person you were after?'

'Ugh, no,' Grace sighed again, leaning back. 'I would have thought they'd be here, but I can't sense any energy at all.'

'Well, it does feel like we are in the middle of nowhere.' David looked around at the surrounding trees and empty white landscape.

'Yes, but this is where they always came at around this time. I was sure they would be here.'

'Well, let's keep looking then, they can't have gone far,' he replied, however, he soon discovered he was talking to himself. Grace had vanished.

After a few seconds, he spotted a faint glow coming from further down the stream and he quickly swivelled on his fence to rejoin her. He appeared above a wooden bridge which stretched over the now roaring river. The water crashing down a small cascade into the misty lake below. He was about to say something, but the look on Grace's face told him to stay silent and as he looked over the water, his stomach churned.

There was something floating on the lake.

He slowly spun on his fence once again to get a closer look and then he saw it. A body bobbing in the water. The boy couldn't have been much older than him and looked exactly as Grace had described. A young man of muscular build with bushy brown eyebrows and wild curly hair. Only now, there was a huge gash on the side of his milky head.

David wiped his face and scratched his arm, doing his upmost to keep it together. The sight was harrowing and after what Grace had been explaining to him about the lost souls; to think this sort of thing could even happen

68

made it difficult to take. He's experienced sadness before, but no one deserved to end up like this.

'An example of why we are needed.' He heard Grace whisper in a sad tone behind him. 'Not everyone can deal with the pressures of modern life. The more the world evolves, the more it takes its toll. Their power goes out and their light fades, until there's nothing left of them.'

'This is...' but he couldn't think of the right words.

'Happening too often,' Grace added bitterly. 'The G.A.F needs to do better.'

'What can we do?'

'We can...' Grace closed her eyes at first as if stopping herself from saying anything, but they soon burst open again and she looked directly at him. Her eyes glistening intently as if creating a new bond of trust. 'Okay, I'm going to come clean with you. These last few situations you've tagged along on. They were tests. I needed to know how your mind worked before I could trust you one hundred percent.'

'Trust me with what?' David leaned in intently.

'I am looking for someone. Someone who can help all of this.' She gazed back down to the body. 'And possibly get you home.'

David's ears pricked up.

'But they...' Grace was suddenly cut off as a tall scrawny G.A spontaneously appeared on the lake. Their greasy brown hair flapping behind them as they ran across the water on their fences. Their legs trembling when they approached them.

'Hello?' Grace questioned. 'Are you okay?'

'T-the Idlers,' the G.A spoke in a scared Spanish accent. 'They've changed.'

'Changed? Changed how?' Grace asked strongly.

'They've turned violent. I see them, clipping G.As in the library like mercenaries.'

'What? Are you sure?'

69

'Si! They are clipping anyone. Anyone who helps too much.'

The angel held her shaking hands to her mouth and David caught Grace's worried eyes. The G.A was utterly terrified. Surely this wasn't what the G.A.F should be like? Angels too scared to help people? The worst thing was, he didn't know how to help, but thankfully Grace did.

'Right,' Grace spoke boldly. 'Here's what you're going to do. Lie low. Find an isolated location with no people around to influence. The Arctic Circle, Amazon Jungle, Sahara, somewhere they won't think to look for G.As and after a few days, they'll lose interest, okay?'

'Si. Okay. Okay, I go now.'

The G.A prepared to jump over her fence when suddenly a crimson light lit up her aura. She screamed loudly as the energy completely engulfed her until... pop! Like a faulty firework the G.A imploded. Her light fading into the atmosphere and standing in her place was a dim demonic figure emitting red radiation. A blade buzzing in the bushy black-bearded Idler's hand.

Both David and Grace stood completely still, speechless. David could sense the rage building up within Grace as her aura got brighter. Her eyes narrowing.

'You!' The Idler pointed at Grace. 'Your energy is familiar. You have broken rules and must be clipped.'

'Oh, I don't think so,' Grace replied through gritted teeth.

The Idler repositioned his blade and held it out like a soldier preparing for battle, but then, he creepily tilted his head at David. 'You! Your energy... you are to come with me.'

David stood perfectly still.

'Why?' Grace interrupted.

'I do not have to answer to you!' the Idler snapped. 'You, come with me!'

David shook his head. 'N-no. I'm staying here, with her.' He stepped closer to Grace, clenching his fist with anger at what he'd just witnessed.

The Idler looked confused at first. Their eyes veered to the side as if he was listening to something and then a smirk appeared on his face. The tingling in David's hands grew stronger, shooting up his arms like an electric current to his neck and in that second, time slowed down. The river below began to trickle rather than flow and he could hear his own breathing.

The Idler's blade spiralled in the air towards Grace, but without a second thought, David grabbed her shoulders and pulled her out the way. The blade planted into his left shoulder causing him to stoop down onto one knee. Its agonising energy burning his skin like cauterising a wound. Time returned to normal as the crimson light brightened over his body and when he turned round, he saw Grace trapped in what looked like a crimson aura. Her body trying to fight it, but it looked hopeless and before he could try to help, the Idler took her away over his crimson fence.

Grace! With his emotions running high, he grabbed the blade and yanked it out of his shoulder. Its handle burning his palm like a hot plate. He dropped it on his fence and watched it disappear before turning his attention to the snow and water around him, wishing he could put it on his burnt skin. The crimson light eventually faded away along with the pain and his body gradually eased as if the toxic energy was evaporating off him.

'Grace!' he muttered, groggily getting to his feet. 'Grace!'

Chapter 9

How can Stephen be of any importance? He's a nobody! He doesn't even know who he is, let alone any purposes he may have! Diego scowled as he paced up and down the platform. The vortex whirring behind him. *If I had known all this sooner, things would have been a lot easier. Why now? What is a M.G?* He stopped to peer over his shoulder at the G.A sitting further along the platform. Their hands bound to a small metal pole with crimson energy. *He knows!*

In a cloud of smoke, Diego spun around and marched over. He stood in front of the G.A like a prison guard with his chest puffed out and his hands cupped behind his back. 'You!' he bellowed. 'Are you conscious?' He stared down at the G.A, tapping his fingers together while he waited for a response. 'Perhaps you need waking.' He prepared a buzzing hand and went to strike them across the face, but before his palm made contact, they spoke.

'What, do you want, Diego?' the G.A asked, breathlessly.

'You know me?'

'I know you. I also heard you talking to Amb. Ermêl. Words of advice. Stop now. Before it is too late.'

Diego chuckled sinisterly. 'You foolish old man. Why would I want to do such a thing? Look at me!' He stepped back to admire his new form. 'Who would give up this sort of power? This is what I was destined for. Now I can finally put the G.A.F back in check. Maybe do even more.'

The G.A raised his head and through his thin grey hair, Diego could see his face for the first time. Peculiarly, he had one golden iris and one blue. 'You have no idea.'

Diego sniggered at the warning and squatted down with folded arms. 'Lionel, was it?'

'Linus.'

'Oh, that's right, sorry, you were pretty forgettable. However, I do remember what you were talking about with the Idlers. What business do you have with them, us? What is a M.G?'

Linus didn't reply and reverted back to looking at the floor.

'I see, okay.' Diego wiped his face. 'Okay.' He prepared to stand when he suddenly cracked a punch against Linus's cheek. The moment his fist made contact his hand electrified, like a bug zapper catching its prey, and it felt good! 'Want to tell me now?' he asked aggressively. 'I could do this for eternity.'

Linus, however, remained silent. Unfazed.

'Alright then! Have it your way.' Diego prepared to strike again when a crimson fence appeared ahead. An Idler returned to view and tossed a body onto the platform. The thump causing it to vibrate beneath his feet.

'Stephen?' he shouted eagerly, stomping over towards the G.A, but he soon spotted their blonde hair and quickly changed direction towards the Idler. 'Who is that?' he yelled straight into the Idler's face. 'That's not Stephen!'

'No.'

'Then why are they here?' He turned away and grabbed the G.A's jacket to turn them over. 'You!' He shoved them back down.

'Diego,' Grace replied weakly. 'You've gotten even uglier.'

Diego's lip twitched as he stared at her sickly yellow eyes.

'So, you've become an Idler now? Interesting, but not surprising with a heart like yours. No wonder innocent G.As are being clipped. What's wrong with you?' Grace spoke, sitting up and crossing her legs on the floor.

'What's wrong with me? I am only fulfilling the Idlers work as it should be done. Those being clipped are those who have broken the rules. The true crime is that they had been getting away with it for so long. We're merely catching up on the workload.'

'You really are a rubbish G.A aren't you. Do you even know what it stands for anymore?'

'Irrelevant now.'

'Irrelevant? Are you an angel or not?'

Diego sniggered at her remarks and simply held out his arms. 'Clearly I'm something better.'

'Oh, I see. Showing off your true colours,' Grace tutted. 'Good for you. I suppose it's ironic isn't it.'

'What is?'

'All this time you've been wanting to banish G.As to Idle when in fact, it is you who belongs there.'

Diego's snigger fell from his face. His aura pulsating. 'And so do you!' he hissed. 'Why are you here? Why did you bring her here?' He turned back to the Idler.

'The G.A they were with. They had unusual energy.'

'Unusual energy? What does that mean? How unusual? Was it Stephen?'

'No. I don't think so. But they were different.'

'Different?' Diego nodded sarcastically. 'Well, that's answered a lot of questions... you Idiot!'

'I caught the G.A to question her. I did not want to involve myself with the other.'

'What, why not?'

The Idler didn't respond.

'He's scared.' Grace leaned forward. 'The Idler is scared.'

Diego looked back at the Idler's twitching eyes and gulped. *What have they got to be scared of? They're making us look weak!* In a flash, Diego returned over to Grace, grabbing a hold of her jacket collar and dragged her across the platform towards, Linus.'

'Get off!' Grace yelled, flailing her arms out, but she was too weak against his energy. He threw her across the floor, her head smacking onto another metal pole which

74

rose up from the platform and while she laid there dazed, he tied her up just as Linus was.

'What are you doing?' Grace shouted.

'Weren't you listening? The Idler is going to question you about your friend. Then, and only then, will I allow you to be clipped. We both know you've been evading it for far too long anyway.'

'Oh, shut it, Diego! Have you not got any more children to neglect?'

Diego threatened to blast a crimson fist at Grace, but she didn't even blink. He left his fist hovering for a few seconds to try and call her bravery's bluff, but she stayed strong and it was he who spun away. 'You!' he shouted, returning to the Idler. 'Find out what you can and create a fence for me. I want to now what all the fuss is about.'

Chapter 10

While staring down the cascade, David held his wounded shoulder feeling completely lost. The pain still burning away at his collar bone. The images of the combusting G.A and Grace being taken haunted his mind, making him angry. How could such things happen in a place like this? After everything Grace had shown and taught him about the G.A.F, the fact these Idlers existed and acted this way... it was more unbelievable than the G.A.F itself. The fun and games of being a helpful guardian had finally run its course as now he was experiencing the ugly side. First there was the body in the water and then, for what happened afterwards. He suddenly saw the full picture and understood Grace's predicament. The afterlife was no different to normal life. Good gets quashed. Bad goes unpunished.

He squeezed his shoulder tightly while he thought about it, wincing at the pain shooting across him. There had to be something he could do, but without Grace here to guide him, he was clueless as to how. Without her there was definitely no chance of him getting back. Who was the person she was trying to tell him about? Every pulsation in his body told him to go after her. Look for her. Save her. 'But how?' he said, looking up at the greying snow clouds. 'How?'

An eerie buzzing sound disturbed the air and David looked out over the lake. A crimson fence was glowing in the mist. He immediately walked towards it with his hands firmly by his sides and when he saw a dark figure appear, his legs began to wobble. Surprisingly, as he got closer, he noticed it wasn't the same Idler as before. This one wasn't completely engulfed in the darkness, but surrounded by a dark smoke pouring off their body and contaminating the mist into looking more like clouds of ash. Their tie matched their eyes and it was they who spoke first.

'Who are you?' they thundered, making David's entire body twitch.

'Where's Grace?' David shouted back.

'Ah, so it is you.' The Idler strolled closer. His aura giving off a sense of villainous supremacy. 'You are the one the Idler is scared of?' he chuckled.

'What are you talking about?' David scowled, looking at his own image. 'What have they got to be scared of?'

'That! Is a very good question.' The Idler flicked a finger at him. 'Look at you. A young, wimpy boy... Oh, well, you haven't even been here long have you?'

'What makes you say that?'

'I can sense it!' the Idler said, waving his right hand in the air around him. 'Your energy is a little off, but weak, you are nothing like me.'

'From where I'm standing that's a good thing. Who are you?'

'I am Diego.' His face went serious. 'And a word of warning, boy. Do not insult me or I will have you clipped. You are lucky to be in the G.A.F as it is because it is quite clear to me that you don't belong here. Why don't you go to Yutopia and save us all the hassle!'

David gulped heavily as he endured Diego's threats. His arms now shaking as much as his legs. *What's his problem?* His instinct was to disappear and avoid the confrontation, but he had to remember he wasn't doing this for himself. 'I'm not going anywhere without Grace.'

'Oh!' Diego laughed, putting a hand to his forehead. 'Of course, that explains why your energy is tainted. You have been conniving with a criminal.'

'A criminal?'

'One of the biggest in the G.A.F!' Diego exclaimed. 'Running around trying to save all those stupid lost

77

souls... it's ridiculous! She should have been stopped decades ago!'

'What's so wrong with helping lost souls? Someone should!'

'Should they?' Diego raised his eyebrows. 'Why? They are lost for a reason. They are too weak to achieve anything. Too weak to be influenced. Why waste your energy on them when any action done is merely prolonging the inevitable?'

'The inevitable being?'

'Depression. Deprivation. Death. Take your pick. Grace would tell you the same.'

David fell silent.

'The only ones who try to help lost souls, are those who were lost souls themselves. It is their way of trying to be something more... it never works. If it was up to me, such people would never become G.As. Their lives are proof that they can't help anyone because they couldn't help themselves!'

'No.' David shook his head. 'You're wrong. Lost souls are the best people to become G.As because they value the help more than those who lived their lives under the influence.' He tensed as he watched Diego's aura flare up, almost becoming radioactive as he could feel the prickling energy react with his skin like the blade had.

'This is your only warning! Obey the rules of the G.A.F or go to Yutopia. Grace is gone and if you persist with your stupid mindset so will you! I hope I don't see your face again! For your sake.'

David glanced down at the crimson fence as Diego began to disappear over it and right there and then, he knew this was going to be is only chance. He took a deep breath and raced towards the dissolving energy. Diego had already disappeared over it, but some light still remained and he just about managed to get a toe to it before it totally faded. The energy scorched his foot like stepping on hot coal and spread over him like a wildfire, searing his skin to the point he thought it was going to melt off his bones.

The crimson fence re-appeared beneath him and wanting to escape the pain, he tumbled straight over. Falling into an abyss.

Chapter 11

Consumed by darkness, David continued to fall down a bottomless pit. A rancid odour, like burning sewage, attacked his airways and made his eyes water sour tears. Despite his attempts, he couldn't create a fence to break his fall, nothing was happening. It was like the darkness had absorbed all his energy and instead replaced it with fear.

Eventually, a crimson glow appeared below him and he braced himself for what was to come. At first it was like falling through toxic cobwebs as the energy clung to his body and stung him as he passed through, making his skin itch all over, until finally... smack!

He hit the rocky floor face down. An excruciating pain trampling over him as if his body broke on impact. He coughed and spluttered violently at the intense stench lingering in the humid air, trying to cover his mouth with a heavy arm to stop it from entering his lungs. 'Grace?' he choked. 'Grace?' He tried to move, but his body was having none of it as if it was demanding to use this time to rest and fix itself, but he knew he couldn't wait. Grace needed him, so, through gritted teeth, he put mind over matter and pushed himself up. His arms and legs shaking beneath him as he got to his feet, rocking groggily on the spot, while hunched over to ease his aching diaphragm.

Once his breathing was back on track, he tenderly brushed the dusty rubble from his suit and took a couple of hesitant steps. 'Ow!' he hollered, feeling as though he'd just entered a patch of nettles. *What was that?* He shook his hands to try and disperse the irritation which was already spreading up his arm. 'Can't go that way then. Where am I?'

A flash of crimson suddenly illuminated the cave from behind him and he quickly spun round to see an army of tiny crimson specks crackling ahead, like a swarm of baby jellyfish in an ocean abyss. 'I guess it's this way?' he gulped. He wiped some dirt from his forehead and walked towards the little lights. 'Argh!' he grunted, jumping backwards again as he was zapped in the chest. More irritation spreading across his torso. *Great! What am I supposed to do now?* he thought, scratching his tingling chest. Another flash of crimson illuminated the cave from further up and this time, it was followed by a scream. A scream which made David's entire body shiver.

Grace!

He stared at the sinister specks in front of him. *I've got to get through!* He took one last deep breath and moved forwards. His teeth gritted in agony as he endured the zapping pain again and again, like being pricked by electrocuting needles. He squeezed his fists tightly with every sting that struck his body and the further he got, the more intense it felt. Although his body cried out for help, his mind persevered. Even to the point when he was desperate to stop, fall to the ground and give up, he kept going. Sweat sliding down his face. He burst through a patch of them, clenching his jaw and crunching his eyes closed so he wouldn't make a sound as the energy stung his entire upper body, but then, the pain vanished. At first he thought he might have made it past them all, but when he opened his eyes again the crimson sparks were still visible, they just weren't affecting him anymore. Of a matter of fact, he didn't feel anything. His body had gone completely numb. Unsure on what was happening, he reached out a hand to wave it through the next cluster of light in front of him and that's when he realised... his hand was glowing red.

What? David inspected his hand thoroughly and quickly saw that the glow was over his whole body. It was as if he had been absorbing the energies on his way through and now they had fried all of his nerves and senses.

Another burst of crimson flashed up ahead. This time a lot closer and yet again, a scream followed. A signal to David he didn't have time to question what was happening. Without the energy's threat of pain, David moved faster and broke out into a run as he travelled down the cave, wobbling slightly with every step as he couldn't feel the uneven rocks beneath him. Another flash of crimson shot through the cave, temporarily blinding him as he came to a skidding halt. Then, as his eyes refocused, he saw a pair of giant doors standing before him embedded with glistening rubies.

He approached them carefully, holding out a hand as he scanned for some handles or a button to open them with, but he couldn't see anything. *How do I get inside?* he thought, placing his hands against the thick steel and leaning into it, hoping to somehow push them open, but the doors weighed a tonne and wouldn't move. *This isn't helpful!* He rolled up his jacket sleeves and tried again, huffing and puffing as he put his whole body weight into it. His new red aura suddenly flickered, lighting up the rubies on the door and finally, it budged open. A pool of ominous red light flowing out of the gap. David stared at the light, taking deep breaths to prepare himself for what might be inside and then, he squeezed through.

Once inside, he found himself standing at the top of a metal staircase overlooking a humongous dimly lit room, like a photographers dark room. The light source being a giant bowl of energy in the centre, buzzing loudly on the ceiling like a demonic beehive. The whole place had a horror movie feel to it and it was making his skin crawl.

He slowly tip-toed down the stairs while gazing out at the thousands of strange counters that were randomly dotted about. What really caught his attention, though, was the swirling vortex on the far side opposite. It was the size of a ferris wheel, located on top of a platform and on it were three dark figures, but only one seemed to be moving. *She must be over there.*

A deep crackly voice suddenly bounced around the metallic room and David dived down behind one of the counters at the bottom of the stairs. His knees smacking onto the cold metal grates. He rubbed them vigorously to ease the pain, noticing that his aura had now dissolved off him and into the red atmosphere. 'That's not ideal,' he whispered, sitting on his haunches. Without the crimson aura for comfort he remained low, staying below the counters as he quietly weaved his way across the room, doing his best not to cough as the dusty air tickled his throat. He could still hear the voice up ahead, but he was too far away to hear what they were saying. What he could hear though, was every slap and thump that rang out, making him wince angrily and pick up the pace.

There was only a couple of counters left now between him and the stairs to the platform and so he stopped to think of his options. He didn't actually know what to do once he got there because he couldn't fight. He'd never fought in his life and this hardly felt like the time to start. He cautiously poked his head above the counter to get a better look and to his relief, he spotted her. 'Grace!' he gasped.

She was bound to a metal pole. Wafts of light floating up off her body, like a distinguished candle. There was another G.A up there too, next to her, but he didn't recognise them. Whoever they were, their yellow aura was very dim and they didn't appear to be conscious.

A loud squeak suddenly pierced across the room as the legs of the counter he was leaning on scratched along the metal floor. The noise making his heart beat erratically as he immediately ducked back behind it and held his breath as he heard the Idler's crackling energy come closer. He kept as still as possible, but he knew he was going to get caught. There was nowhere to hide. He pressed his back up against the counter's base, but ended up falling through. The counter was hollow. A thin sheet covering it from top to bottom and without hesitation he hid beneath it. Something brushed over his head as he scrambled under and dropped the cloth behind him. He sat silently huddled underneath. His eyes fixated on the buzzing footsteps stepping around him. The Idler was already here and standing where he had been, looking back however, David's body fell weak. He covered his mouth with a shaking hand as he felt his stomach churn. An arm was dangling in front of him.

He stared at the metal frame above, now understanding that these weren't counters, they were autopsy tables. His head suddenly jolted to the floor beside him as he saw a crimson glow seeping beneath the sheet. The disturbing sound, like a static tv, fuzzing in his ears. His heart tried to escape out of his chest as a dark hand began to slowly lift up the cloth.

'We've got the M.G!' a female voice suddenly shouted.

'Where?' the Idler replied eagerly. Their hand quickly retreating from the cloth.

'The library! Come, Diego wants us all there.'

A flash of crimson lit up the cloth as the voices disappeared, leaving David nestled beneath the table, like a scared child hiding for their life. He did his best to calm his trembling body. To try and get his heart rate down, but the fear of being caught was taking a while to drain away. His breathing still shallow as if there was a shortness of air to breathe. He closed his strained eyes, thankful that they were called away and was not at all curious as to who it was they were after.

84

Chapter 12

'This way!' Diego bellowed his orders at the Idlers. All five of them pacing around the bookcases like a hunting party. Their blades fizzing at the ready. Stephen their prey. The library fell into further darkness which each one of their buzzing footsteps, following Diego's directions as he tracked Stephen like a wild animal on an island. His right-hand outstretched ahead of him as he used it to sense Stephen's fragmented energy. It was proving much easier now as more and more G.As vanished from the area. All of them disappearing at the powerful sight of the Idlers. Fearful they were the ones they were after, but little did they know just how insignificant they were right now.

The pulsation in Diego's hand grew stronger and his body tensed with anticipation as he knew they was closing in. 'Come now, Stephen,' he called out, licking his lips. 'I just want to talk. It seems you're more important than you think.'

'Go away!' Stephen replied from close by. 'You left me alone! So leave me alone again!'

'I can't do that. I have new orders now. Come quietly and I'll take it easy on you.' There was no reply this time, but it didn't matter now because he knew Stephen was close. He slowly placed his palm against the bookcase in font of him. His grin growing wider as his hand heated up to the point of boiling. Stephen was on the other side of the bookcase and like a squad leader, Diego clenched his fist to signal the Idlers to stop. He then slowly spun on the spot and held a long finger to lips while gesturing to the blonde Idlers to go around, making it clear to them what his plan was. To approach from every corner and trap Stephen in the centre. It was obvious Stephen wasn't going to escape because his energy was weak and if he

85

could cross a fence he would have done so by now, meaning he was there for the taking.

Diego chuckled at how easy this was turning out and quickly forged a fence of his own, appearing a good twenty feet in the air as he moved round the bookcase. His eyes flaring up at the sight of Stephen sitting defeatedly in the shadows below. There was no reason for him to be this high. Stephen's capture was all but imminent, but that didn't mean he couldn't have a bit of fun first. He could see all the Idlers in place from this height. Their crimson glows closing in and he rubbed his hands together at a job well done, thinking of the praise awaiting him once he brought Stephen to Limbo. Although, he wanted to be the one to do it.

He leapt off his fence, hoping his emphatic entrance would scare Stephen to death or an angel's alternative anyway, but as he hurtled down, something was wrong. The shadows around Stephen turned bright. A bright emerald green. The Idlers stopping abruptly at the strange sight and as Diego thundered onto the carpet. The light had faded away... and Stephen was gone.

Diego clenched his shaking fists and pounded the bookcase in a fit of rage, causing hundreds of files to fall. 'What was that?' he shouted angrily at the Idlers expecting them to know the answer. 'Where did he go?'

Chapter 13

The voices had been gone for a few seconds now and David slowly lifted the cloth to assess the area. He listened intently for any ominous sounds, but the only noise he heard was from the buzzing above and so he swiftly exited from under the table. His body still feeling faint as he shuffled out on his haunches, wanting to keep as low as possible to be on the safe side. Despite being alone in the room, he still felt like he was being watched. As if there was a pair of hidden eyes somewhere keeping him on high alert like a fawn in a field, expecting danger at any moment. He gradually got to his feet, glaring in every direction to inspect the shadows. His eyes widening at the thousands of other tables in the room. All now clearly with bodies on. Were they angels or people? Where did they come from?

A loud buzz crackled across the room, making his body shudder and cause him look up at the giant bowl on the ceiling. His eyes drawn to the crimson energy swirling inside of it like a bottled up storm. So many questions in his mind, but he knew there was no time to investigate. All he wanted to do was get Grace out of there. He put all his thoughts to one side and ran towards the staircase, jumping up them two at a time onto the platform and then sprinted over to Grace. She had gashes all across her face and body with puffs of light weeping out of them. 'Grace? You okay?' he asked.

'David?' she croaked weakly, lifting her head. 'What are you doing here?'

'I'm here for you obviously!' He went to undo her binds, gritting his teeth in agony as he endured the familiar pain he'd experienced in the cave.

'But, how did you get here?'

'The same way you did. Now come on, I don't know how long we've got.'

'Where did the Idler go?'

'No idea. They left because of a M.G or something?'

'A M.G?' Grace's eyes widened as she rubbed her free wrists.

'Yeah... why?' David quizzed. 'What's a M.G?'

'They're who I was trying to tell you about. Who I've been looking for!' Grace replied.

'A mortal guardian,' a tired rusty voice spoke.

David turned to face the other G.A further along. His head face down to the platform with his eyes closed.

'Linus!' Grace exclaimed, sliding over to him on her knees. She grabbed the binds to try and free him, but yelped as she touched the energy.

'I got it,' David said, heading over to help.

'I'm so sorry, Linus, I didn't realise it was you,' Grace said, putting a hand on his shoulder.

'It's okay,' Linus replied, breathlessly. ' I wouldn't have expected you to, considering what they were doing.'

'The M.G?' Grace asked. 'Are they really here?'

'Yes, they're here and now the Idlers are after them.'

Grace covered her mouth with her hand, but David couldn't tell what emotions were flowing off her. It was like a mixture of panic, shock and excitement. 'What's a mortal guardian?' he asked, finally breaking through Linus's binds.

'A mortal, with angel qualities,' Linus spoke again, putting his hands on his lap. 'They have the ability to move between worlds freely, before death.'

'That's insane.' David frowned.

'It's a miracle,' Grace added. 'A miracle that has been forgotten about over time because no one has ever witnessed one before.'

'If no one has witnessed one, then, how do we know they are real?'

'Because... ' David frowned when Grace stopped mid-sentence as if changing her words. 'Some believe. I mean, the very prospect of their being someone out there who can keep the balance and be a bridge between worlds with the power of influencing fate itself. It is worth believing. The M.G can get rid of those stupid Idlers and bring peace and freedom back to the G.A.F. Allow G.As to do their jobs properly. Look out for everyone equally. They have the power to get you home.'

David's eyes lit up, but before he could say anything it was Linus who spoke next.

'Speaking of Idlers, you need to get going. They will return soon.'

'Yes, yes, we must go,' Grace said as David helped her to her feet. 'We can continue this later. Linus, come on.'

'No, I'm not going,' Linus coughed.

'What? Why not?' Grace asked.

'My only task was to protect the M.G and now, the events that are to come, they are outside of my control. I have done my bit.'

'But we can't let the Idlers get them!' Grace exasperated. 'They'll clip them and then they'll be gone for good.'

'It's your task now. Not mine.'

'Why is it ours?' David asked.

'Because that is what's written... isn't it Grace.' Linus finally opened his eyes to look at them both, revealing his dual coloured eyes of gold and sapphire. 'You need to go.'

'No, Linus, you're my only ally here. I can't lose you. How will I get by?'

'You'll be fine. You know what to do. Find the M.G. Protect them, teach them. Just as we spoke about once before. Don't let them get influenced by the wrong ones.'

David stood beside the tearful Grace, biting his lip helplessly. He did his best to follow what they were saying, but right now, he felt like a third wheel. He slowly turned his head to the bowl of energy again as the energy began crackling louder. Almost like it was warning them something was coming.

'Grace, we've got to go,' David said, putting his hand on her shoulder, but she was quickly pulled away from his touch as Linus started whispering something in her ear. He tried to listen in but all he heard him say was, 'just incase, take this.' David stared at the pair of them with sunken eyes. Noticing Linus pass her something small which she quickly tucked into her trouser pocket.

'Now go. Before they return. I'll be fine,' Linus spoke louder, finally letting Grace go.

'Okay, okay, which way?' Grace wept.

'Which way?' a voice thundered across the room. 'You're not leaving?'

David gripped hold of Grace's wrist and pulled her behind him as a figure appeared on the platform. 'You again!' he loured at Diego entering into view.

'Yes.' Diego pointed a long finger at him. 'How did you get here? Do you not remember my warning, boy?'

'I remember, just don't care.' David shrugged.

'Hmm, perhaps this will make you care. Clip him!'

'Linus!' Grace shrieked, reaching out a hand as Linus's body suddenly lit up in a bright sapphire, glowing brighter and brighter to the point where he was no longer visible within the twinkling energy, and then, the light burst into stardust. Linus was gone.

'See, that could be you.' Diego continued to march forward. 'If only G.As could just listen properly and follow the rules, then these things wouldn't happen.'

'You're a monster!' Grace shouted.

'No I'm not. He'd run out of use. Just like you have. There's been a place in Idle for you for a long, long time.'

'So you keep saying!' Grace shouted back.

'The only reason we kept you around this time was because of this one.' Diego flicked his head at David. 'But, now you're both here, might as well get this over with.'

David continued to shield Grace as Diego got closer. His eyes widening as he spotted a blade appearing in Diego's hand.

'Do you even know what you're doing?' Grace asked.

'I'm following orders.'

'To what purpose? What are you gaining from acting like this?' But Diego remained silent. His snarl fading from his face. 'You have no idea do you. You're blind to it all.'

Suddenly, a wave of energy shot out of the blade towards Grace and David immediately swivelled on the spot to take the blow. The energy crashed into his chest like a taser and he collapsed to the ground. Rings of crimson flowing over his body like constricting vines.

'Well, that was stupid.' Diego scowled, his red eyes glaring down at him. 'And who do you think you are to question me?' Diego bellowed at Grace. 'You want an answer? How about power. Control. Everything happens for a reason and no one needs to know what that reason is. It is fate! And that's all there is to it!'

'Whatever you are trying to achieve, you wont succeed. Idle is for failures and as an Idler... well, you're the perfect role model for them aren't you.'

There was a eerie quietness in the room.

'Perhaps,' Diego finally growled. 'But we both know you are too!'

David could only watch as Diego stepped over his restricted body, grimacing at the electrical pain scorching his skin. He rolled his eyes over his head to see Diego and four other Idlers close in on Grace from every angle, but yet she seemed reluctant to run. She just stood there bravely, her aura flickering, her hands held out in front of her preparing for the inevitable attack, but surely she didn't have a chance?

Desperate to do something, he urged his body with all his might to break free, doing his upmost to break through the sizzling coils. His blood boiling in anger. His jaw clenched. Steam floated off his head as if the bowl of energy on the ceiling was a hot red sun cooking him alive. Its rays making his body go hotter and hotter... Bang!

The energy exploded off him and out the bowl like a crimson flash bomb and surged across the room like a solar storm. The coils fizzled away off his body and he sprung back to his feet. He immediately ran towards Grace who had been knocked over by the blast, as had Diego and the other Idlers.

'Grace,' he said as he picked her up. His body instantly cooling the moment he touched her. Her body was so light it was like carrying a pillow. 'I got you,' he whispered. He stood there anxiously. His legs shaking as he didn't know where to go. This was their domain and he had no idea which way was out.

He suddenly heard groaning and his pulse quickened as he saw Diego slowly getting back to his feet. The vortex behind him whirred into life, spinning faster and faster. Bolts of crimson shooting out of it like unstable fusion. He saw Diego summon his blade back and head straight for him. Almost diving in slow motion and when David looked at Grace's unconscious body in his arms, only one thought came to mind. He had to risk it. *I hope this works.*

Just as Diego shunted the blade towards them, he jumped into the vortex.

Chapter 14

David immediately found himself floating across an infinitive inferno. The blazing heat incinerating his body and causing his skin to flake off and combust into crimson ash among the flames. Bit by bit, he watched as a little part of him disappeared. His feet and ankles were the first to perish and now his knees and shoulders were quickly disintegrating too. Despite the conditions however, his insides were growing cold. It was as if his very soul was being excavated out of him and being persuaded to join the other millions of ghostly screams which were sweeping through his ears.

He held Grace as close to his chest as he possibly could, wishing he could still feel her warmth against him, but the conditions were too extreme and she too, was beginning to perish. Despite his attempts, he couldn't shield her from what was happening. His eyes sizzled as if the heat was evaporating his tears before they even had a chance to form and he gazed down helplessly at her sleeping face. An angel in his arms and yet he was incompetent of helping her. He needed a miracle.

Eventually, his hands disappeared into the furnace and Grace began to drift away from him. He did everything he could to retrieve her, but he was trying to move limbs that were no longer there. It didn't stop him trying though, with only one arm and his torso he dived down towards her, reaching out an invisible hand in a desperate attempt to catch her again.

A pair of giant crimson eyes suddenly appeared in the flames below them. Eyes of such villainy, David thought he could feel himself combusting there and then. The hallowing screams got louder and soon he saw a strong current of souls swirling downwards like water in a drain, and Grace was very close to it, making David swim harder and faster. Even when he had no arms left, he still felt as though he could reach her and after a few more seconds, his miracle appeared.

There was a fence. A blue sapphire fence. It was so close to him he could hear it chiming like a glass harp melody. He looked down at Grace's falling body. Only her head and shoulders now visible and he knew he had to try. He jolted his head towards the fence, feeling the strain of all his neck muscles and head butted the rail. The sapphire glow immediately engulfed him. It's energy reconstructing his nerves and bones until he was simply a glowing crystal skeleton, but he had control again and he pushed himself away from the fence and swam straight for Grace, cutting through the inferno like an indestructible icicle. He hooked his arm under Grace's shoulder and pulled her away from the deathly current, fighting its watery suction as he powered back towards the fence. The pair of eyes watching him the whole time. He grabbed hold of the fence rail and carried Grace over to escape the tortuous nightmare and passed out on the other side.

Chapter 15

Once Grace and the boy had decided to perish in the vortex, Diego returned to his favoured island. He prowled along the charcoal sky with his hands cupped behind his back, half-hoping Stephen might have been here, but he was left disappointed. He'd ordered the Idlers to continue monitoring the library and report any findings of his whereabouts, but since their last encounter there he seemed to have vanished off the radar.

Diego replayed the moment in his head, gripping his wrists tighter as he thought about how Stephen had got away. *He was trapped! I had an Idler on every corner of that bookcase. I had him covered from above. How did he escape? What was that green light?* He hated the fact he didn't know and worst of all, he hated how Grace was right. He didn't know what was going on. He didn't know what a M.G was and he didn't know why that made Stephen special. He shouldn't need to know either, but now there were too many mysteries for his liking. Once he'd been blessed with this spectacular Idler power, he thought he'd be on top of it all. Be the angel to fix things and control the G.A.F as needed, but he still felt second best to all the other G.As who were running around cluelessly and the more he dwelled on it, the louder his energy crackled.

Suddenly, his ears pricked up as he sensed a sinful energy. A rule was being broken and this time, he wasn't going to stand by. He swivelled on his crimson fence and appeared above a sandy coastline, glaring around the vicinity in search for G.As. To his left was the busy clay-red promenade, lit up in an aquamarine glow from the faint fairy lights hanging overhead on both sides. At first there was no sign of a G.A, but then a sudden tingle flowed over his fingertips and he darted his head towards the beach. 'Got you.'

There was a G.A over the shoreline and Diego immediately strolled over to them. His hands tucked behind his back. 'Uh-Hmm.' A smirk spread on his face as he watched an older G.A fearfully bolt up on his yellow fence and nervously fold his arms over his gut. 'What's happening here?' Diego spoke strongly.

'N-nothing...' the G.A answered. 'I-I'm just looking over those people.' He pointed at the small group of young adults partying in the shallows of the sea. Their loud music blaring out.

'I don't think that's true.' Diego raised his eyebrows.

'W-what do you mean?'

'Energy has been overused here. I can sense it, and the group you speak of, their minds are too focussed to be influenced. So who did you help?'

'I...'

'Was it her?' He pointed at the lonely figure of a tall slim girl further up the beach. Her body wrapped up in a pink sarong while sitting at the water's edge. 'I can tell her energy has been influenced. So, what did you do?'

'I... I persuaded her to come here,' the G.A replied almost apologetically. 'I guided her here to meet her sister. She is from a broken family and I am trying to help... re-rebuild.'

'I see, and is that what their fate suggests you do?' He watched the G.A's eyes twitch frantically. 'I thought not.'

'P-please, I have not done much. Fate was leading them here eventually, I promise. Her sister, she is not right. She is very lost. I can help both.'

'I understand.' Diego nodded.

'You do?'

'Yes, I do. The thing is though, that's not what you're here for, is it?'

96

'N-no, b-but I must. Her sister is on the path to Idle and I can change that, through her. You see?' The G.A pointed to a younger girl trekking across the sand in their direction. She had no shoes on her feet and was wearing a pair of ripped denim shorts with a dirty black crop top. 'She comes here most nights.'

Diego stared at the younger sister and focussed on her energy. She was on the path to Idle alright. He could sense the sinful anger inside of her. Whatever her past was it had moulded her well and now her mind was closed off to any influences.

'How strange.' He smirked, sensing an opportunity.

'W-what?'

'She can be helped, you are right.'

'Really? Oh, thank you, thank you.' The G.A put his hands gratefully over his chest. 'I knew.'

'Not by you, though.'

'Qué?'

'We must help her on her current path, fates path, and you have disobeyed the rules of the G.A.F in attempt to deviate her from this.'

'No, no!'

'Yes. Therefore, I hereby banish you from the G.A.F.'

Before the G.A could defend himself, Diego flicked his wrist and stabbed them in the chest, causing their body to implode in a burst of crimson light.

'Stupid do-gooder,' he spat as he put his blade away. 'Now, lets see if I can correct this.' He rubbed his hands together and swivelled around on his fence to get closer to the girl in the sarong and appeared just in front of her over the gentle sea. 'Let's have some fun.'

He pointed his palms down at the waves. Crimson smoke pouring down his arms and into the water. It had been a long time since he'd tried controlling an environment. Once upon a time it would have been a regular occurrence, especially during the early days when naval warfare and sea explorations were more common, but like many things, these abilities soon dwindled. As the G.A.F progressed through the years, a G.As abilities diminished, but now, with this power surging through him, he felt stronger than ever.

Soon, the sea within a two-metre radius of him began to swish around as if it was reaching boiling point. The energy he'd poured in acted like a physical presence in the water and he watched it excitedly as it mimicked his movements, manipulating the sea at his will. He then clashed his hands together, causing a pair of waves to collide with a mighty crash. 'Amazing!' he chuckled.

Still focussing on his energy, he swung his arms back and forth to push the tide further and further up the beach. The waves creeping closer to the girl's feet the faster he moved, thrashing about as if there was a shiver of sharks in the water.

An abnormal energy lingered in the air as his actions attracted the interest of the party of people further down and he knew he'd have to stop soon. The amount of energy he was using was beginning to drain him anyway, but he couldn't stop. He didn't want to. So obsessed with the power he wanted to keep going. He wanted to generate the highest wave possible. Maybe even wash the girl into the sea. The very thought caused his mind to flash back to the monstrous waves he used to sail through when he was alive. The amount of seaman lost to the ocean's hunger and that's when he stopped. He released his control of the water and caught his breath as he watched the sea calm back to a mere trickle up the sand. *That's not the way to resolve this.*

He stared at the younger sister in the crop top and synced with her energy again. Now sensing room for influence as she had obviously seen her sister waiting for her. This was the moment the G.A was waiting for. To infiltrate her mind and convince her this reunion was going to help her. To get them talking and bring her off her path, but he knew that wasn't right. Her sister wasn't meant to be here and so this reunion shouldn't happen. It soon didn't matter, however. 'Go on. Go for it!' Diego sneered.

The girl continued to approach her sister, who was oblivious to her presence and inspecting the water by Diego's feet, but rather than saying anything, she slowly knelt down to pick up her sister's light blue handbag and just stared at it in her hands.

'Go on!' Diego urged her. 'Go on!'

Suddenly, a curious bystander who'd been venturing over to investigate the sea for themselves saw what was happening and shouted. 'Oi! That's not yours! Quick! She's stealing her purse!'

The young girl immediately ran away with the purse clutched in her grasp as a couple of people chased after her, making Diego chuckle as he watched her evade everyone and disappear down the narrow streets of the market on the other side of the promenade. 'Good girl. You'll be just fine.'

Diego transported to higher ground afterwards and folded his arms proudly at his work. Now taking the time to enjoy the ocean view for himself. Although, his moment was soon interrupted as he heard a couple of other G.As talking.

'Well, that was odd. Did you see that, Mary?'

'Yes, very strange. I wonder where Alonso has got to. I'm sure he was here. He kept going on about trying to help that family.'

'Looks like she is too far gone now.'

'Shame really.'

'Yes, it really is, Martha.'

Diego looked down to see a pair of G.As sitting a few metres below him. Both of them older women with white and grey hair.

'It was so close to working too, I honestly thought they'd have patched things up after tonight.'

'It was her path!' Diego growled, jumping down in front of them. His fence buzzing loudly as he slammed his feet onto the crackling crimson rail. He waited a few seconds to soak in the fear on the G.As faces before saying, 'she shouldn't have been influenced!'

'An Idler!' Martha gasped, then she slowly pointed a finger at him. 'Is that?'

'Yes it is, Mary! You're the one who got that little girl killed!'

Diego snarled like a vicious dog.

'Was this you as well!? What is your problem?'

He glared at them bewilderedly, unable to get a word in.

'Where's Alonso?'

'What did you do to him?'

'Like everyone else who breaks the rules, he has been banished!' Diego finally spoke.

'No!' Both G.As put a hand to their mouth.

'You are a disgraceful angel!' Martha spat.

'It's your kind that cause this world issues you know,' Mary added, pointing fingers. 'Peace will never remain as long as there are people and angels like you around. Why can't you just let us do our jobs properly!'

'I mean, honestly, what do you hope to gain by all this?'

The two ladies leaned forward with scowling faces awaiting Diego's defence, but he had grown tired of the same conversation. How many more times did he have to explain the rules? How many more times did he have to remind everyone what the G.A.F's actual job was? It was easier to just stay quiet, and act accordingly.

He quickly flicked his wrist to wield the blade back in his hand and threw it into Mary's chest. Her fence and body immediately burst like an overpowered lightbulb and then he glanced at Martha, watching her squirm on her fence. 'Do what you must,' she croaked. 'This wont end well for you.'

'I beg to differ.' Diego summoned his blade back. 'It's not going to end well for you.' Again, he threw the blade, smiling as he watched her light vanish from the sky. 'Good riddance.'

'Diego!' Amb. Ermêl's voice screeched in his ears and he was suddenly transported back in front of the vortex.

'What?' Diego thrusted his arms in the air.

'You know what! I told you not to clip G.As!' Amb. Ermêl shouted through the speeding energy.

'But they were breaking the rules. Is that not what an Idler's job is?' Diego argued.

'An Idler's job is whatever I say it is! The balance of the G.A.F must remain! I cannot risk awakening Divinity. Not yet! Only G.As who break rules of a severe nature get clipped.'

'What, like Grace? How long were you going to let that stupid angel get away with it for!?'

'Enough!' The room shook as sparks flew out of the vortex. 'Do not test me Diego. Remember I got you out of Idle. I can put you back!'

Suddenly Diego found himself being sucked towards the vortex as if it were a black hole. Helpless to its gravitational pull like metal to a magnet. 'Is this what you want to experience?' Amb. Ermêl's voice echoed out as Diego now found himself floating inside the giant inferno. His Idle energy defenceless against the scorching heat as he watched his skin melt off his hands and that wasn't the worse bit. The crackling infinite fire began to morph in a lash of flames while he spun like meat on a spit. The continuous sounds of gun shots and explosions roared out among the screaming. Two fiery silhouettes running around him. A father and son, blasting their pistols, swinging their swords.

'Remember the rule son. What is our one rule?' He heard his father's drunken words.

'Don't feel. Just do.'

'That's right. That's how we survive. It's us against the world, son. We are all that matter.'

'No. No stop this!' Diego murmured, but there was no escaping for his arms and legs had disappeared and he had no strength to move.

The fire quickly caved in on itself like a tsunami to create a new scene depicting a boat and knowing what was coming Diego tried to close his eyes, but he couldn't. It was like his eyelids had been scorched off, forcing him to watch.

The same two silhouettes of flames were now running up and down the deck. A sinister fire roaring in his ears as he pictured the shipwreck they had just caused. 'Hurry son!' His father shouted, wanting him to hide the loot they'd stolen in the keep. 'Hurry!' His father was about to take the helm when an intruder burst out of the fire as if jumping from the wreckage and kicked him to the deck. Their sword drawn. He watched the fiery figures fight furiously. So much aggression in their attacks as one was desperate to kill the other. A couple more swings and the intruder collapsed. His father finishing him off right in front of him. A cry of agony bellowing out.

The intruder's silhouette then vanished into the abyss of flames as his father toppled the body over the side. 'I'll be back son,' his father said as he jumped off the boat into the flames. Fulfilling his obsession of not leaving any survivors and a few seconds later another body was dumped on board. A child. His father walked past the small silhouette towards him and handed over his sword. He reluctantly took it. Stepping closer and closer to the cowering silhouette. Despite it now being flames, Diego could still picture the young girl's face. So innocent. So scared. He watched his silhouette back away, shaking his head, but his father insisted and when he still didn't comply, a scuffle broke out. His father pulling him about like an empty sack and throwing him down on the deck to steal the sword back. First he slashed the sword at his neck and then raised it above the girl and in that split second, Diego had grabbed the intruder's sword and plunged it into his father's back. He collapsed hysterically onto his knees as he watched his father die in front of him.

Diego wanted it to end there. It was as though it was only his eyes left as he couldn't even conjure any words to speak, but the fire continued to torture him and showed him the aftermath of the girl approaching him. She tried to comfort him, but staring at his distorted silhouette it was like he was feeling the pain all over again. He remembered how angry and confused he was. How disjointed his mind had become, like something had snapped inside his very soul.

He watched his silhouette shove her away and grab her by the hair. He dragged her flailing body to the edge of the boat and pushed her back onto the flaming wreckage before sailing away. His father's body still on board. The child's sobbing cry calling out for miles and miles. *'Please. Don't leave me! Please!'*

In that moment the fire seemed to race past him and he smacked down onto the metallic platform, like being spat out of a monster's mouth. Diego laid completely still, staring at his reconstructed body. His Idle energy returning as if its electricity had kickstarted his heart. He eventually managed to pick himself up and dusted down his suit, he aligned his sleeves and straightened his tie just as Amb. Ermêl spoke once again. 'Have you learned your lesson.'

'Yes,' Diego hissed not looking up.

'Good. I admire your desire Diego. That is why you were chosen for this. The time will come for us to cleanse the sky, but not yet! Focus on the M.G!'

'The M.G... Stephen vanished in a puff of green smoke... why do we need him? Surely he's useless to us with a blank mind?'

'His mind is blank for a reason. That's why his file is hidden here.' Like a villainous spotlight the energy on the ceiling shone down over a vacant table and illuminated a file. 'It's his essence I need.'

'Essence? What do you mean?' Diego asked, teleporting over to the file and flicking through its pages.

'You want to control the G.A.F? Restore it to its authoritative glory? First I need to be freed.'

'You are a prisoner?'

'Yes. Stuck here in my own realm. Unable to escape. Unable to influence. The M.G holds the energy from all the realms that imprisoned me and with it, these chains can be broken.'

'I see,' Diego said still reading the file. 'So what now? How do I find him?'

'Green smoke, you say...' there was a slight pause. 'It seems a little more patience is required, but a moment will present itself soon. So make sure you are ready.'

The voice disappeared and Diego was left alone. His experience in the inferno had left his body and soul beaten and bruised as he slumped back to the floor, dropping the file. Those images. Those memories. They had been buried for so long, but you can never truly escape your sins. Never.

Chapter 16

'Ugh!' David sat up holding his pounding head. His body warm and tingly as if he'd just got out of a hot bath. 'What was all that about? Where was I? I...' he stopped mid-sentence as a wave of excitement washed over him. 'Yes!' he said, patting his legs and chest. 'I'm back. I'm back!' However, realising he was alone, he quickly scanned the dark room in search for Grace and sighed in relief when he saw her laying a couple of metres away. He slid across the slate floor to check on her and hovered a hand over her dim body, caught in two minds whether to touch her or not, but in the end he thought better of it. She was clearly breathing and that was good enough for him. Rest was what she needed and besides, her glow was already getting brighter. *She'll be fine. No need to worry,* he told himself.

He rolled away and put his head in his hands, rubbing his tired eyes. It had all been non-stop since they found the boy in the river and it was beginning to take its toll, but once again he was in an unfamiliar location and he wanted to investigate. He picked himself up and began to explore the odd circular room. It was approximately ten metres in diameter and had a horrible dungeon feel to it as there were no windows or doors in sight. The only source of light came from a ghostly white glow in the centre which he headed towards and the closer he got, the more he could feel a calming breeze being emitted from it, like walking outside on a crisp spring morning. Now he was within touching distance he could see a peculiar opal orb half-embedded in the stone floor which looked like a shrunken moon the size of a beachball. Its energy gently wafting over him. The orb was so mysterious and wonderful he couldn't help but want to touch it and as he crouched down to place his palms upon it... it burst into life.

The orb flashed the bright colours of orange, purple, red and green. Illuminating the room into four equal segments with sparkling gems corresponding to the colours outlining each one. There were even twinkling diamonds now circling the orb itself. 'This is cool,' David said, heading over to examine the quadrants more closely like an adventurer discovering a lost temple.

Firstly, Grace was now laying in a quadrant outlined by shiny emeralds, with an image of an oak tree illuminating in the middle of the stone wall. Next, going anti-clockwise was a quadrant surrounded by amethysts with an image of a whale, followed by a citrine zone with an image of a bottle. The last quadrant was glistening in rubies however, the image on the wall remained dark. 'Strange.' He went to run his hand along the carving to try and figure it out, but before he put his hand on it the green quadrant suddenly turned fluorescent with a mighty bang. The light blinding him. 'Grace?' he called out, trying to shield his eyes as he went over. 'Grace?'

The second he stepped inside the glow he was sucked into an emerald whirlpool and fell down an infinitive green sky, being propelled about like a parachute caught in crosswinds, until eventually... thump.

He landed on a glistening green fence stuck high in the sky. The ground barely visible beneath him. *Not sure how much more of this I can take,* he thought as he sat up, rubbing his winded stomach. *I'm never getting home at this rate.*

From this height it was like he had entered a new world. A large lime green sun beamed down from the moss-coloured sky and lit up what looked like a meadow below him. Tall bushy trees circled it from about two hundred metres out with a lonely oak tree in the very centre.

A small bird suddenly swooped past him, causing him to lose his balance and fall off the fence. With a hint of panic he braced himself for impact, but puffed out in relief as he landed on the cushioning olive green grass by the oak tree. It was like he'd fallen into a painting as the selection of colourful wildflowers scattered around him dazzled like an impressionists artwork; consisting of yellow buttercups and daffodils, white daisies, purple corn-cockles, blue columbines and red poppies. All vividly standing out from the greenery with their own unique floral perfume which tickled his nose. A tame breeze blew through his hair as the small bird came back into view again. A green-breasted robin. It hopped across his legs and round the tree trunk bringing his attention to Grace who was laying in the grass amongst a patch of daisies and dandelions. Small lilac and blue butterflies fluttering above her body with the robin perched on her left wrist.

'Grace?' he whispered, squatting down beside her. Her injuries now non-existent as her glow had fully returned and now, she looked more beautiful than ever. He went to move some stray hairs out of her eyes when they suddenly fluttered open and he quickly shuffled back.

'David?' she spoke groggily, rubbing her forehead as she rose. The robin now flying away into the sky. 'Where are we? What happened?'

'Umm.' He scratched his shoulder. 'Quite a lot has happened to be honest. What's the last thing you remember?'

'I... remember being in Limbo. You were there... Linus, gone,' she choked up a little. 'There was a bang and... that's it. Now I'm here. Where are we?'

'I have no idea. I was hoping you knew.'

'It looks like.' Grace sat up to get a better look. 'No it can't be. How did we get here? How did we escape Limbo?'

'I don't really know that either,' David replied, sitting down and resting his back against the tree trunk. 'I picked you up and jumped through the vortex thing. That was a weird place I can tell you. Then, we ended up in this really peculiar room,' he laughed almost hysterically. 'Gems everywhere with these weird cave drawings on the walls and then we got sucked into a green portal and... here we are.' He looked back into Grace's confused eyes. Her eyebrows raised and mouth slightly open. 'Yeah, I know the feeling,' David chuckled.

'I... what?' Grace exclaimed. 'I don't know about the room, but the vortex... David that was the Inferno of Sin.'

'The what?' David widened his eyes at its sinister name.

'Inferno of Sin. It's the way to Idle after death. Rather than entering the Tavern, those who die, 'evil' shall we say, go through there and are tortured with the sins of their past.'

'Oh, I see. Well. We're here now.' David changed the subject not really knowing what to say.

'Yes we are.'

David picked at the grass as they rested quietly for a bit, but after a while he couldn't help but ask. 'Grace. When am I likely to get back?'

'Back?'

'To my mum,' he emphasised. 'I have no idea how long I've been gone already and If I'd known it would have taken this long, then...'

'Then what?' Grace interrupted him. 'Would you not have helped me?'

David stared at her large questioning eyes and knew that wasn't the case. He would have always offered to help her because that's who he is. He just wished he'd get the reward of it sooner. 'No, I would still have come. I just...'

'I know.' Grace reached out a hand on to his foot. 'But at least now you know who we are looking for and why. You understand the magnitude of this?'

'I do.'

'Good. Because, honestly David, I know we haven't known each other long, but I'm beginning to think I can't do this without you.'

David felt a lovely warmth elevate his mood. 'Thank you.'

'Once I figure out where we are, I'll make a plan and get us back on track, I promise. I just. I wouldn't mind resting for a bit.'

'Okay.' David bit his lip. After everything that had happened he understood her wanting to rest, but did they really need to? Why couldn't they crack on? The sooner they find this M.G the sooner he could get home. 'I'm going to take a look around.' David got to his feet. 'See what I can find out.'

'Alright. Don't go too far,' Grace replied, laying down as if she was enjoying a summer picnic.

'Okay.'

David headed through the long rustling grass. A light buzzing coming from the bugs hidden inside. Under different circumstances this place would have been amazing to spend time in, especially with Grace. He pictured himself laying beside her by the tree and looking up at the mossy sky. Her hand in his. Then, he got to grips with what he was feeling. 'Come on, David. Sort it out,' he told himself. 'She's an angel and you need to get home. That's it. Be of use then go. Don't get attached,' he sighed heavily. 'It wouldn't work anyway.'

Putting his thoughts to bed, he suddenly saw something poking out of the grass. Something that looked like a tail? He slowly stepped backwards not wanting to disturb anything he shouldn't, but it was too late. A loud growl reverberated through the grass and David raced back towards Grace, not daring to look back.

'Are you okay?' Grace called out, seeing him run.

'There's...' David got within an arms length of Grace when something suddenly leapt out of the grass and caused him to fall to the ground on his back. Grace's hands were now on his shoulders as if she was trying to pull him away. His body tensed up at the sight of the lioness. Its deep emerald eyes glaring at him. Its body rippling with green energy. Its large pointy ears twitching as it stalked towards them, licking its lips.

'Go!' David shouted at Grace.

'Not without you!' she replied just as strongly.

The Lioness crept closer and closer. Close enough that David could feel its strange minty breath on his face. The smell of grass and flowers floated off its coat and then, it licked him.

Grace dropped her hold on David in a fit of giggles as he screwed his face up at the slobber dripping down his cheeks. The animal now sitting down in front of him like a playful pet.

'I wasn't expecting that,' David said, wiping his face clean. He then watched as the lioness disappeared in a puff of green smoke and in its place stood a tall, lean woman. She was laughing excitedly in a strapless forest green dress, which twinkled beneath the lime sun. 'Did I get you?' she asked, walking towards him.

'Yes. A little,' David replied, staring at her wrinkled face plastered in pale green lipstick and eyeshadow. The same colour as her headdress which was also covered in tiny animal symbols.

'Good, I like a bit of fun.' The woman smiled. 'My name is Rev. Lionesminntat. Don't worry, I know it's a bit of a mouthful, you can call me Rev. Li.' She winked.

David and Grace shared a curious look as if the same question was on their minds and it was Grace who asked it. 'Rev. Li. Where are we?'

'My Dear, this is Eden.'

'Eden?' David questioned.

'Yes, that is what I said young man.'

'I'm surprised your name isn't Eve then,' David joked, but quickly regretted it.

'I'm nothing like that silly woman thank you and If you call me that again I'll eat you!' Rev. Li bared her teeth playfully, or so David hoped.

'I thought this was Eden.' Grace smiled. 'But there has been no mention of this place in over a century so I presumed it had gone.'

'Oh no Dear, not gone. Just well protected by its guardian.' Rev. Li winked again.

'Its guardian being you, obviously?' Grace said.

'Obviously.' Rev. Li shook her head proudly. 'And you two are more than welcome here. All I ask is that you don't harm the environment or its inhabitants otherwise I will cast you out, okay?'

'Okay,' David said.

'Okay,' Grace also replied. 'Why does Eden need a guardian?'

'All four realms have guardians My Dear and this is mine. After certain events it was decided to keep this place hidden from prying eyes. So now, only those in need of Eden are invited in.'

'We are in need of Eden?' David asked.

'Oh yes, I believe you are.' Rev. Li's smile grew wider. 'Shall we all get going?'

'Where to?' Grace asked.

'I didn't bring you here for nothing, Dear. Things are beginning to happen, just as they did before.'

'Yes,' Grace said tearfully. 'Linus told me, before...'

'I know, Dear. I know. Must have been difficult for you.' Rev. Li put a hand on Grace's shoulder, making her emerald beaded bracelet rattle.

David, meanwhile, just stood there quietly rubbing his shoulder. He had no idea what they were talking about and didn't know whether he was allowed to ask. The pair of them seemed to be having a moment and he didn't want to interrupt it, but at the same time, he didn't like being left out. As the two of them kept talking he tried to keep up with the conversation, but he couldn't concentrate and just stood there patiently. Half expecting, half hoping, they'd explain things to him in a minute or so, but the next thing he knew, Rev. Li had transformed back into her lioness form and began to walk away with Grace on her shoulders.

David scowled at them as they headed off into the long grass, his body shaking from pent up energy as he wanted to shout at them. What were they doing? Did they expect him to follow? Perhaps he should do his own exploring and meet up with them later?

'Are you coming, David?' Grace's voice called out.

I suppose I am, then! 'Yeah, I'll catch up,' he called back. *Don't know where to or why, but sure. Not like I've known what's been happening this far... I just want to go home.*

Chapter 17

Ever since they left the meadow and entered the surrounding woodlands, David knew there was something special about Eden. There was a source of magic in the air connecting him to everything as if he'd gone inside natures consciousness. The dusty dirt beneath his feet; the squeaking squirrels leaping overhead; the lime-light streaming through the thin trees. He could feel their energies linking to his, like small streams joining a rolling river, making him feel fresh and clean.

What started out as a leisurely walk however, soon turned into a tiring hike as the woodland expanded. The skinny beech and ash trees faded away and were being replaced by denser firs and spruces. Some towering up so high they blocked the light from shining down through the canopy. It was now obvious he was in a greater scaled forest with pinecones and pine needles scattered across the earthy floor. It was like something equivalent to the baron lands of Siberia as even the temperature was dropping by the second and snow began to fall.

Grace and Rev. Li had disappeared a long time ago and he was having to rely on the faint footprints in the mud to follow them. At first it didn't bother him too much, but the more congested the trees got, the harder it was to keep on track. His suit jacket kept getting tangled up in the spiky branches and the amount of times he lost his footing on the raised roots was beginning to annoy him. The noises didn't help either as the cute sounds of the woodland had turned more sinister, especially with the haunting owl hoots echoing around him and it always felt like there was something watching him, or someone. The whole experience was now putting him on edge as all he wanted to do was get out or at least see Grace and Rev. Li again. It felt like ages since he last saw them. How did they even know he was still following and not lost somewhere? Nevertheless, he kept walking, knowing it was the right thing to do and assumed he'd catch up eventually.

While wrestling his way round a thick trunk, he suddenly slipped on its roots and clumps of snow fell on his head from the branches above. 'Urgh, great!' he said, untucking his shirt to shake out what was sliding down his back. The amount of snow on the ground had increased a lot in the past few minutes and there were now more paw prints visible, but they weren't the same as Rev. Li's. He slowly got up and gazed around at the surrounding trees. Had he been following the wrong ones?

'Grace? Rev. Li?' he called out, but the trees were quick to swallow up his words. 'That's not ideal.' He rubbed his shoulder and continued on the route he was on, ignoring the unfamiliar trail. The snow continued to fall over him more constantly now and got deeper and deeper with every crunching footstep. His legs began to tire from dragging them through the powder, which was now up to his calves. Even the wind appeared against him as it got stronger and colder and tried to blow him backwards.

'Grace?' he called out again, hoping they hadn't gotten too far ahead, but there was still no reply. *I assume they know I've fallen behind. Will they come back for me or shall I keep going?* David stopped to think about it for only a second as he knew what the answer was. *Come on David, keep going.*

He wrapped his jacket around his shivering body and tried to ignore his cold wet feet which were beginning to get uncomfortable. Thankfully, he could now see a green glow up ahead and as he exited the tree line he saw Rev. Li once again with Grace still on her shoulders.

'There you are,' Rev. Li spoke. 'We wondered where'd you'd got to.'

'I'm still here,' David replied without looking at them. 'Two legs is obviously slower than four. Especially when you don't know where you're going.'

'Perhaps you should try using all four of yours then,' Rev. Li said.

David frowned. 'What do you mean?'

'Just a thought.' Rev. Li started walking away. 'Come on. Got a fair way to go yet.'

'Where exactly are we going?' He looked up at Grace's vacant expression. She looked as though she'd been crying. *Whats going on with her?*

'You'll see when we get there. Come on.'

David followed a few paces behind as he crossed the tundra terrain, gazing out at the white mountains in the distance to the East. After a short while though, the mountains appeared more like enormous glass glaciers, reflecting the last of the sunlight before the sky got dominated by more snow clouds. Without the sun around, the walk was more like an expedition to the North Pole as he trekked through a blinding blizzard with tiny icicles stabbing away at his skin. His arms clutched around his shivering sides to try and conserve some warmth. His energy was so low he didn't try to speak. He didn't even think as he was totally focussed on putting one foot in front of the other. Already, he'd fallen behind Rev. Li. Her glow vanishing into the storm, but as long as he walked in a straight line he should be okay.

A short while later he spotted something out towards where the glaciers were. He moved a numb, furry-feeling hand above his eyes and squinted through the storm, seeing what looked like an igloo camouflaged in the landscape. *That's bizarre.* His thought was quickly distracted however, as he heard loud squawking from up ahead. It was like a choir of poorly playing kazoos and as he walked a little further, he stumbled upon a colony of penguins. They were all huddled up in a circle to protect themselves from the blizzard and he knew if it wasn't for the fact he was freezing, he would have enjoyed the moment a lot more.

The temperature slowly started to creep up again as he left the icy habitat and the winds died down. He wiped the melting frost from his chapped face and stared down at the snow which appeared to be gradually changing colour. Bit by bit the surrounding snowflakes turned into sand molecules and the white landscape turned golden. The glaciers turned to dunes as the lime sun suddenly exploded back up from the horizon, turning his body from freezing to melting in a matter of seconds.

This is ridiculous, he thought as he took off his jacket and undid his tie, wiping the stream of sweat pouring off his forehead. 'Why are we putting up with this? Why is it so far away? Why... just why?' he tried to laugh, but he was exhausted and placed his clammy hands on his thighs for a quick breather. A herd of camels suddenly sailed past him with a loud grumble as if they were judging him. 'Alright, alright,' he called over to them. 'I'll keep going.'

He puffed out his cheeks as he watched a small scorpion scatter past and then, he began to move again, dragging his heels through the sand. Funky shaped cacti appeared around him like a plant-based crowd cheering him on. He chuckled deliriously as he pictured their branches waving joyfully at him and he raised a hand of acknowledgment to them all, turning as he walked to make sure they could all see him. 'At least someone is supporting me,' he laughed, wiping a dollop of sweat off his chin.

Eventually the desert had transformed into something more like the plains of Africa. The cacti were no longer present and were instead replaced with the tall, dry grass of the savanna. Its crispiness scratching away at his arms. However, he was just thankful he was walking on solid ground again and his feet weren't sinking with every step for the sand was now a dusty mud track. It took him a little while to adjust to the new terrain, so much so, he nearly fell over as a loud trumpet noise echoed over the plains. A flock of yellow barbets taking to the sky as a result. *No way!* He picked up the pace as he approached the brow of a small hill and immediately came to a stop. 'Oh, wow!' he said, collapsing to the ground.

The lime sun lit up the vast busy grassland below, scattered with thick baobab trees. Herds of zebra, buffalo and wildebeest were grazing between the small shrubs as far as the eye could see. A troop of ostriches sprinting through them and leaving a trail of dust in their wake. What he was really in awe of though, was the parade of elephants authoritatively marching along like the generals of the animal kingdom they are.

'It's quite something isn't it?'

David turned around to see Rev. Li taking a seat next to him in her human form. Her dress sparkling brightly in the sun.

'Where's Grace?' David asked.

'Don't worry, she's around. I thought we could all do with a little break.' Rev. Li closed her eyes to soak in the sun's rays. 'She's over there if you wanted to speak to her.'

David looked over to his right to see her happily stroking the leg of a giraffe while it ate leaves from a wide acacia tree. 'Is she alright?'

'I should think so, why do you ask?'

'She looked upset earlier.'

'Don't worry young man, she is completely fine. There is a lot happening right now. Especially for her.'

'The M.G?'

'Yes, among other things, and she has found herself in the heart of it, as have you. She just needed a bit of time to talk it through.'

'Could she not have spoken to me?' David picked at the grass near him.

'She could have. She still might, but her past is a sensitive one. Best to let her go at her own pace.'

'Yeah. Okay.' David looked back over at her, smiling when he saw her laugh. 'That's kind of what I thought.'

'How about you?'

'Me?' David quizzed. 'What about me?'

'Well, how are you coping with all of this? You've been on the same journey as her. Is there anything you want to talk about?'

'No, not really. I'm always alright.' He smirked.

'Hmm.' Rev. Li opened an eye to look at him.

'I'm just curious as to what's happening and where we're going. It seems everyone knows more than me and I'm just here for the ride.'

'Well, maybe you are. Maybe, that is why you're needed.'

'Am I'm needed? Didn't feel that way when you left me behind back there.'

'We didn't leave you behind, young man. You need to learn to speak up.'

'Speak up?'

'Yes, that's what I said. No point in feeling hard done by if you don't try to make it easier for yourself. You could have asked us to slow down. You could have asked for a lift. You decided to suffer in silence.'

'I see,' David tapped the ground.

'And as for not being needed, where would Grace be now without your help? Something to think about.'

David turned away to look back at Grace as Rev. Li slapped her legs and got back to her feet. 'Right, think we ought to keep going.'

'Really?' David moaned playfully. 'It feels like I've trekked across the globe. We must be getting close now?'

'Close? Yes,' Rev. Li laughed. 'Were in environment six of seven. One more to go,' she said, turning back into her lioness form. 'Would you like a ride this time?'

'Umm, you know what, I've gone this far, I'm sure I can handle one more stint.'

Rev. Li tilted her head. 'Very well. Grace!' she roared. 'Ready to move?'

'Yep! Coming.'

David watched as she came bouncing towards them like an excited child, catching the sparkle in her eyes as she walked past. 'Are you still going to walk?' she asked. 'There's room for you too.'

'No.' David smiled. 'Honestly I'm okay walking. We haven't got much further to go apparently.'

'Okay, if you're sure.'

He watched her climb back up on to Rev. Li's back and as the two them headed down the hill, he followed shortly after.

Soon he was standing at the edge of the safari savannah and wished he'd taken them up on the offer as his feet slipped and slided on the sludgy mud. He fought his way through some giant felty ferns. Their flimsy leaves sticking to his sweaty skin, but eventually, he stumbled into the new environment. He quickly realised he was in the tropics based on the humid air laying on him like oil and the brightly coloured birds chirping from the jungle treetops. He slowly made his way through what looked liked an overgrown garden, swiping the thick dark-green vines out of his way which drooped from the mossy branches. A group of small golden marmosets swinging loudly across the canopy above.

Despite the testing temperatures and horrible weather conditions he'd been through, this was the worst one yet. Not only did he find it difficult to breathe with the humidity, but the climate was more prone to bugs and insects which he was constantly having to bat away. High pitched buzzing followed him everywhere he went as if they were literally in his ears and every now and again, he'd think he could feel them crawling on his neck and arms, leaving him paranoid. Right now, he was desperate for a shower, wanting to clean himself up, cool down and wash away anything he was potentially sharing his body with, but there was no chance of that.

While batting away the bugs yet again, he spotted a shadowy part of the jungle. A weird glow hiding within it. He headed over to investigate, doing his best not to slip over and once he was there, he saw the glow was coming from a huge patch of peculiar plants. All of them different shapes and sizes, standing from four to forty feet tall. Although they were stunning to look at, some of them also looked very unfriendly. There were some with ugly warty leaves; some that were brightly coloured and covered in pox and some even had a luminescent goo seeping from their stems. The scents they were giving off was clogging up his nostrils as it smelt like a concoction of honey infused petrol.

'I see you found the medicine garden,' Rev. Li spoke standing behind him.

'Medicine garden?'

'Yes, that's what I said. It's quite unbelievable to think what could still be on Earth with the absence of man. In here holds the cures for anything and everything.'

'Strange to think of them as cures when they look so dangerous.'

'Yes, true, but no matter how ugly or evil things may seem, there is always good inside. You just need to understand how to get it out.'

David nodded, understanding the message Rev. Li was trying to deliver. 'Where's Grace?' he asked, noticing she was gone again.

'Oh, she's at the end of the journey. I figured I'd come back for you just in case the final leg was too much.' Rev. Li winked.

'Thanks. Think I've done pretty well to be honest. Would have been quite easy to give up walking through all of that.'

'Yes, well, I've never known any other G.A to do it.'

'Really?'

'Oh yes. Most barely make it out of the woodlands. Some don't need to of course, but I usually have to carry them to their destination.'

'And what is our destination?'

'Come on.' Rev. Li smiled, flicking her tail. 'Time to find out.'

David turned away from the plants and walked beside Rev. Li through the remainder of the jungle until they hit a wall stretching across the environment's perimeter. It was covered from top to bottom in mint green ivy, with colourful exotic flowers of pinks and golds scattered across it. 'Where now then?' he asked.

'Now, we go up.'

'Up?'

David watched Rev. Li leap straight to the top of the wall and disappear without turning back. 'Just like that, then.' He wiped the sweat from his face with a heavy arm and approached the wall. He grabbed hold of a thick vine which hung down from the ledge and slowly began to climb, but he had no grip from the soles of his shoes and immediately fell onto his behind.

'Ouch!' he said as if someone was listening. 'Let's try that again.' He took off his shoes and placed them against the foot of the wall. This time getting all the grip he needed from his sweaty socks on the rocks. It only took a minute or so for him to scale the wall and when he reached the top he pried himself up and rolled onto his back, grateful to finally be at the top. Up above he could see more flowering plants arching over him and continue further on like a garden tunnel and there at the end, was a

121

cabin. Lime light funnelling down upon it as it was situated at the bottom of a circular pit cave.

David rolled onto his front to get a better look and saw Grace and Rev. Li, in her human form, sitting on the cabin's porch waiting for him and so he quickly jogged over. As he approached the pair of them, he stared at Grace's neck. She was now wearing a necklace he hadn't seen before. It had a gold chain with a small diamond pendant hanging from it, like a little vial with small wings either side of it.

'Well you two, we're here,' Rev. Li said.

'We're here... so what's inside?' David asked eagerly.

'I understand the pair of you are looking for the mortal guardian?' David and Grace shared a look of excitement. 'Well, inside is the last one to have seen them. They could help you with your search to understand what's happening.'

'Why didn't you tell us sooner?' Grace questioned harshly.

'Because this requires patience. The angel inside is not well.'

'How so? Why are they in Eden?' Grace asked.

'Eden has been re-established as a place for troubled souls to seek sanctuary from the G.A.F. There are G.As hidden in every environment and use Eden's energy to help with their rehabilitation. Help them think clearly about what it is they want. It is for everyone,' Rev. Li said sternly. 'Everyone.'

'Okay.' David frowned. 'And why is this G.A in rehab? What happened?'

'Let's find out,' Rev. Li replied. 'Brace yourselves.'

David rubbed his shoulder as Rev. Li walked up to the door made of tree bark and knocked. 'Cedric?' she called out, gently pushing it open.

David and Grace followed her inside, cautiously entering the dimly lit room. Only a small amount of lime light shone in from two windows either side to reveal a single table and chair to the right and a large rug laying between a green-cushioned sofa and a lit fireplace. A green fire dancing on the crackling logs.

'Cedric?' Rev. Li called out again. 'Cedric?'

David winced as the floorboards squeaked beneath them. Why were they being so careful? Who was this person? He assumed to be greeted instantly, but somehow it was like they were entering a predator's den.

'Who's there?' a deep, rusty voice shouted out.

'It's me, Cedric, and I have brought guests,' Rev. Li answered.

'Guests?'

'Yes, they are here to help. To help fix what happened.'

'The M.G?'

'Yes,' Rev. Li spoke like a nurse to a troubled patient, clearly trying to remain calm and not scare them.

'Okay.'

David's body tensed as a large figure hobbled towards them from a dark corner and stepped in front of the fireplace. His suit was dirty and creased. No tie around his neck. His hair wild and black like the stubble dotted across his wrinkled jaw. His eyes closed.

'We're looking for the M.G,' Grace said softly. 'Rev. Li says you were the last one to have seen them?'

'Yes... yes I was.'

'Do you remember where?' Grace stepped forward.

'At the the end of my blade.'

David's body suddenly fell cold and he quickly held onto Grace's wrist as Cedric's eyes flicked open. Crimson iris's staring back at him.

'I killed them.'

Chapter 18

Cedric didn't say another word after that. Instead, he slowly shuffled away to sit on the sofa and stare into the fireplace. Grace meanwhile, just stood perfectly still, her lip quivering. David could tell she was distraught. Angry even, but looking at Cedric, how frail he was, it was almost impossible to hate him. He seemed genuinely broken, like a veteran haunted by his actions in war. Did he know what he was doing? Was he following orders? It didn't seem to matter. The M.G was dead and with them, so were Grace's hopes for the G.A.F, as were his for getting home. What was he going to do now? How was he going to get back? He wanted to ask Grace. Ask if there was another way, but how could he think of himself in a moment like this? It would be highly insensitive wouldn't it? Even if he did just trek across the entirety of Eden for her.

Before he knew it, Rev. Li was ushering the pair of them out the cabin to leave Cedric alone and she closed the door behind them. Grace immediately walked off and paced around the grass with her hands on her head, while he stayed at the top of the porch.

'They can't be dead. They can't be.' Grace shook her head. 'Did you know?'

'No,' Rev. Li spoke calmly, joining her on the grass. 'That was the first time he said that. When he first came here, he kept mumbling about a M.G and something about being tricked, but he never said what happened. What he did. He just surrendered his blade and his council started.'

'He's an Idler! You could have guessed he'd done something bad! Why is there an Idler in Eden?'

'Because he is lost and requires help,' Rev. Li spoke super calm.

'Ooh please! Idlers are renowned for being lost! That's why they belong in Idle!'

'Like the lost souls you have been helping?'

'That's not fair.' Grace pointed a finger. 'The lost souls I help are sad, defeated, struggling. They are not evil!'

'Evil? You know Idlers have just as much right to be in the G.A.F as G.As? That is how it was designed. To be balanced and fair.'

'But it isn't fair! Is it?' Grace blasted hysterically. 'I'm tired of seeing the light go out of people. I'm tired of looking over my shoulder every time I want to help someone. The world is falling apart and all we can do is watch! That's why the G.A.F needs the M.G!'

'I agree.' Rev. Li nodded. 'Do not think I was happy when an Idler was granted haven here. Why do you think I located him on the very edge of Eden? I too, feared the Idle realm would still influence his mind, but over the years he has proven me wrong and I am obligated to help all lost souls. No matter where they are from. As I said, everyone is welcomed here.'

'Okay, okay.' Grace surrendered her argument. 'He does appear harmless.'

'Yes, he is. He is obviously devastated by what happened and he has been patiently waiting for a moment to make amends ever since... just like you.'

David's ears pricked up at that comment and he took a seat on the wooden step. What did she mean by that? Why did Grace need to make amends? Was Diego right? Was Grace a criminal who was now only doing good to try and balance the books? Had she been an Idler? He stayed quiet and continued to observe the the two of them talk.

'That's not totally fair.' Grace wagged a finger at Rev. Li teary eyed. 'I just don't understand how the M.G could be dead. Linus said he had been protecting them and since he... went. It was down to me to takeover. I can't have failed already. Not again.'

'Maybe Linus was protecting them in the G.A.F? Why does it matter if the M.G is dead?'

'Why does it matter?' Grace raised her voice. 'Because they're supposed to be the bridge between the worlds. They're supposed to be the one to re-enable the G.A.F to do what it was made for, through teachings, guidance. To stop the Idlers interfering. How can they be a mortal guardian without their mortality?'

'Even after death, we are all still here,' Rev. Li said slowly as if spelling something out for her. 'It doesn't matter where someone is. They are still the same person. They still have the same beliefs, the same attitudes, the same fate... the same power.' Rev. Li stepped closer to Grace with every example. 'They may not be able to walk on Earth anymore, but they would still be powerful enough to influence fate itself. To influence the realms. To change things. Providing they don't get wrongly influenced themselves.'

'Yes.' Grace nodded quietly. 'Okay, yes, I understand.'

'Remember what we spoke about on the way here.' Rev. Li put her hands on Grace's shoulders. 'There was two stages last time. Neither of which were your fault and now, Cedric's actions have brought you closer to them. Think of it that way.'

David rubbed his shoulder as he watched Grace and Rev. Li embrace like mother and daughter, similarly to when they were in the meadow, and again, all he could do was watch and to try absorb as much information as possible. From what he could gather, this M.G seemed to be a very complex character and until they found them, he wasn't going to understand what all the fuss was about. Unless... David turned back to the cabin. *Maybe I could get some answers myself?*

While Grace and Rev. Li were still occupied, David crept back into the cabin and closed the door. He doubted they would notice him missing as they were too engrossed in their own conversation and besides, he was tired of being left out. Cedric obviously knows a lot about it and now was a good opportunity to finally get on the same page.

Not once did Cedric acknowledge his presence as he walked around the sofa towards him. He just stared into the fire as if in a trance and it made David uncomfortable. He could feel his mouth going dry and the hairs on his arms slowly raised. How could someone appear so harmless and yet... have murdered someone. The contrast made Cedric unpredictable in David's mind and he wasn't sure he trusted him. How could he when he knows he killed someone? He'd seen what the other Idlers were like. What they did to Grace. *What am I doing?* he questioned himself, *I shouldn't be doing this.* He went to leave, but quickly stopped as he remembered his promise. *I'll do whatever it takes to get home.*

Before he could change his mind again David stepped round the sofa, keeping a safe distance away from Cedric. 'I need to know about the M.G,' he squeezed the words out. 'We need to find them.'

Cedric didn't move and so David tried a different approach. 'Rev. Li said something about you being tricked?'

'Tricked... yes.' Cedric nodded slowly. 'I was tricked.'

'How so?' David asked hesitantly.

'I... don't talk about it.'

'Okay. I understand. I don't like talking about things either.'

'Why not?'

'My mind is for me.' David shrugged. 'I deal with things in my own way, for better or worse.'

'Same.' Cedric turned to face him like a possessed puppet. 'Certain things can't be understood. Certain things can't be helped.'

'Like, what happened to you?' David asked cautiously, hoping he'd opened a door into Cedric's mind.

'Yes. That is why I don't talk about it.'

'Again, I understand. You don't have to talk about it.'

'No... but I can show you.'

David frowned as he watched Cedric disappear into a room to the right of the fireplace and when he came shuffling back in, there was something in his hand. Something small, glowing purple. 'What is that?' he asked.

'A Yutopian bead,' Cedric answered, staring at the gem no bigger than a marble. 'The Reverend gave it to me to help with my council.'

'What does it do?'

'Yutopia is a realm where you can live however you want based on what is in your mind and memory. For me, this bead gives me the energy to travel back to the moments of my past. To the moment that can help me reconcile with my actions. To help me understand what happened.'

'That's... cool,' David gulped. As happy as he was for Cedric to be more open and seeking help, he was well aware of what he was about to see. Did he really want to witness a murder? 'How, umm, how does it work?'

Cedric held the glowing gem out on his palm. 'Put your hand on top of it, but only think of the gem. It must be my mind it connects to so we get sent to the right place.'

David took a deep breath and slowly placed his hand over the bead. He stared at the glowing amethyst between their palms and waited anxiously for whatever was going to happen. 'What now?'

In that moment, he felt the bead pop like a bubble and his hand went wet. A stream of chilly lilac water came gushing down his arm and on to his shoulder before cascading down to his feet. It began to fill up his body as if he was a human container with none of it leaking on the floor. The water level rose to his knees and he could see the same thing was happening to Cedric.

'How high does it go?' he asked, but his voice was drowned out by the water continuing to flood in, rising and rising up to his chin. His heart quickened as the fear of drowning took over his mind. He gasped one last breath of air before he was totally submerged and with his lungs on the cusp of bursting, the water exploded, surging outwards as if an underwater mine had been detonated. Every detail of reality was washed away and he was left totally immersed in the middle of a lilac ocean, alone. Amazingly, he was able to breathe as normal despite the feeling of being underwater and there was a calming smell of lavender helping him to relax. 'Cedric?' his voice gargled, but Cedric was nowhere to be seen.

He began to swim ahead in a breast stroke motion, looking around at the purling lilac. His body rippling in a weird watery form while reflecting the ocean's light. *Is this Yutopia?* he thought, gazing around. His eyes suddenly veered towards a giant bubble spontaneously floating upwards in the distance and he could hear something echoing out of it like music in an aquarium. The closer he got however, the sooner he realised it was a voice, like a narrator setting the scene for what was to come.

'Tonight is the night Cedric. Tonight, you fulfill your purpose. Tonight, marks the birth of a new era.'

As David swam through the bubble the ocean drained away behind him, leaving him stranded on an amethyst fence made up of blobbing soap bubbles. Some of which drifted away from the pack and out into the watery world ahead where everything looked so distorted, like a plum-coloured hologram being shown on a lilac sea. It took a minute or so, but eventually his eyes adapted and he could see he was standing outside a house on the first floor. A tall violet figure appearing through the window. He wanted to get a closer look, but his feet wouldn't move.

Instead, the fence floated closer towards the windowsill by its own accord as if it was on a programme. Clearly mimicking Cedric's movements from that night and reminding David he was in a memory and merely a guest in Cedric's shoes. He had no control.

From this position David could see the figure standing by what looked like the bottom of a bed and they stayed there for a while. It was almost like they were watching over someone and even when they appeared to leave, they stopped again in the doorway for a further few seconds. It was as if they were savouring the moment for as long as possible and then, like flicking off a light, the scene went dark. The fence slowly drifted down a level to show the same figure coming down a set of stairs and pause briefly in a hallway before entering the next room.

There was something about this next scene which made David more curious. As he watched the figure walk towards the corner of the room, there was a second figure sitting on a sofa which caught his eye and he didn't know why. There was just something about them. His eyes got drawn back to the first figure however, as they slowly stepped into the centre, their hips shaking. *Their dancing!* David smiled. He watched them hold out their hands to beckon the other to join them, but in the end they had to pull them off the sofa and in that moment, they both began to dance. They twirled and swayed like a pair of loved-up teenagers. It was beautiful to watch. *If only there was sound,* David thought, but all he could hear were the bubbles beneath him. Despite this though, he still tapped his hands against his thighs, trying to guess the beat of music from their dancing. Right up to the point when they stopped, and kissed, embracing one another so closely their two shadows became one.

'Oh, come on,' David sighed as the fence floated away again. This time moving to the side of the house and his chest suddenly tightened. He watched the figure exit outside and head over to a small car to the right of the building. They sat in the car for a moment or so before starting the engine. Visible scuff marks on the rear wheel arch as they drive away. *No. No. It can't be.*

The whole world suddenly flipped on its head, like turning the page of a storybook, causing him to sway on the bubbles as if he was on a rocking ship. His vision blurred briefly while the figure got out of their car. Trees behind them. The fence then floated a couple of metres parallel to the figure as they headed up a hill running adjacent to the woodland. Their shoulders shivering as they reached the top and once they were there, they hopped up onto a lonely fence rail and just sat there.

David gripped his pounding head. His stomach churning like wild ocean waves crashing together in his hollow body. His fence circled the figure manically, spinning and spinning like a rogue roundabout and suddenly, it stopped. A crimson glow came upon David's hands and he stared at them horrified, feeling like someone's puppet as they raised above his head uncontrollably. Higher and higher until finally, they plunged down. The crimson glow invaded the figure's violet shade and surged through their watery image, turning them a fluorescent magenta. The light growing brighter and brighter... pop!

Like a bursting water balloon, the figure imploded, but just before they disappeared. Just for a millisecond. David got a glimpse of their face. Their eyes.

The memory came to an abrupt end and the whole world drained away to transport David back to the cabin. He gasped loudly as the water gushed out of him and back into the bead. His weak body collapsing onto the floorboards.

'No, no, it can't be,' David whispered, clenching his fists as he felt a horrible heat take over his body. His eyes stinging. 'You killed him.' He glared into Cedric's crimson eyes. 'You killed my dad!'

Chapter 19

David felt his blood boil. His head burning. His body trembling with rage as he tried his upmost to keep it all together, but there was no holding this back. The emotional floodgate was open. 'You killed my dad!' he yelled. His smouldering eyes trying to combust Cedric's very existence from his sight. He threw a rampant fist at him, catching him across the jaw and sending him flying into the cabin wall. Cedric remained poised, sitting defeatedly on the floor as if wanting to be hurt and David was willing to oblige. He was the reason for all his hurt. His mother's hurt and he needed to pay.

He stormed up to Cedric once more. A strange superior strength taking a hold of him as he managed to lift Cedric up and pin him against the wall. His fist hovering at the side of his face waiting to strike like a snake on its prey. 'I thought angels were meant to be the good guys!' he hissed through spitting lips.

Cedric chuckled. A glimmer of life sparking back in his eyes which made David even angrier.

The cabin door burst open and Rev. Li roared inside in her lioness form. She swiped David away from Cedric with a heavy paw, causing him to tumble back to floor, but he quickly got up unscathed. His arms and neck electrified with hate.

'Stand aside,' David threatened.

Rev. Li growled monstrously, baring her large teeth to protect Cedric as if he was her cub.

'David!' Grace came hurtling into the room to stand in front of him. 'David, what's going on?' she said, holding his cheeks with her hands.

'He killed my dad!' David shouted. 'He...!'

'Okay, okay.' Grace's hands got stronger as she tried to get David to look into her eyes, jarring his head from left to right to stop him squirming and eventually, they caught hold. Grace's glowing iris's compelled him to calm down. His rage sizzling out as her energy took ahold of him. 'Your dad was the M.G?'

'It, it seems that way,' David replied more civilised.

'Okay,' Grace whispered. 'It'll be okay.'

Rev. Li retuned to her human form as David started to relax.

'What was his name?' Grace asked, trying to distract him.

'Stephen,' David gulped, holding onto Grace's wrists and closing his stinging eyes. 'Eight years. For eight years I thought he left us, but...'

'Okay. Okay,' Grace continued to comfort him.

'Did you say, Stephen?' Rev. Li queried.

'Yes.' David scowled.

'Short, round, brown hair. A bit... bumbly?'

'Yes.' David frowned. Where was she going with this? He watched her eyes twitch as if she was working something out and then her eyes burst wide open.

'He's here.'

'What?' Grace exclaimed.

'There was a G.A in the library of that description. The same name. The Idlers were after him and so I invited him here. The timelines add up to his energy levels... so it could be...'

'Where?' David spoke strongly.

'He's in the woodlands habitat, but-'

Before Rev. Li could say anything else, David had already flown out the cabin door and sprinted off as if his life depended on it down the grassy tunnel. His fingers tingled as the realm's energy connected to his. The grass and plants bending towards him as if passing him extra energy on the way, enabling him to run faster and faster. He could feel his body absorbing it all, making him go numb once again. He quickly approached the end of the tunnel and launched himself off the edge, hitting the ground unscathed. A twinkling emerald aura now surrounding him and he wasn't alone. His aura had morphed around him to form a wolf rippling in the green energy. Although, David didn't react. He was a man on a mission. A mission to find his dad and when the wolf briefly looked back at him with its friendly, yet serious face, he could tell their minds were in sync.

David's legs pumped like a machine. The wolf acting like his personal fuel source, recycling all the energy he was using back to him so he wouldn't run out of steam. Within seconds they had bolted out of the tropical ferns and entered the savannah, leaving dirty dust clouds in their wake as they raced across the grassy plain. Overtaking the stray wildebeests and cheetahs with ease. They were rapidly approaching the larger herds of animals, but rather than changing course, the wolf howled loudly. Its call travelling out further than any lion's roar and the animals quickly parted from miles ahead. It wasn't long before they pounced up the hill and entered the desert. Sand flying behind them like a jet trail. A pack of vultures rasped into the air as they came ploughing through and just like the savannah, the desert was soon far behind them. Now they were gliding across the tundra ice like a speedy apparition. One blink and they were gone.

A grumbling snowstorm was sweeping in from up ahead. The snow now hurtling through him relentlessly, but David wasn't bothered. Nothing was going to stop him. He felt no signs of fatigue. His muscles weren't tight. His lungs weren't losing breath, he couldn't even feel the beating of his own heart. It was as if he was made of pure energy. No different to the wind rocketing through the landscape. Even his mind was clear as all he could think about was seeing his dad again, hearing his voice and feeling the touch of his hand on his shoulder. The idea of being able to talk to him again. To confide in him and settle this storm in his fragmented head.

The forest boundary was getting closer and closer and before he knew it, he was weaving around the thick tree trunks and dodging the outstretched branches. His feet skimming off the powdery surface and not leaving any tracks. A few more seconds passed and finally, the snow had melted away. The trees became less congested and the lime sun now streamed through the woodland like he remembered from before. The whistling wildlife from the open canopy calmed his mind as he slowed down. *Where now? He's here somewhere,* he thought, placing his hands on the wolf's back, but now he'd reached his destination the wolf's energy slowly disintegrated from around him. The lime rays instantly warmed his body like a strong embrace as he got his senses back. The transformation didn't faze him though, as he still felt the urgency. He spun around in a circle trying to guess the right way, knowing if he walked straight ahead he would end up back in the meadow.

'Come on! Bit of help here!' he exasperated, holding out his arms and right on queue, the wind suddenly picked up around him. It swirled through his hair and down his arms towards his fingertips as it was his own personal breeze. *Strange.* Every time he moved his hand, it was like the wind was changing direction. It was as if it was acting like compass to lead him where he wanted to go and so he followed it, hastily walking in an easterly direction. He skipped round the trees on the dusty mud trail until finally, the feeling stopped. The air on his fingertips suddenly felt as though it was travelling upward, tickling his fringe, and so he came to an abrupt stop and turned his attention to the branches above. His heart beating faster as he expected to see something within the foliage, but there was nothing there. He continued squinting upwards. Adamant he was missing something. His eyes growing tired from looking up at the bright limelight. 'Oh! Come on!' David shouted, looking away and blinking manically to get rid of the eye floaters he'd occurred. 'That wasn't all for nothing. There must be something here!'

He looked again. Solely focussing on the one spot where he believed the wind was blowing to. *What is it! What's there!* Even if he couldn't see it, he could sense it and eventually, his belief paid off as a large group of leaves suddenly began to glow. He stood back in awe as they revealed the outline of a small treehouse hidden at the very top of a large beech tree. The excitement was getting to him now. His whole body went jittery as he ran closer to the trunk and grabbed hold of one the branches to pull himself up, but his eagerness got the better of him and his hands slipped. He fell and smacked his back on the dirty ground, wincing in agony as he heaved back to his feet and dusted himself off. 'Let's try that again.'

'Hello?'

David froze at the sound of the voice. His breathing deepened as he tried to find the confidence to look up.

'Hello? Is someone there?'

'Y-yeah!' David called back stepping away from the tree. 'It's me!' He peered up to try and get a glimpse, but the leaves were too congested where the treehouse was.

'I'll come down. Hold on.'

David paced around in a circle with his hands on his head. An uncontrollable smile painted on his face. He was going to see his dad! He was finally going to see his dad again! The very thought made his body glow with happiness.

Like a hidden elevator, he watched his dad slowly flutter to the floor on a giant leaf. The sight was so surreal David didn't know what to do. A rare tear dripping down his cheek.

'Hello?' Stephen asked apprehensively.

'Hi,' David stepped closer.

'Are you okay? Are you here to help?'

'Help?' David frowned. 'It's me?'

'And you would be...'

'Wh-what?' David's body fell weak. 'Seriously?'

'Sorry, are you a helper of the Reverend? It's just, I don't know how these things work.' Stephen stepped closer with a Yutopian bead in his hand. 'Its supposed to help me with my past... or something, but its not doing anything.'

'You...' David gulped. 'You don't know who I am?'

'Umm, no, sorry. Why? Have we met before?'

David stared into his dad's lost eyes. There was nothing there, but emptiness and confusion. He immediately turned away. After all these years of wishing to see him again. Wishing to talk to him again. Here they were face to face... and he didn't recognise him. His dad didn't know him. *This isn't right. This isn't fair.*

'Sorry, are you here to help or are you lost?'

'Oh, I'm lost alright.' David wiped his face and looked up to the sky. 'I've been lost for a very, very, long time.' He slowly turned back to face his dad. His legs shaking. His mind pounding. His eyes tearful, but there was no point in confiding in a stranger. 'But I'll be alright. I'm always alright.' He turned away again, wanting to leave and escape this torture, but he stopped at the sound of his dad's voice.

'Hey, wait!'

David continued to stare at the ground not wanting to meet his dad's empty gaze again. He grimaced as he felt his dad take his hand and tuck something inside it. 'Here, I think this will do you more good than me.'

When his dad stepped away to head back to the tree, David opened his hand to see the Yutopian bead glowing in his palm. 'I'm not so sure,' he whispered back.

All of sudden Rev. Li hurtled into view with Grace on her back. 'How did you get here so quickly?'

'I ran,' David replied.

'Is that him?' Grace asked, running over.

'Yes.'

'What is it? What's wrong?'

'He... it doesn't matter.' David smiled weakly, not knowing what to do with himself.

'He doesn't remember you, does he?' Grace sympathised.

David shook his head.

'Of course he doesn't young man,' Rev. Li spoke soothingly. 'He has been in Idle. It's a miracle he's here with us now.'

'Idle?' David queried.

'He was pierced by Cedric's blade. An Idler's blade. Only one thing happens after that.'

'Idle is a cruel place,' Grace continued putting a hand on his shoulder. 'It's a place of penance where your mind slowly erodes away until you forget why you're there. Who you are. You're just... idle.'

'I see.' *But it doesn't help me.*

Grace briefly rubbed his shoulder before running down the path after his dad.

'Are you okay, young man?' Rev. Li asked, swishing her tail.

'I'm always alright.' David smiled. 'Let's hope Grace gets what she needs from him.' He began to walk away again.

'Are you not staying?'

'I don't think I need to do I? Just, give me a roar if you need me.' David tucked his hands into his pockets and headed back through the trees. Where to, he had no idea, but anywhere was better than here.

Chapter 20

Diego strolled through the empty library, twirling his blade in his hand like a guard on patrol. After his little cull, the G.As had finally become aware of his presence and seemed to be avoiding him at any cost, some even fleeing to Yutopia, and he couldn't be happier. This is what he wanted. At last the G.A.F seemed to be operating as it should. All it needed was an act of authority and the G.As quickly fell back in line, like peasants in a kingdom. Those who were incapable of following the rules were either forced to Yutopia or clipped and made examples of.

Finally, he was beginning to feel in total control and with the other Idlers on the lookout for Stephen, it was only a matter of time before they could move their plan along. *How did he escape us?* Diego scratched his chin with his blade. *The only green light I've ever known is that of Eden... but that realm's gone. Hasn't it?*

If only he knew Stephen's backstory, perhaps there was something he could use. Something to lure him out, but his file was as empty as his mind. Clearly he had a strong mind as a mortal because no G.A looked out for him, either that or his file was erased. All it said was that he was the M.G and clipped while still mortal, thus stating the obvious.

All of a sudden there was a strange rustling sound, like wind blowing through grass and Diego stopped in his tracks. There was a faint green glow reflecting off a bookcase to his left and he sprinted towards it. *Not this time!* He spun round the corner and stared at the emerald fence. A sinister smile spread across his face. 'Idlers!' he bellowed, all of them appearing beside him over their buzzing crimson fences. 'We're in.'

Diego led the way into Eden, stepping over the fence and onto a pile of crunching dry twigs. The four Idlers close behind him with their blades at the ready. He knew the stories about this place, but it was supposedly locked up long before he even joined and now, looking up at the mossy sky, he knew the stories didn't do it justice. There was such tranquility in the air he almost felt guilty being here, but he knew he didn't have a choice. Stephen was his target and he knew he was here.

He prowled down the track quietly, listening intently to his surroundings for any clues and it didn't take him long to hear voices. 'This way.' He smirked. 'And remember, this is Eden. It is a sacred place. Do not harm the environment or it will be the end of you. Understood?' All four Idlers nodded back at him and he continued onwards, doing his best not to let his crimson glow give away his position, and after a few more steps, he saw him. 'Got you.'

Stephen was standing flabbergasted beside a large beech tree, appearing to be arguing with... *Grace? How did she get here? She should be gone!* He scanned the area for the boy she had been with, but with his absence he quickly assumed he had perished in the vortex, but why hadn't she? He continued to look around and quickly spotted a beastly looking creature rippling in green energy. It was something he'd never seen before and with it sitting on the earth like they were on sentry duty, he knew this wasn't going to be a simple task.

'Listen up,' Diego said quietly, facing the Idlers again. 'We need to get the M.G back to Limbo whatever the cost. I don't trust this creature so I'll go first and distract them while you get into positions. Two of you on the beast. Two of you on Grace.'

'What of the M.G?' The blonde-female Idler spoke.

'He's mine.'

Diego left the Idlers there and went in closer, squatting behind an ash tree where he could hear them talking more clearly. He listened closely, waiting for the opportune moment to enter.

'But you're the mortal guardian!' Grace said dramatically, waving a necklace at him. 'We need you.'

'I don't know what to tell you.' Stephen shrugged. 'Even if I am this person, I wouldn't know how to help you. I don't even know how to help myself. I don't have a memory.'

'That shouldn't matter! You're still the same person. You still have the same values? The same beliefs? There must be a part of you that knows what I'm saying?'

'I understand what you're saying, but I've been having conflicted feelings about everything since leaving the Tavern. I knew I should have stayed there.'

Grace threw her hands on her head. 'There must be a way to restore his memory? How about a Yutopian bead?' She turned to the beast.

'I had one of them,' Stephen quickly replied. 'It doesn't work.'

'Because you have no memories.' Grace sighed, tucking her necklace away in her pocket.

'Oh, this is priceless.' Diego snarled in his hiding spot.

'What about his file?' Grace asked again.

'Nope, tried that too, it isn't there.'

Here we go. 'Perhaps I can help with that.' Diego stood up and strolled out of the trees. The beast instantly got down on all fours and aggressively growled at him.

'How did you get here?' Grace shouted aggressively.

'How did you get here?' he asked back.

'She was invited,' the beast barked. 'You however are trespassing in a protected realm.'

'Calm down,' Diego teased. 'I am only here for him. Come on Stephen.'

'He's not going anywhere with you.' Grace quickly stood in front of Stephen.

142

'Do you want your memory back or not?' Diego spoke to Stephen directly. 'Look, I'm sorry if things got a bit hostile between us, but I said I would help and now I am.'

'How will you help my memory?' Stephen asked.

'I found your file and it was quite the read. I'm sure you'll enjoy reading it, too.'

'Where?'

'In Limbo. Come with me and we'll go get it. Let's put all this nasty business behind us, hey?' He watched the cogs turning in Stephen's eyes and could tell he was tempted.

'He's using you,' Grace interfered. 'He has an alternative agenda, don't fall for it.'

'Come on! I haven't got all day,' Diego said, but Stephen remained still. 'Very well, how about this, you come with me now and I won't clip your friends.' He clicked his fingers and sneered as the blonde Idlers popped into view and grabbed hold of Grace. Their crimson energy swirling around her with two blades resting under her chin, likewise with the beast, the black Idlers stood either side of it with their blades readied for action.

'What do you want from me?' Stephen asked. 'Ever since you changed colour you've wanted me for something, like back in the library that time. Why?'

'It turns out you're more useful than we first thought, Stephen.'

'How?'

'Come with me and we'll find out together.'

'Stephen, don't listen to him,' Grace choked.

'Oh, will you shut up!' Diego thundered. 'Can't you see this is out of your control? Stephen, I'm going to make this really easy for you. Come with me, get your memory back and fulfill your purpose, or stay here and be clipped with these idiots. What's it to be?'

143

Silence bestowed the woodland. A disturbing breeze rustled through the branches above while everyone had their eyes on each other, weighing up their attacking options. Diego was certain he'd won Stephen over, but with the beast staring at him so viciously he didn't dare make the first move.

A sudden snap came from above and Diego watched a squirrel fall amid the leaves. The animal headed straight towards the black-bearded Idler and before he could say or do anything, the Idler swished his blade. The squirrel hit the ground, sliced in two.

An enormous roar thundered through the trees as the beast stood on its hind legs and stamped its huge paws down upon the Idler causing them to explode in crimson smoke. The beast's energy clearly much more powerful than he realised as it completely distinguished Idle's energy.

'Run Stephen!' Grace yelled as the beast pounced at the blonde Idlers to free her.

'Stop him! Get him to Limbo!' Diego bellowed, but Grace was too quick to grab Stephen and drag him away into the trees with the remaining Idlers after them. The beast meanwhile chased close behind, roaring and snarling its algae-coloured teeth which quickly snapped shut around the black-female Idler's torso as if devouring her.

Diego gave chase too, wanting to keep the events happening in front of him to remain undetected, while keeping Stephen in view. He could see his fellow Idlers in pursuit through the tree line, the beast close on their tail. It didn't take long for it to catch up and within seconds it had pounced upon the blonde-male Idler and consumed their energy too. Its jaw crunching down on his neck until he was just a cloud of crimson dust.

I can't lose him. Not again! 'You!' Diego shouted to the remaining Idler. 'I'll take care of the M.G. Lead the

monster away.' The Idler obliged without a second
thought and veered off further into the woodland, the
beast immediately following and leaving Stephen for the
taking. The trees suddenly disappeared and Diego found
himself in a meadow. Stephen and Grace in his sights.
Come on! I got ya! I got ya!

'Keep moving, Stephen!' He could hear Grace say, but
it was obvious the man was tiring. He was slowing down
at a lovely rate and soon he was right up close. Grace must
have been aware of this as she turned on the spot to face
him, clearly trying to buy Stephen some extra time, but it
wasn't going to work. Firstly, Stephen had already pulled
up just behind her and he also knew she was no match for
him. With a flick of his wrist he summoned his blade.
'Now you're gone for good!' he hissed. He went to shunt
the blade into Grace when a firm frail hand grabbed his
wrist. 'Who dares...?' he trailed off, staring at another pair
of crimson eyes behind a curtain of black hair. 'Who are
you?'

'There has been enough clippings for one day,' the old
man said. 'Get the M.G and we'll go.'

'We?' Diego pointed the blade at him. 'Where do you
think you're going? Why don't I clip the pair of you now
and take the M.G for myself?'

The old man swayed towards him almost zombie-like
and whispered in his ear. 'Trust me. Idler to Idler. Let's
go.'

Diego retreated a step to observe the man more
clearly. Who was he? Why was he interfering? He peered
back over at Grace and scrunched his face up. 'Stephen!
Lets go!'

'Cedric? What are you doing?' Grace seemed to weep,
but Cedric didn't reply. Instead he pondered over to
Stephen and pulled him by the wrist towards a crimson
fence which spluttered and fizzed like a dodgy cable.

'We're not through yet!' Diego sneered at Grace with a twitching eye. 'Your luck will run out.'

'You're despicable,' Grace spat, rubbing her neck. 'Whatever you're doing. I hope it fails and you get your comeuppance!'

'I wish the same for you.'

Grace appeared to make one final attempt at stopping them, but only managed to graze Stephen's trouser pockets before they all disappeared to Limbo.

Chapter 21

Rev. Li's roar thundered through the trees and David swiftly made his way back. He sprinted along the dusty mud path, half-hoping they'd discovered something positive for him. Had his dad's memory come back? Had they figured another way to get him home? The thoughts refuelled his otherwise empty self, but when he arrived the area was empty. 'Where are they? This is the right place isn't it?' he said. There was a disturbed crackling energy in the air and he then saw the red dust on the ground. *No!* David's heart skipped a beat and with a flick of his wrist he sensed the direction of the villainous energy and raced towards it. Soon seeing Rev. Li's fresh paw prints on the mud. He kept going until he entered the meadow and there he saw Rev. Li in the distance swishing her tail.

'Reverend!' he shouted, skidding to a halt. 'Reverend! What happened? Is everyone alright!?'

'Idlers!' she growled, stamping her paws. 'Trespassing in my realm! I wont stand for it! It's an act of aggression!' She stamped once again causing tiny tremors.

'Where's Grace? Where's my dad?'

Rev. Li's body language changed as she turned to face ahead of her and David could see Grace's head over the grass. A look of anger and sadness on her face. Her bare neck red from where she'd been rubbing it.

'Grace! Are you okay?' David said, striding towards her. 'Are you hurt?'

'I'm fine,' Grace replied quietly. 'Honestly, I'm fine.'

'What happened?'

'Diego and Cedric took Stephen.'

'What?' Rev. Li questioned, now in her human form. 'Cedric? But he... how?'

Grace silently held up Rev. Li's bracelet and slapped it into her hands. 'I found it in the grass. I guess he dropped it when he left.'

'That sly...' Rev. Li clenched her fists over the bracelet. 'He used this to create a fence for them. That's how they got here.'

'I guess once an Idler always an Idler,' Grace spoke bluntly.

'What about my dad?' David asked hesitantly. 'What are they going to do to him?'

'No Idea.' Grace shrugged not making eye contact. 'Nothing good. Should have left you alone to beat up Cedric,' she sniffed. 'At least you would have been useful then.'

'What do you mean by that?' David frowned.

'Where were you?' Grace said loudly, darting her head up to him. 'Where were you?' she asked again getting to her feet and getting in close. 'Whatever it takes is what you said to me. Whatever it takes. Well guess what, while we were getting attacked and your father kidnapped you were off moping in the woods! Now the M.G is gone. Probably for good once they are finished with him!'

David stood perplexed. He hadn't seen this part of Grace before. Did she have a right to be angry at him? Was this really his fault? Anyone would think it was her dad who'd been killed, brainwashed and kidnapped.

'What is their plan?' Grace turned to Rev. Li. 'You must know. What do the Idlers want with him?'

'To free Amb. Ermêl,' Rev. Li said quietly.

'Whose that?' Grace asked. Her back now to David as if cutting him out of the conversation.

'They are the realm guardian of Idle. She has been banished for a long, long time due to her obsession with fate and the G.A.F. She believes it can't function on its own and used to summon Idler after Idler to help control

148

it until she went too far. With the M.G's essence she can return and if they do. The G.A.F would be doomed.'

Despite the severity of Rev. Li's words, David didn't react. Grace's words were still rattling in his mind. How had he messed this up so badly? His mum. His dad. Grace... It seemed he couldn't do anything right. Grace, meanwhile, took the news much worse. Her hand shaking over her lips and he wanted to say something helpful, 'dad wouldn't do that. He wouldn't allow such a thing to happen.'

'But he's not your dad, young man. Not anymore. His mind is gone and he has been exposed to Idle's energy from being in that realm. All Diego has to do is make him remember where his power lies and that's it. He could steal it if he wants. That's what Cedric tried to do those many years ago.'

'So, what can we do?' Grace said strongly smacking her hands together. 'What is there for us to do? I mean, we can't go back to Limbo. We can't fight him... We need to prepare for the worse,' she said defeatedly. 'If we can't stop them, we can warn everyone. Every G.A. Perhaps even...'

'Raise an army?' Rev. Li queried. 'Think about what you are saying Dear.'

'What other choice do we have? We can't let the G.A.F succumb to such evil because the Idlers may not stop there.'

After a brief silence David spoke. 'I'm with you.'

'No.' Grace waved a dismissive hand in David's direction, making his heart wrench. 'Sorry, but you had your chance. I can't trust you at the moment. Your mind is clearly not up to the task. Oh, and for the record. You'll never get home now.'

David exhaled slowly, feeling more alone now than he ever has before. He caught Rev. Li's eyes for a brief moment, but even she had no words to say. He felt Grace was being very harsh, but maybe those words were needed. Not only that, but finding the M.G seemed like a life long obsession of hers and so to lose them this way... he understood. Even if it was at his expense.

'Well,' David said. 'If I'm not needed then, I'll leave you to it.' He created a yellow fence and disappeared over it. He had no idea where he would end up, but anywhere was better than here.

Chapter 22

A mighty clang rang through Limbo as Diego propelled Stephen onto the platform. A sinister smile on his face as he watched him tumble over. He then strolled back over to him, pushing Cedric out of the way to get to him, and grabbed him by the scruff of the collar. He turned him over so he could lour straight into his tired, feeble face, 'so, Stephen, you're the mortal guardian?'

'So I keep being told.' Stephen squirmed in his grip.

'How?' Diego chuckled. 'I mean, how can someone like you, be a legendary figure like a mortal guardian? It's ludicrous!' As he spoke a metal pole rose from the platform and he bound Stephen to it from the waist.

'Thanks. Thanks, Diego. Is that why you've brought me here? To insult me?'

'No, that bits just for fun.' He shoved Stephen backwards, causing him to hit his head. 'We know why you're really here. You're here to help me.'

'Help you?' Stephen scoffed, rubbing his head.

'Yes, you see, the power you unknowingly hold is the key to freeing someone. Someone who can fulfil what the G.A.F is craving for.'

'Sounds fantastic,' Stephen sighed uncaringly. 'Then what?'

'Total, Idle, domination,' spoke a different voice.

Diego slowly turned round to see Cedric standing behind him. 'Who are you again?' he asked.

'Cedric. Also, I must say, well done on capturing the 'M.G." He air quoted. 'It's good to be in his company again.'

Diego scowled at Cedric's strange behaviour as he walked past. 'Look. You may have been an Idler before, but since you deserted your role for a sunny day in Eden, I don't think you qualify as my equal. As far as I am aware you are my prisoner as much as he is.'

Cedric shuffled towards Diego. His eyes unblinking. His hot, sweaty face only centimetres away from his and in one split movement, he grabbed him by the throat.

'How dare you!' Diego thundered, but Cedric was too strong to break free from. It was as if their aura's had somehow locked together.

'You may be the chosen one, but it was my duty first. I am the one who got this stone rolling and I will be the one to see it through. After all, I am the one who clipped him.'

Diego was finally released from Cedric's grasp and he took a large step back to readjust his suit. Not taking his eyes off Cedric. Every zap of his energy was telling him to clip Cedric there and then. How dare he disrespect him like this. It may have been his duty first, but it was his duty now. His destiny, but yet there was something about his violent nature he liked. 'How are we the same, you and I? Why aren't you like the other Idlers who... well it seems they are gone now.'

'Those idiots.' Cedric shook his head smiling. 'I am nothing like them. They were the product of a bargain when Amb. Ermêl was first imprisoned. Me, I am pure, proper, Idle. The last of my kind.' Cedric continued the conversation as he headed down the staircase. Almost familiarising himself with the home he had abandoned all those years ago. 'It appears you somehow managed to slip through the cracks of the realms and have harnessed the G.A.Fs energy too. Well, I cannot do that.'

'If you are still for the cause, why hide in Eden?' Diego asked.

'I clipped a mortal on Earth.' Cedric rolled his eyes. 'Those acts get recognised by higher authorities. Luckily, the G.A.F is all about second chances.' He waved his arms around at the surrounding bodies. 'So, I went to a safe space. Spoke my confessions, said I saw the error of my ways and the benevolent reverend granted me pasture into Eden. Once I was in, I figured I would bide my time. I knew my past would come back to me at some point and, here I am.'

'I see.' Diego strode across the platform to keep parallel to him. 'So, the mortal guardian. What went wrong? Why did this... buffoon.' He scowled at Stephen. 'Not give us his power?'

'I don't know. Once clipped the blade should have absorbed his power instantly. It would have been compatible as there would have already been an Idle energy within him, but it never happened and once he was in Idle... his mind was as good as gone. Wait!' Cedric clicked his fingers and teleported back onto the platform over a crimson fence. 'There was a G.A... Linus!'

'What about him?'

'He was always there. Watching me like a weary warden as if he knew what was going on. I could never clip him because I was sure he was working with Divinity. I hated him nonetheless, but I bet he knows something.'

'He's gone. The Idlers clipped him.'

'That was a mistake.'

'Excuse me?' Diego cleared his throat, straightening his tie.

'I think he meddled with their fate. His fate.' Cedric pointed at Stephen. 'And I think I know how.'

'Tell me,' Diego asked eagerly, with raised eyebrows.

'No.'

Diego bit his tongue. No? How dare he say no to him.

'If Linus was still here I could have made him tell us.' Cedric sneered over his shoulder.

'We extracted as much knowledge from him as we could, besides there was a rescue attempt which needed to be stopped.'

'You just didn't interrogate him properly.' Cedric sneered, his hand illuminating in a crimson glow and then, he lashed a fiery fist across Stephen's face. His cheeks still rippling for seconds after with a large gash carved in the skin. That single punched appeared to knock out all of Stephen's bravery as he had no witty banter to say. No silly remarks. Instead there appeared to just be fear in his trembling eyes.

'Do you know why it didn't work!' Cedric asked Stephen, smacking him once more, so hard it even made Diego flinch. 'Ah, of course, your mind is frazzled. I should know that as I was the one who sent you there.' Cedric patted Stephen on the top of the head as he walked away, but he didn't stop talking. 'You are not to remember the night when you abandoned your wife and son. The night when you took your last lonely walk up that cliff. The night my blade carved through your very existence.'

Despite his initial thoughts, Diego was somewhat impressed with Cedric. He exampled the ferociousness of what he expected an Idler to be and it was a pleasure to witness. The soft, sinister feel to his words left an unnerving rashness in the air. Even he didn't know what he was going to do next, but as it turned out, it was his turn to influence. Acknowledging Cedric's hints, he retrieved Stephen's file and tossed it at his feet. 'I told you I would get it for you,' he bragged. 'Now you owe me.'

'Owe you' Stephen mumbled angrily through his busted lip. 'Look at me! If it wasn't for you I would still be in the Tavern minding my own business. Not... here, being beaten like a criminal for no reason.'

'But it isn't for no reason. It's saving the G.A.F, Stephen,' Diego hissed, gliding over to him. 'You may not think it, but it's the truth. Remember what I said to you when we were on duty? The world is caving in on itself. It's being neglected by the very people living on it and as G.As were hopeless at saving it. Instead, we sit by and watch it happen and the G.A.F is too 'good and pure' to do what is needed.'

'But it was your lack of actions that hurt people!'

'There is always someone who gets hurt. Dies. Is sad or troubled. It's the way life is and fate shouldn't be manipulated to change that. It's a fact, not everyone can be happy. Not everyone can thrive. We may come across as the bad guys, but we are necessary. We are the only ones looking at the bigger picture and have the means and strength to do what is right.'

After that, everyone stayed silent. Stephen appeared to be contemplating his words as if he had finally gotten through to him. The static sound waves from the crimson energy however, was causing an unnecessary tension, especially with the vortex sparking and whirring also. The silence wasn't welcomed and he was about to slam his foot on the platform to get something back when finally, Stephen picked up his file. Diego took a slight step back, catching Cedric's approving eye as they waited to see what happened.

Very slowly, Stephen raised the file to his face and as soon as he opened the first page, their energies had already begun to sync. The file lit up like a glow stick which spread down his arms and around his head, almost to the point his face was no longer visible. He watched Stephen's body jump as the file suddenly flicked through all its pages as if it was haunted, causing Stephen's head to jolt about as he downloaded all the information. The file then fell from Stephen's hands and the glow faded, but not completely as Stephen's aura was much more vibrant now. The wounds on his face had healed up and there was an element of surprise in his expression to suggest it worked.

'I-I remember,' Stephen muttered.

'And? Are you the mortal guardian?' Diego asked.

There was a brief pause, but eventually, Stephen replied. 'Yes. I am.'

'What?' Cedric blasted. 'Then how do we access your power? Why didn't I retrieve it when I clipped you?'

'I don't know.'

'You don't know?' Cedric thundered.

'Nope. Not a clue,' Stephen replied smugly.

Diego was about to takeover the interrogation, but before he could act Cedric had already made his move. He yanked the crimson binds off from Stephen's waist and threw him over a crimson fence.

'What are you doing!?' Diego snapped following him over.

'I'm tired of playing games!' Cedric growled. 'This is where he was clipped.'

Diego looked around over the fields. A broken fence laying on the cliff edge highlighted by the afternoon sun.

'And there is his home!' Cedric pointed. 'If he doesn't tell us what we need to know, I'll make sure everyone who lives there perishes and his home will become rubble.'

'No!' Stephen shouted. 'No, you can't!'

'We can!' Cedric gripped Stephen by the throat to quieten him down. 'And we will!'

'Hold on!' Diego held out a hand. 'Look we have the M.G, he has his memory. We can win him over.'

'Can we?' Cedric glared at him.

Diego met his strong gaze and refused to back down, even when Cedric burst into a bellow of laughter. 'You see. You're not pure Idle.' Cedric sneered. 'Fine. It's your duty now... isn't it. If you want to keep Amb. Ermêl waiting, be my guest. You have until the sun disappears over the horizon.'

'Stop giving me orders!' Diego thundered.

'I'll give you whatever orders I feel like!' Cedric bellowed back. Their voices echoing out like rival storms. 'Remember, I am pure Idle! You are a hybrid and as much as you think you belong here, think again. You were an experiment which worked in our favour. That is all.'

Diego's body boiled once again as a huge mountain of steam clouded over him. He was craving for a fight to prove his worth, but Cedric quickly disappeared back over a fence, leaving just one person he could take his anger out on.

Chapter 23

Everything appeared bleaker now through David's eyes. The world below was playing out like a video in greyscale. As if the rain was washing away all the colour it had left to offer. Even his fence was twinkling dimly under the tame sun.

The people bustling about in his familiar town were oblivious to all of this. As far as they were aware the world was probably still as bright and colourful as it had always been. He could tell from their energies and faint yellow auras they were enjoying themselves. In one way it was quite nice to see people happy, but on the other hand, it felt alien to him. Witnessing joy had become a rare thing for him, especially after what he'd been through. He thought things were tough before he died, but it hadn't got any easier. Since then his seen dead bodies; been attacked by evil angels; nearly burned alive in a sea of fire; came face to face with his dad's murderer; then found his dad only to lose him... again. Think that was probably enough to drive anyone insane. The only good thing amidst it all was meeting Grace, but now it seems he's burnt that bridge too.

A loud sigh left David's mouth as he continued to watch over everyone. Despite the amount of happy auras there were still some sad ones. One in particular which caught his eye was a woman walking fast down the street with her earphones in. She was clearly trying to shut the world out after having a bad day at work or something equivalent. There was a lot of angst in her energy so when he sensed a gap in her thoughts he influenced her to focus on the music and before he knew it her aura changed as she began to play an air guitar and nod her head aggressively at the beat to relieve some of her pent up stress. Her happiness became contagious as she influenced another lonely soul to join her as if they were listening to the same music. *At least I've made a difference to someone.*

Suddenly, another fence appeared in a whir of energy and to his surprise it was Grace. Without saying a word she came and sat next to him, quietly observing the street too with her feet swinging off the fence. After a few tense seconds she finally said, 'how are you doing?'

'I'm okay,' David replied without looking at her.

'Do you want to talk about it?'

'I don't think so. I understand I was in the wrong. I should have been there to help, but I just wanted a bit of space after... you know. I'm sorry.'

'What? No, that wasn't what I meant.'

'What?' David turned to look into her twinkling eyes.

'Don't worry about that, it's me who should apologise, I was in the wrong for being so mean to you. I'm asking if you are okay because of your dad.'

'What about him?'

'The fact he didn't remember you? The fact Diego and Cedric took him away? I can't imagine that was easy?'

'Oh.' David rubbed his wrists tightly. 'No, it wasn't easy, but I'm okay.' *Kind of have to be.*

'Really?'

'Yeah.' David shrugged. 'It isn't the first time he's been gone. I mean, there was a moment when I thought, you know, I had him back, but all well.'

'And you're okay with that?' Grace frowned.

'Of course not!' David scoffed, wiping his head harshly. 'But what is there to do? What can I do? You're right, I am useless.'

'Useless!' Grace scowled. 'David you rescued me from Limbo. Got us into Eden. You're the one who actually found the M.G. Don't be so hard on yourself. That's how you got here in the first place.'

David bolted up right as if insulted by Grace's words.

'Oh, come on, David. I sensed it the first moment we met. It wasn't an accident you joining the G.A.F. You don't care about yourself and until you do, you will always feel that way.'

David turned away back to the people below unsure on how to react. She wasn't wrong as such, but it doesn't mean he wanted to hear it. *It's difficult to care about yourself when you think the world doesn't.*

'You are so concerned with helping people and doing what is expected you've been neglecting yourself. I noticed it mostly in Eden.'

'Why Eden?' David asked quietly.

'Because while Rev. Li and I were talking, you just followed. Did nothing. Didn't catch up, didn't get involved. We weren't isolating you, we were waiting for you to join in.'

'I see.'

'David, your energy and heart is too strong to be a spectator. That's why I really believed we could have got you home.'

Home. A word that brought a warmth of cosiness to him as if he was wrapped up in his mum's purple blanket. How he wished to be home. To be seen by his mum. To talk... he closed his eyes to stop himself tearing up. 'I've made a mess of everything.'

'It's not you whose messed up,' Grace sighed, putting her hands together over her lips. 'This whole thing is my fault.'

'How do you mean?' David questioned, hoping she'd finally tell him what she's been holding back all this time. What she was secretly talking to Rev. Li about in Eden. Although, as much as he wanted to find out, he was suddenly distracted as he saw his mum stepping out of the café's berry red door with a hot beverage in a takeaway cup, most likely a milky cup of tea. She was wearing his dad's large navy coat which he used to wear when walking

Bud, highlighted by the number of mud stains on the right shoulder where he used to clean his hands after throwing a stick. There was a tired look on her face as if she hadn't slept in while and he watched her take a seat on the bench and he carefully synced with her energy. A sad aura wafted over her. One of concern and worry... and hope. Hope that her son was okay. Hope that he would return. Clearly thinking by staying in the town where he worked three jobs and visited the café, she would see him.

'Is that your mum?' Grace asked softly.

'Yes,' David replied flatly.

'She has a very caring nature.'

David smiled. 'She does. She would refer to me as her guardian sometimes you know. So did my ex-girlfriend for that matter,' he fell quieter. 'I have the letter to prove it as well.'

'Come with me.' Grace stood up and held out her hand. 'There is something I want to show you.'

David looked at Grace's glowing hand. Part of him didn't want to leave. Thinking the least he could do was continue to watch over his mum, regardless of the silly rule Grace had explained, but at the same time he didn't want to risk bringing anymore Idlers here. Not only that, but he sensed Grace was going to show him something important. So, he took one last look at his mum as she sipped her drink while watching the world flow past. *Sorry mum. I'll be back. I promise. I'm still here for you.* He turned back to Grace and took her hand as she led him over her fence.

They were now standing over acres of grassy fields. At first he thought he was back in Eden, but the energy didn't feel right. The sky was much cloudier and the fields stretched out as far as the eye could see. Banks of subtle wildflowers curved with the hilly landscape and a few hundred metres behind him was a large house, like an estate home.

Up ahead, he could see Grace waiting by a large oak tree and when he got closer he felt a sudden chill. With the grey sky looming down on it, the tree looked haunted. There were no leaves on its black bark and numerous branches had snapped off. Some laying in a heap at the bottom of the steep bank it stood on. He peered up at Grace who was now standing above a thick branch hanging a metre or so off the ground, her face full of sadness while she gazed outwards over the fields.

'Is this what you wanted to show me?' he asked.

Grace turned her head to the right as if gesturing to him to look at something and as he slowly peered passed her, his eyes widened. In front of him, gently blowing in the breeze were two large splinters of a fence rail standing in the shape of a cross.

David gulped, looking at the hallowed image. 'Is this... you?'

'No.' Grace shook her head, wrapping her arms around her chest. 'It could have been, but it's not.'

'Then, who?'

'It is a friend of mine.'

Many questions filled his mind, but he had no idea where to start. Many words tried escaping out of his mouth, but none managed to and luckily they didn't need to as Grace started talking again.

'I was much like you. When I was still alive,' she began, looking back over the hills and playing with something in her hand. 'I never felt like I fitted in. Thinking everything was against me. Even back in my time the world was a tough place to survive in, especially for a young lonely girl.' She smiled weakly. 'Unlike you, even my family weren't too keen on me. So I spent my days out here, playing in the fields, being one with nature and always wondering where my life was going to take me. But it didn't take me on the path it should have. I didn't let it.' Now close to tears Grace held out her hand to reveal

162

a Yutopian bead innocently glowing on her palm. 'Please,' she cried. 'I want you to see.'

David hesitantly held out his hand and placed it over the bead. Immediately feeling it 'pop' between their hands and the cool water rushed over him just like it had in the cabin. He didn't know if he was ready for this. Especially after what he witnessed last time, but Grace was entrusting him with her past and he wanted to show he cared.

Before he knew it, he found himself swimming back in the lilac ocean. Only this time it looked as though he was standing in the same place, only not on fences. This time he was free to move around. The violet outline of the tree was still in front of him, with a small figure sitting on the branch. At first he thought it was Grace, but they looked different and he soon saw it was actually a young boy. Another figure then came running into view following a small bird and he immediately knew this was Grace. Especially when they stopped beside him because even in a distorted shade of violet, her eyes stood out to him. He watched her appear to communicate with the boy and eventually she went up to sit beside him. Smiles on their faces.

The scene washed away in a current of ripples and he was now standing in the middle of what seemed like a ballroom. Plum figures dancing everywhere in synchronised fashion with a lonely shade of violet in the corner. Again it was Grace, but she looked older now. He could sense her sadness through the watery energy as everyone seemed to be ignoring her. Then, from nowhere, someone was asking for her hand and she hesitantly took it. The two of them danced about and David followed curiously as the boy didn't appear to be the same one as before. They appeared much older and his suspicions soon came true as in the next scene Grace was back at the tree with the first boy. The two of them appeared to be arguing. *A love triangle perhaps?* David thought.

As the next scene came washing in it looked like a ceremony was going on in some sort of barn. Grace was at the front holding the hand of the man she danced with. *She made her choice then.* The image didn't last long however, because as soon as the crowds cheered them kissing, David was transported to a small one room shack. Two figures wrestling. A fight. David's eyes widened in horror as the man appeared to slap Grace's face and toss her onto a bed. He didn't want to watch anymore, knowing the reality of what was happening, but then something strange happened. While the scene played out, random objects in the room began flying about. A cup. A saucepan. Shoes. The man was then blown across the room and looked to have been knocked out against the fireplace. The shack's door swung open wildly and Grace made her escape.

What did he just see? Was Grace about to be... what happened to the man? It was almost supernatural as if a... G.A had got involved.

David put his hands on his head, anxiously waiting for the next scene and he was now back at the tree, only now it was burnt out. There was no one on the branch and sitting on the bank in front of him was a sobbing Grace on her knees. The cross now in view.

He reached out an arm, wishing he could comfort her. *Oh Grace.* He watched her move her hands as if getting something from her pocket and then raised it to her mouth. He didn't know what it was, but he understood what she did.

The watery-lilac landscape drained away and David gasped for air with his hands on his knees. He took a few seconds to comprehend what he'd seen before peering up to see Grace's weeping tropical eyes. Lost for words.

'It turned out,' Grace spoke instead. 'My marriage was a sham of my mother's creation. The boy you saw who once sat here, they tried warning me, but I didn't listen. And then it was too late.'

David wanted to go up and hold her. Wrap his arms around her to try and squeeze the sadness out, but then she said something which answered so many questions. 'He was a mortal guardian.' She wiped her tears away. 'Because of my... actions. They died. Knowing the only way to protect me was from above and in doing so they broke the laws of the G.A.F. Linus told me all this after I...' she gulped, making David weep himself. 'That's why I do what I do. I break the rules to help people just like they did for me. And all this wouldn't be happening now if they were still here. Which is why I was so determined to find the next one.'

'Grace, I am so sorry,' David said softly. 'I can't imagine...'

'It's okay,' Grace whispered. 'It was a very long time ago,' she sniffed. 'It's funny though, your dad may be the M.G, but it is you who reminds me a lot of my friend. My... they were my guardian.' She smiled weakly again, wiping her face clean and put the Yutopian bead away. 'I'm going back to Eden now,' she said more strongly. 'Rev. Li has offered me a place with her for the time being and to be honest, I need some time away too. A lot has happened. Hopefully you'll return to us when you want to. If you want to.'

Grace quickly spun round on the fence before David could even open his mouth and he found himself alone again, digesting Grace's tragic story. What she had to deal with. The burden she'd been carrying and yet she was still so strong. He turned back to the grave, feeling himself getting emotional. This could so easily be him. His body fell weak as he pictured his mum on her knees by the grave, sobbing loudly as she could be doing right now in his absence. How many other mothers, fathers and friends have gone through something like this, like Grace had too? How had he allowed himself to be one of them? He gripped his head tightly and turned away. He rubbed his eyes harshly to stop anymore tears from formulating in his eyes. *This is it! Time to grow up!* David thought harshly. *You said you'd do anything. You said you'd help. You said you'd get home. You promised!* David clenched his fists and channelled the energy from his yellow fence, using it to purify his mind and give him a new found strength. Strength to keep going. Strength to fight. Strength to do the right thing. 'I can still fix this. For mum. For dad. For Grace... For everyone!'

He slowly took a step, trying to connect to Rev. Li's energy to re-enter Eden and eventually his fence turned emerald. 'Good first step,' he said, puffing his cheeks out, but he couldn't take the next one. He couldn't go over the boundary. Something wasn't right. His body twitched uncomfortably as if he could hear someone in distress, like someone was calling out to him.

He quickly jumped across the fence, praying he was wrong. His feet landing on grass.

Chapter 24

'Just tell me!' Diego thundered, glaring into Stephens stubborn eyes. 'You know what's going to happen if you don't. Is it really worth it?'

Still, Stephen remained silent. His body paralysed from the crimson energy invading his fence and body. 'Why are you being like this? Is this your mortal guardian power? Do you think you are better than me, too?' Diego snarled, slashing his blade across Stephen's thigh. 'I don't care what power you supposedly have. You're nothing. I mean, look at you.' He chuckled, waving his blade up and down at Stephen. 'You're still as useless as when I first saw you. How are you expected to make a difference.'

Stephen mumbled something back so Diego lowered the intensity of his energy as if turning down a dial to let him speak more clearly. 'What did you say?'

'You... you don't need power to make a difference,' Stephen said slowly. 'You just need the right beliefs... and a strong will.'

'That's it?' Diego chuckled. 'That's what you are going to say. Wow, I really do pity you Stephen.'

'I pity you.'

'Oh really? And why is that?' Diego folded his arms.

'Because you're trying so hard to be someone your not that you can't actually see what you're getting involved in. You want the G.A.F corrected, I get it. I understand, but do you really think what you're doing is going to lead to that? You're being played and you don't even know it.'

Diego's top lip twitched. He stared at the blade in his hand. His crimson aura. Stephen's bound body and suddenly, it all felt alien to him. As if he'd snapped out a trance. 'What other way is there?' he grumbled. 'No one listens. No one acts. Now I can act. Look at me, a responsibility comes with this energy.'

'Then give up the energy. You heard him, you're an experiment. That's all.'

Diego looked back at his blade. Was Stephen right? Was he being played? This isn't exactly how he thought things would go. He just wanted the G.A.F to be better. For angels to follow the rules. The more he thought about it the looser his grip became on his blade. To the point it was going to fall out of his hand, but he couldn't let go. The power was too great to give up. He clenched his fist back around the handle and slammed it into Stephen's shoulder causing him to yell. 'If you ever! Try to influence my mind again, I will clip you so slowly you'll feel like you've entered Idle a hundred times over! Understand?'

He pulled the blade back out and stepped backwards over the cliff. 'The sun is now gone, Stephen. Last chance to do the right thing. Tell me how to harness your power and your family will be spared.' He held out his arms. Crimson smoke spiralling around them and forming two tiny tornados on each palm. 'No? Still refusing to do the right thing... and you call yourself a guardian!'

In one split-motion, Diego thrusted his arms up. Zaps of crimson flickering over his suit as his energy soared up into the nighttime sky. The tornados swirling possessively among the darkness and tainted the clouds red. Feeling its monstrous presence in the atmosphere, Diego slapped his hands together. A colossal crash cracked over the land. A catalyst to create a storm and within moments Mother Nature took over.

The clouds continued to mimic the explosive sound every couple of seconds. The electricity in the air becoming more visible as it crackled through the cloud cover like live wires, and in a flash, lightning struck. The lonely broken fence below burst into flames which quickly spread to the grass and slithered along like a sizzling snake. Diego watched with fixated eyes as the fire continued down the hill towards a cornfield. Its trail staying ablaze as if the crimson flames were following a line of oil and within a matter of seconds the flames were on the house.

'Come on, Stephen. It's now or never.'

But with tearful eyes, Stephen remained silent.

'Very well.' Diego spun away in a huff to the watch show nearer the house. Not understanding how it had come to this. *He's such a fool!* He took a seat on his fence when, something caught his eye. *No! It can't be!* He quickly spun on his fence once again to get a closer look. *Impossible!*

Chapter 25

David raced across the grass towards his house. The soles of his shoes pounding on the solid Earth, praying his mum wasn't home yet. His eyes focussed on the monstrous fire attacking his home like a luminous kraken trying to sink a ship. A devilish creature in a hellish setting beneath the crimson sky.

Without hesitating, David propelled himself through the flames and broke down the back door, landing on his haunches in the kitchen. He coughed and spluttered as he inhaled the toxic smoke seeping through the window frames. The heat attacked him like fiery fists covered in napalm and it stuck to his clammy body, just like the energy in Limbo. He warily looked out the window on his left as sweat seeped into his stinging eyes and all he could see was the intense crimson flames trying to break in. *This isn't normal. What is happening!* He forced himself up, hearing Buddy's ballistic barking. 'I'm coming!' he shouted, straining his leg muscles as he stumbled through the kitchen and into the hallway that was dimly lit by the red smoke he was choking on. He spotted his dad's muddy coat hanging up by the front door and thought his heart was going to burst there and then. 'Mum!' he yelled. His throat as dry as sandpaper. 'Mum!'

With is body on the verge of collapsing he tried to create a fence, trying anything to escape the treacherous conditions, but nothing was happening. 'Mum!' he shouted again desperately. He dragged himself to the bottom of the stairs and suddenly Buddy's barking got louder. *He never goes upstairs!* David boosted an ounce of energy to begin climbing the stairs, believing his mum was up there too. 'Mum!' He heaved his heavy feet up. His energy draining faster than water down a plug hole. His suit melting against his skin like rubber on tarmac and making him wince in agony, but there was nothing he could do about it. With his arm covering his mouth, he got half way up when the house suddenly shook. Picture frames came crashing down onto the landing as he fell off balance and into the scorching bannister. 'Argh!' he yelped, shaking his hand wildly. The barking got more frequent as if Buddy could sense him coming and David could hear it was coming from his mum's room. 'No time to stop. No time to stop!' He raced to the top just as a second quake struck the house and the stairs crumbled away behind him, leaving his left leg dangling over the smoky pit below. Through blind panic and adrenaline, he hauled himself up onto the landing and went straight to the bedroom, barging through the door. 'Mum!' he shouted, trying to look through the dense smoke. 'Mum!'

Finally, he spotted her lying on the bed unconscious in her jeans and white blouse. Buddy barking frantically beside her. David immediately scooped up her warm body and headed out the room. 'Come on, Bud, stay close,' David said.

Diego was perched as close to the house as he could get. Still commanding the raging fire and trying to compress it as tightly against the house as possible to force the boy out, but there was something blocking him. His hands shook from the tension in his arms as he put all his effort into it, but still the flames were being kept at bay. There was too much smoke to see what was happening inside, but it was as if something was fighting back, or someone. 'This isn't possible!' he grumbled through gritted teeth. 'Why can't I... argh!' He slammed both his hands down and the house shook with a tame rumble. 'Huh.' He smirked. He did it again. His body and fence illuminating brightly as he summoned as much energy as possible, desperate to get this over with before Cedric returned, and then, the flames burst, like a match on petrol, and he stopped. He glared around the fire in search for the boy. The smash of breaking glass came from the upper floor and when he moved higher, for a very brief millisecond, he swore he saw a light blue glow sparkle from the roof. 'What's that?' He leaned in to get a better look when suddenly, a strong force hit him over the back of the head.

'Whose there?' Diego bellowed out, swishing his blade about as he stalked over the garden. 'Who dares attack me?' Another force struck his back and he quickly spun round, but there was no one there. 'Show yourself!' He snarled angrily, huffing through his nostrils. He listened intently to his surroundings like a bat on the hunt and soon, he heard humming. The sound growing louder and louder in his ears and this time, he timed his move to perfection. He spun round once again and launched himself at the yellow energy, tackling an angel over the fence and appearing further away from the house. His aura spilling off his fence and wrapping the culprit up like a bandit in rope. Small yellow sparks lit up the night as they tried to break free, but there was no escape from his energy's clutches. He readied his blade as their light crumbled off their body and just as he was about to strike, he saw a pair of hateful golden eyes.

'You!' Diego shouted. 'It is always you!'

David kept his mum close as he got to the top of the stairs, staring at the fiery wreckage debating what to do. The pressure of time fizzing in his mind with every flare up of flames. Buddy was constantly barking next to him as if telling him to get on with it. 'Alright, Bud! Alright,' David said. He jumped down onto a segment of the broken staircase still sticking out of the wall, but it immediately snapped beneath him. His adrenaline ran wild as he clenched his mum tightly, preparing to get burned in the fire, or worse, but suddenly, before the fire touched him, his feet landed on something else. The new solid ground immediately propelled him out of the front door like a springboard and he landed on the crunching gravel. He didn't stop to see what had happened as he thanked his fortune they were okay and he carried his mum further away from the house, placing her on the nearby grass in the recovery position. He put a hand under her nose to check she was breathing, but he couldn't feel anything. 'Come on, Mum!' he urged her. 'Come on! I don't know how to help. I...' He put a hand on her chest and felt her weakening heartbeat. 'No! No! I'm not having it. Come On!' Like a river of emotion, David channelled all his energy through his arm as if he was still on the G.A.F's fences. His hand shaking aggressively and suddenly, his palm began to glow. Through the light he could feel her heart strengthening. His own chest tightening. He winced at the sharp pain building up inside of him until he could take no more and stopped. His light instantly going out. He quickly put his hand back to her nose and when he felt her breathing a wave of relief washed over him. He didn't relax however, as he could still hear Bud barking inside. He forced himself back up onto his wobbling tired feet and raced back towards the house. 'I'm coming, Bud!' He tried to get up onto a fence to retrieve some energy, but he was too exhausted. Barely able to put one foot in front of the other. 'Come on, David! Come on!' he spurred himself, but his body was totally depleted. He needed to rest, but he couldn't allow that. He had to fight it. He had to. He couldn't stop. Not yet. 'Bud!' He looked up, wiping the sweat from his melting face as he dragged himself towards the house, passing his dad's burnt briefcase which had somehow found its way outside. His eyes reverted back to the house and a wave of panic crashed into him as he could see flames now on the upper level. 'Buddy!'

'Why have you come here?' Diego shouted ferociously.

'To stop you!' Grace yelled. 'How can you justify this?'

'It is my duty!'

'Duty? Diego, look at what you've done!' Diego peered back over the fiery wreckage. 'You once spoke about how it was wrong to intervene with the world and now you're the universe's biggest hypocrite.'

'Pah! Out of all the illegal good deeds you've done this is nothing!

'You're actively harming people!'

'And?' he bellowed back. 'You alone must have saved over a hundred lost souls which you shouldn't have. I am merely balancing the books. Besides! It is my orders!'

'Orders! Why are you so fixated on orders and rules rather than the greater good.'

'This is the greater good!'

'Is it?'

'Of course it is! If this is what it takes to put the G.A.F back on track, then I will do it a thousand times over!' Diego gripped the blade tighter in his hand and looked at Grace's flickering body still trapped in his energy, laying before him at his mercy and then, it dawned on him. He didn't need her approval or her respect. He didn't need Cedric's approval. He knew his power, his fate, and that was all that mattered.

'What are you laughing at?' Grace spat tiredly, her fence now nothing more than a single rail plank.

'All this time I've been seeking respect from the likes of you. To be seen for the powerful angel I am and now, I don't care,' he chuckled. 'It's not a contest. My fate can't be changed. It's an inevitability and I will clip every last G.A who tries to change that, including you... and the mortal guardian.' He saw the light in Grace's eyes spark up. 'Oh yes, quite the game you all played, whether you knew it or not I'm not so sure, but what I am sure of, is that it's coming to an end...'

He turned to the house, the flames now devouring its structure. There was something moving sluggishly in the grass and a wide smirk spread across his face. He released his energy from over Grace and squeezed her chin bullishly. 'You speak to me as if I'm a failure, when in reality, you are the one who has failed, in everything you've tried to do. And this... this is the epitome of your failures and one I want you to see... before I clip you, too.' He unleashed a blast of crimson energy upon her causing her body to seize up and then he vanished over his fence.

David halted. There was something nearby. Something he could sense. His body shivered despite the heat coming off him and he slowly crumpled onto his knees, gazing out nervously around him. Someone was watching him. He tried his best to ignore it, forcing his legs to get back up. 'Buddy!' he called once more, but he quickly stopped again. Whoever it was, they were close, now feeling more like a ghost than an angel and he couldn't shake the horrible feeling churning in his stomach. With his fists clenched and his eyes closed he finally managed to create a fence and scrambled up onto it. Bang!

'Bud!' He was too late. All of a sudden the roof of his house exploded. Thick red smoke poured up into the sky and David collapsed defeatedly onto the fence. Glass and debris scattered around him. The feeling of imminent danger rushed through his veins and in that same moment his fence began to glow green.

Within the next few seconds he found himself being engulfed by the green light and he was ready to concede. He waited to be swallowed up and taken away, but then he heard barking. He raised his heavy head and watched Buddy scamper out the house, bravely jumping through the fire and that was motivation enough to get his third wind. David rolled out of the green glow and ran back onto the grass to give him a hug. 'Bud! Whose a good boy!' he said, ruffling his collies head, but Bud still wouldn't stop barking. 'What is it?' David croaked.

Bud began growling at the air above and David hesitantly stepped back up onto a fence. A demonic energy ringing in his ears. A buzzing blade hurtling towards him in Diego's grasp. David stood petrified, but strong, preparing to defend himself and his family from the attack. A look of pure evil etched on Diego's possessive crimson face. He reached out a hand in an attempt to block the blow when a flash of gold suddenly lit up between them. Grace's holy eyes dimming. The crimson blade protruding through her chest and without a word, she fell forward into David's arms.

'Grace? No... no!' David held her tight. A rampant flood of emotions swirled through him like a mighty maelstrom. All the power he had left inside of him suddenly woke. His fence and aura turning luminous. He glared at Diego's menacing eyes and with his storm knocking at the door desperate to get out... that was it. David unleashed a thunderous cry. All his energy spilling out like a tidal wave and smashed into Diego, carrying him away far into the distance. The blade evaporated off Grace and the flames extinguished from the house. The night fell dark and quiet.

'David,' Grace said quietly.

'Ssh, I got you.'

Numerous popping sounds filled the air as a small group of G.As appeared on the scene, all of them rushing about to see what they could do.

'Hey!' David shouted at them. 'Look after them and get an ambulance here!' He pointed at his mum stirring on the floor. 'Keep them safe!'

'We will,' a G.A responded. 'Services are already on the way. She'll be fine.'

He leaned over Grace as she laid on her fractured fence. Pockets of light fading away into the atmosphere. 'I'm going to get you out of here.' While keeping her tight against his chest, he picked Grace up and spun on his fence to appear over the reservoir. Their fences of emerald and gold glowing off the tranquil water, enlightening the reeds and lily pads on its surface.

'Grace?' David said quietly. 'Talk to me. What can I do?'

'There's nothing you can do,' she whispered back.

'What about Eden? If I get you back to Eden you'll heal like last time? Rev. Li will know what to do.'

'No.' Grace shook her head.

'Then, what do I do!? Tell me what to do! Because I cant just-'

'It's okay, David.'

'No. This isn't okay.' He looked up at the starry sky as Grace put a soft hand to his cheek. 'I don't understand what's happening... what's... what's going on? I've already lost dad. Nearly lost mum and Bud... now you... I can't lose you. I can't lose...'

'You'll never lose me.' Grace smiled.

David could feel his eyes getting watery. 'Man, I thought I'd blocked all this out,' he sniffed.

'It's okay, David. Let it out.'

He looked into her glistening eyes and it suddenly felt like the lid of his emotions had fallen off and everything came gushing out at once. 'You were right earlier,' he cried a little. 'About me not caring about... myself, but for so long now, I've just felt so empty. And when I did feel something, my mind was so separate from my heart I found it easy to disregard the feelings and block them out. Forget about them. My walls have always been so strong, so strong I've almost been numb to it all... then I met you...' His jaw trembled. 'And you broke those walls down. I have no idea how it happened or why, but you did and

177

now these emotions are running riot within me and... you went and did this.'

'I had to,' Grace whispered. Tears dripping from her eyes.

'No, no you didn't. You-'

'We both know that's not true.' Grace smiled again. 'You know, deep down I knew it was you. If only I'd listened to myself sooner, but now you know your purpose. You are the mortal guardian, David, and it's you we can't afford to lose. Something is coming and it will be down to you to stop it. To protect those in need and those emotions you speak of... use them. They'll make you stronger.'

'How can I do anything without you. I can't go back to feeling alone. I can't be broken again, it'll... kill me,' he tried to joke.

'You're never alone David. Not now, not before and certainly not after. I'm always here.' She gently prodded his temple. 'As are we all and always will be.'

He clasped her hand tightly and lowered it in front of his chest, leaning forward so their foreheads kissed.

'What if I'm not as strong as everyone hopes?'

'David, you're stronger. You just need to believe you are.'

Grace's glow began to fade more.

'No... no yet.'

'Ssh, it's okay,' her voice whispered. 'It's okay. I'm still here.'

Her hand slipped away from his as he helplessly watched her face turn into pure light.

'Grace?'

But there was no answer. Grace's body dimmed down into tiny drops of light in front of him, like huddled up fireflies. Their golden glow shining off the water as if Grace's essence was still there, and then they swooped around the reservoir, brightening up everything in its path like magic dust. The water beneath him swirled smoothly as if the last of Grace's energy was putting on a wondrous display for him. He felt her presence one last time as the trail of light spiralled around him, revitalising his tired, beat up body. A warm sensation flowing off his lips before the light turned sapphire and continued up into the night sky, like tiny stars returning home.

A single tear trickled from David's eyes.

Chapter 26

By the time Diego came to, he was back in Limbo. He was sitting on the metallic floor with the whirling vortex directly in front him. His body ached and his eyes were sore, but as he tried to raise a hand to rub his face, he couldn't. 'What?' he growled, clenching his fists to try and break free of the crimson binds. 'What is this? What's happening?' He cast his eyes to Cedric's smug face as he shuffled past him. 'What is this?' he asked him directly. 'Release me at once!'

'Why?' Cedric tilted his head playfully. 'Can't you do it?'

Diego tried to lash out at him.

'I told you, you aren't pure Idle. You have weaknesses. Your Idle energy is dwindling due to your moral code of the G.A.F.'

'Morale code?' Diego scoffed. 'I have no obligation to the G.A.F. Not anymore.'

'And yet, you're no longer connected to Idle, so where do you belong now?'

'But... I was doing it. I was fulfilling my Idle duty. The plan you set out. The house burned. Stephen watched... where is Stephen?'

'He's here. Somewhere. We couldn't risk him trying to influence you again. The last thing we'd want is for your allegiance to Stephen cause you any issues. We can't let you use the little Idle power you have against us.'

'Allegiance?' he chuckled. 'What allegiance? He's a moron. An idiot. A waste of space, even more so now. You know he's not the mortal guardian?'

'Yes.'

Diego stared at him. 'How?'

'I was there. I saw the real mortal guardian. The same boy who saved his mother is the same boy I spoke to in Eden. Curious how these paths interlink. What I also saw, was you letting him get away.'

Diego double blinked. 'I... It's not like-'

'Not only that, but you couldn't even clip the G.A Grace, who has been a thorn in our sides for centuries.'

'Yes I did! I watched her perish with my own eyes! She wont be causing us issues anymore.'

'Perhaps, but your actions resulted in her dying as a martyr and therefore, although she is no longer present in the G.A.F, she is immune and protected from the Idle realm. Would it not have been better to know she would suffer a bit more? After all the chaos she has caused us?'

Diego remained silent. For the first time in a long time he felt as though he had done something wrong. Surely not, though? Surely the fact Grace is gone was enough? Surely the fact they knew the boy was the real M.G things would only work out from here on in? But yet, here he was, practically on trial for his actions.

'If it was up to me you'd be clipped,' Cedric added. 'But Amb, Ermêl, they are more intrigued.'

'You've spoken to them?'

'Oh yes, we go way back. I have been a loyal Idler for a very long time. Anyway, being their first experiment, they feel you may have one final chance to prove your worth. That you have the capability of being a true Idler. And if you succeed, you will be rewarded. Fail, and Idle will not be kind to you.'

Diego sat up straight. He hated the idea of being given an ultimatum by this brash senior Idler, but he knew he had to oblige. 'What do I do?'

'First, break free of your binds. Second, clip the mortal guardian. It's as simple as that. I will be here, waiting for you to pass the blade with his essence on to me, and then, together, we'll do the deed.'

Glaring at Cedric's haunting face, Diego had already begun, using his hatred of the Idler in front of him. The hatred of the situation. The hatred of not being in command anymore. Mixed in with his attitudes of the G.A.F and his own history was all the motivation he needed.

Lose my Idle energy. What nonsense! I know it's within me. I know. This is who I am! They think I am soft. They think I am a push over! Another insignificant pawn in this power play! They can think again! I'll show them!

His body heated up as the energy binding him sizzled over his body like trickling lava. Its power stronger and more reckless than before as if he'd dived deeper into the darkest corners of his mind and once he felt it fully return, he stood. He had broken free of his binds. His body absorbing the energy.

'Impressive,' Cedric spoke, re-adjusting Diego's suit and straightening his tie, 'And now?'

Diego's eyes burned once again as his vision turned infra-red. 'Now, I will clip the mortal guardian and I think I know how to get to him.'

Chapter 27

A few minutes after Grace disappeared, David surrendered to Eden's energy. He was transported back to the meadow and this time it didn't seem so bright or beautiful. The only positive he had was knowing his mum was safe thanks to the angel chatter he could hear. But as for the state of his home, he didn't want to know. Right now, he was just sitting in the grass, plucking out the surrounding flowers and crushing their petals between his thumb and forefinger. A weird prickling feeling niggling into his palm every time.

'Young man, please don't harm my realm.'

David immediately stopped what he was doing as Rev. Li walked over in her human form. 'Sorry,' he said, watching her take a seat beside him. 'I wasn't thinking. I... yeah, sorry.'

'It's quite alright, just don't let it happen again,' Rev. Li said, leaning back to soak in the lime rays with her eyes closed. 'So, you're the mortal guardian.'

David flicked his head to the side. 'You knew?'

'Meh, I had my suspicions. As did we all really.'

'Why didn't anyone say something sooner?'

'It is not our place to say what you are and what you are not. And even if we had said something, would you have believed us?'

'I'm not sure.' David turned away. 'I was pretty adamant I was dead. I did fall off a cliff.'

'Lucky you did.'

'What?'

'That was the key to you entering the G.A.F. Meeting Grace. Nothing like a near death experience to wake up our inner energies.'

'I see. Still. Would have been nice to know what was happening to me.'

'Young man, we must discover who we are in our own time. That's how we become the truest of ourselves. Not to be influenced by other peoples words.' There was a brief pause before she then said something which made David freeze all over. 'Everything happens for a reason.'

'My dad used to say that.'

'He is not wrong. That is how fate works, young man. We must not dwell on what has been. No matter how sad, unfair or traumatic it may have been. We need to learn from it.'

'Learn from it?' David shook his head. 'Learning is what you do after you make a mistake or gave something a try. What is there possibly to learn from losing someone? Multiple people. What can you learn from having them taken away from you? Are you supposed to hold them tighter? Let them go sooner? Care for them more or care for them less? Love them mor-' he stopped. 'You get the idea.'

Completely unfazed by his outburst, Rev. Li continued to sunbathe. 'How long have you had that pent up for?'

'I don't know,' David spoke more relaxed, picking at the flowers again until he realised what he was doing. 'Too long perhaps.'

'Hmm, well, this is more of a place of sanctuary. Works of the mind are more of the Captain's domain in Yutopia, but I strongly suggest you don't go there.'

'Why not?'

'Because your journey hasn't finished here yet.'

'Hasn't it?' David sighed. 'Whatever is happening is beyond me. I thought I could do anything, but now, with Grace gone...' He shook his head. 'I just want to go home, but I can't. Too risky now.'

Rev. Li finally looked at him. 'What you need is self-belief. There are things to be learned, young man, and the sooner you realise that the better. Bottom line is, Amb. Ermêl is likely to return and whatever happens after is down to you.'

'Down to me to do what?' David asked almost begging for guidance.

'I don't know. I wonder what Grace would want you to do as a mortal guardian... and a friend.' Rev. Li got back up and repositioned her headdress before walking away, leaving David to reflect on what she'd said. A single sentence which sparked so much inside of him.

'Where are you going?' David asked.

'I can't be sitting on my behind all day, I have things to do. As have you.'

David watched her walk away and leap over an emerald fence in her lioness form.

What would Grace want me to do? he thought. *Silly question. I know what she wanted. What she wants. She wants to help the G.A.F. Help the world. To stop the Idlers.* 'But how do I do it?' He put a hand to his head and then slowly moved it away again as if inspecting it. *The mortal guardian has the power of all the realms.* He clenched his jaw as he pictured Idle's horrific crimson energy. Everywhere he'd seen it, sadness and misfortune followed. Limbo. The G.A.F. Eden. His home. He couldn't allow it to get any further.

David slowly got to his feet. He crunched his eyes closed and used his emotions of hatred and hurt to channel the energy inside of him. His body radiating heat like an overused engine as he relived the last event. What happened to his dad. His Home. Grace. All of it festering away in his mind and heart like a vengeful sickness. The initial burning lasted a few seconds as Idle's energy awoke from within him and suddenly, he heard a voice. A familiar, sinister voice causing his anger to rise.

'Can you hear me, boy?' it hissed. 'I know who you are. We both have something the other wants. Use my energy to find me and we can resolve this mess you've caused.'

That was it. No thinking required. Like a soldier ready for battle, David stepped over his fence. Not worried about what might be waiting for him on the other side.

Chapter 28

Come on, boy! I know you heard me. Idler to Idler.
Diego paced around the island's perimeter on his crimson
fences. Nesting seagulls squawked at him every time he
passed them as if he was a lurking predator. It had been a
while since he tried communicating with the boy.
Although he had no idea where he was, with Grace gone
and his dad here, he knew it was only a matter of time
before he came. Besides, there was something else he had.

Still bound by Diego's energy, Stephen was placed in
the centre of the island and although he was unable to
move or talk, it didn't stop him making noises. All Diego
had heard since they got here was his incessant
mumbling. He'd ignored it this far, but his patience was
running out. With the flick of his wrist he lowered the
level of energy around Stephen so his head was free from
the crimson aura. 'What?' he said angrily. 'What is it?'

'I have got, the worst itch.' Stephen stared at him. 'It's
right between my shoulder blades if you wouldn't mind
getting your dagger out again.'

'G.As don't get itches!'

'Really? Well I got something... and its annoying. Not
nearly annoying as you, but still, think I got more of a
chance of getting rid of this one.'

'Are you not scared?' Diego strutted over to him. 'You
are still in the coils of Idle energy. Your home is
destroyed. Your loved ones injured if not dead and your
stupid son is about to fall into my trap by coming to save
you and yet you sit there... mocking me!'

Stephen smiled back. 'Scared? Of you? No. You like
me too much to do anything drastic.'

'Like you?' Diego chuckled deeply. 'And why do you
say that?'

'Because you can't let me go.' Stephen continued to smile. 'Think about it. You took me away with you into the G.A.F when you could have left me in the Tavern thing. You tried to help me with my file, but when you failed you took me on your. Then... you abandoned me.' Stephen acted sad. 'But you came back!' His smile reappeared. 'I mean, for sure it was for dark purposes and all. You did attack my family and burn my home... that was a bit much. I didn't appreciate that, but I don't know, I feel as though we have a really weird love hate relationship going on.'

Diego's top lip twitched at Stephen's babbling. What was he on about? Why was he acting this way? Any other G.A in his position would either be begging for freedom or wishing to be clipped to get it over with, but Stephen was putting on a performance. His thrusted his blade at Stephen so its tip was pricking the middle of his forehead. 'Do not mistake my actions for ones of kindest,' he hissed. 'The only reason our paths keep crossing is because of fate, and fate alone, but our ends will be very different. The only reason you're still here is because I have yet to acquire what I need, but once I have it, you'll be sent back to Idle to rot! As will your stupid son!'

He watched the expression on Stephen's face change from pure playfulness to seriousness. 'My son, is not stupid.'

'We'll see about that when he gets here, shall we,' he spat in Stephen's face. 'It's no wonder Cedric never got the mortal guardian essence. You never had it.'

Stephen shook his head. 'Yup. Finally figured that one out hey. Well I'll tell you what I've figured out.'

Diego lowered his blade. 'And what is that?'

'You're not pure Idle. Which to me is the same as not being pure evil. There is a good energy inside of you, Diego, I have seen it. Granted it's in your own weird way, but you should listen to it. You might actually begin to like yourself more.'

Tired of his games, Diego restored the aura over Stephen's head to shut him up. 'I will not be influenced by you!' he hissed, glaring into his frozen open eyes. He spun away in a huff and strolled to the edge of the island, swinging his blade at the seagulls still squawking at him. He then stood completely still. His hands cupped behind his back as he watched the rising sun. Stephen's words rattling away in his mind. *Not pure Idle, I'll show him! I'll show... Finally!*

Diego quickly withdrew his blade, tightened his tie and straightened his jacket. 'I knew you'd come!' he said, running his hand over his head. Having been met by silence however, he slowly turned round and smiled as he saw the boy's zapping ruby eyes glaring back at him. A crimson fence beneath him on the other side of the island. 'Well, well... look at you! Standing on Idle's fences. Must feel quite privileged.' The boy still didn't reply. Stephen on the other hand, was making more noise than ever now and Diego flicked a wrist to intensify the aura's power to try and shut him up. 'Have you come to bargain?'

Seeing what was happening to his dad, David slowly stepped forward. His hands clenched by his sides. His heart racing in his chest, but not from fear, from rage. Without blinking, he walked towards his dad. He had a plan in mind, but seeing Diego's smug arrogant face made his eyes sting and his vision blurred into a tone of sepia. All he wanted to do was release the anger pent up inside of him. Attack him like he had attacked them, but he held it back. This was the first time he felt this kind of power consistently bubble inside of him rather than just being an emotional outburst and he was biding his time.

'Don't want to talk, hey?' Diego smirked. 'Okay, fine, give this a read instead.'

David watched wide-eyed as a file was tossed towards him and he flung his arm out to catch it. His chest calming as he read the title. 'What is this?'

'That, is your file. Thought you'd like to give it a read.'

David scowled at Diego's strange, pleasant attitude. He half expected him to be shooting energy bolts at him by now or at least have a blade at the ready, but there was nothing. He flicked through the pages with steady fingers. Going faster and faster while staring at the document. 'Is this a joke?' he shouted across to Diego. 'It's blank.'

'Of course it's blank!' Diego shouted back, moving forward. 'It has never been touched, used or even seen! You're the mortal guardian.' He air quoted mockingly. 'Your mind can't be influenced. You can't be looked after. As far as the universe is concerned, you don't even exist!'

David's heart sank in his chest.

'Oh, don't look so down beat,' Diego chuckled. 'Don't you see what this means?'

'What?'

'Your file is blank, because your fate hasn't been written.'

David stared back at his reflection on the shiny pages as Diego spoke.

'You don't have a path to follow. You don't have a G.A trying to dictate your every move and action. Every second of every day is yours to do as you please, completely uninterrupted. You, are in charge of your own destiny, like me.'

'You?' David said aggressively, bolting his head up. 'I'm nothing like you and besides, how is this a good thing? My life has been nothing, but difficult and lonely because of this!'

'But that was before you knew about your power!' Diego argued back, still strutting towards him. 'Imagine how different things could have been if you had known this beforehand. If it had not been kept from you. Imagine what you could have achieved.'

David hated how much sense Diego was talking. It was like every word was indoctrinating his soul. Awakening those sinful, unhappy thoughts he'd spent so long repressing and then, he heard the one thing he didn't want to hear.

'Your father would still be alive, that's for sure.'

David bit his tongue as he looked over at his dad. 'What do you want from me?' he shouted, tired of the mental games.

'I want you!' Diego stroked his tie. 'Look, we have the same cause you and I, whether you believe it or not, we are the same. We both know the world is broken. The corruption, the inequality, the selfishness. I have watched over mankind for centuries and with every passing year it only gets worse and I know you understand what I mean. Are you not sick of the rich getting richer? The scandals getting swept under blood-ridden carpets? Everyone in this so called 'entitlement era'? Believing they should have luck and fortune just for the sake of it? Without working for it? It's ridiculous!' Diego was getting more riled up the longer he spoke. 'Its gotten so bad that it's begun to contaminate the G.A.F. All these bloody do-gooders! And they see me as a villain because I am different. I'm the only one doing what is right! Fulfilling the G.A.F's purpose and between us, we could achieve it! Be unstoppable!'

David finally blinked. Shocked by Diego's proposition. 'You want me to help you? Help you clip innocent G.As and neglect innocent people?'

'Innocent is a strong word. Especially when you don't know the people you are referring to. The strongest people need to be risen above the rest. Not every one deserves a guardian. Not everyone should be entitled to a guardian. Only the selective few, the ones destined for greatness!

They are the ones who should be influenced and looked after.'

'Like you?' David scowled.

'I should have been!' Diego growled. 'As should you!'

'And what about the ones left behind? The lost souls?'

'They are lost... nature will take care of them.'

David looked out over the calm ocean. The sun shimmering on its surface depicting a beautiful world and yet to him it still looked gloomy grey. Despite understanding Diego's argument, deep down he knew he was wrong. Yes, the world wasn't perfect, far from it even, but there were other ways.

'All I need, is your essence,' Diego said more civilised.

'I know what you need! I know what you want it for.'

'Good! So you understand that with it I can free Amb. Ermêl and then they can help us fix this faulty world.'

'No...' David shook his head. 'No, you can talk the talk, Diego, I'll give you that, but you're wrong. I've seen and experienced so much in the G.A.F and it's amazing. There's so much to give. Yes it could be better, but through leadership, not dictatorship. Not the way your suggesting. Everyone may not be entitled to luck and fortune, but everyone is entitled to be helped. Regardless of who they are.'

'But not me, clearly!' Diego snarled. 'Or you!'

'Me? I've been helped. I've been helped more than I could have asked for. I was just too late to see it. I know that now.'

'Rubbish! I know how you must have entered the G.A.F. You are tired of it all, right? The helping, but never being helped. The bad luck. The misery. Being a lost soul! You know what I have said makes sense, but there is something inside of you saying it's wrong. The same part which you allow to torture your mind day in and day out as if you like the pain, but deep down, you just want out.'

'I... no, I-' David's fence slowly turned yellow, as did his eyes and aura.

'Yes you do. I can see it in your eyes, even through that weak crimson mask.' Diego moved closer. Both of them now an equal distance from Stephen. 'Perhaps, now is the time to make amends?'

'Amends?' David's ears pricked up.

'Well it seems poetic does it not? You want to disappear... your father here wants to reappear... you can't be more helpful than that.'

'Y-You can make bring my dad back? As in back back? Back alive?'

'I can, yes... with your essence.'

David ran his hands through his hair, gripping it tightly. Was he really contemplating this? This wouldn't just be helping his dad, but his mum too. The thought of them being reunited... it almost put a smile on his face and he... he could be with Grace, perhaps? Be done with all of this. All this expectation. His file showed no path so maybe it meant no future? Should he put this tortuous path to an end? He stared at Diego's cold garnet's. He knew of his plan. He remembered what Rev. Li had said, but you know what, why did it have to be his problem? Besides, there was always a chance another mortal guardian could appear in his absence. History could repeat itself like it had before.

'Do we have a deal?' Diego reached out a hand. Crimson energy swirling around it like a deadly mist.

David stared at it hesitantly. Complex emotions swirling around every little crevice of his brain as if there was a moral civil war in his head. The pair of them stood anxiously like cowboys at a Mexican stand off, waiting for the other to move or say something first.

'Do we have a deal, or not?' Diego repeated.

David exhaled slowly and raised his arm towards Diego's, but he felt something. Another presence. A strange ping, like a tuning fork hitting a wine glass filtered into his ears. He instinctively dropped down from his fence onto the island's rocks just as Cedric swung a blade at him. Flocks of seagulls fled into the sky at David's physical presence, distracting Diego as he made a run for his dad. His adrenaline pumping as he could no longer see anyone, but still feel their supernatural presences in the air. He quickly stepped back up on to an emerald fence and leapt towards his dad. The moment his fingertips hit the crimson aura imprisoning him, the demonic energy dissolved and his dad disappeared in a burst of emerald light. David however, didn't go with him. He collapsed back onto the hard rocks. His body scraped and bruised from the impact. His energy depleted. A cold burning pain ate away through his heart as if he'd been stabbed by a fire poker. He exhaled slowly, feeling the buzzing energy consume him from the inside. *No.*

Diego watched in amazement at the colourful energies of sapphire, emerald, citrine, amethyst and gold transfer onto his crimson blade. The metal illuminating like light through a diamond. The energy suddenly exploded with a mighty bang. Sonic waves hurtling out far over the ocean, like a combusting star. Smoke covered the island and once it settled, the boy was gone.

He stared at the humming blade and raised it up to the sky, a wide grin spread across his face. 'Yes!'

Chapter 29

David stood in darkness. Tiny balls of buzzing crimson blinking back at him in the smoky atmosphere. He wanted to call out, but kept gagging at the pungent stench infiltrating his throat and lungs, like a mixture of bleach and vomit. The odour burned his nostrils as if his nose was corroding off his face. It was a similar experience to when he entered Limbo, only a hundred times worse. The only positive was that despite the unbearable smell he didn't feel as though he was going to be sick, although, he couldn't feel anything. His body felt as empty and hollow as a scooped-out shell, so much so, he couldn't even feel the weight of his suit on his skin. It was as if he was having an out of body experience.

Eventually, he came to terms with his surroundings and managed to ignore the horrific conditions. He gazed around the darkness, trying to figure out what to do next. His ghostly presence made him feel uncomfortable and he hit his numb body rigorously, hoping to feel something, but it was like all his nerves had been singed away. What he did notice however, was that his tie was red and it suddenly dawned on him.

Idle!

A sudden bellow of thunder roared out like a monsters warning. The sky coming to life in a burst of flames and lit the realm in an eerie crimson. Two sheer cliffs appeared either side of him as if he was at the bottom of a mountainous chasm and with forward being his only option, he slowly ventured through the narrow gorge. He squeezed through all the little crevices that came his way, some so tight, he could have sworn he'd cut himself on the sharp rocks, but there was no pain or evidence to suggest it. The only sensation he got was something like pins and needles, which were currently prickling his arms as they scraped against the two large boulders he was trying to pass between. He was about halfway through when the entire sky suddenly snuffed out and left him in darkness once again. This time the pitch-black played tricks on his mind as he thought he could feel things scuttling up his arms and neck, but he was unable to do anything about it as his touch had no impact when attempting to wipe them clean. His anxiety went up a notch as a result and he forced his way through the boulders and kept moving with outstretched hands to try and navigate, placing one hesitant foot ahead of the other as if he was walking on thin ice and scared of falling through. His breathing deepened the longer it went on for and soon the apprehension got the better of him and he had to stop again. He rested his hands on his knees while he caught his breath, trying to make sense of yet another disastrous event. *What's happening? What's happening? What did I do?*

Wanting to sit down, he lowered his senseless body, but immediately lost his balance on the uneven ground and fell forward. He tumbled down a gravelly slope at some velocity until he crashed against something solid at the bottom. His whole body now sizzling as if he was being fried in an oily pan, causing his sleeping muscles to spasm helplessly. Even if he could speak, he wouldn't be able to explain the pain surging through him right now, both mentally and physically, and when it was finally over, he simply curled up on the floor and laid completely still. Half hoping the darkness would just swallow him up. His empty eyes wanting to cry.

Was this fair? All he ever wanted was to be the good guy and help people, yet his actions have led him here. Maybe it was his own fault. Maybe he shouldn't have let Diego influence him as much as he should, but he wanted to help his dad. Wouldn't anyone else have done the same in his position? It's so difficult to know what is right or wrong when the stakes are so high and right now, he didn't know if it was the right choice. Maybe he did deserve to be here. He'd let everyone down. There was no going home from this.

The sky thundered down upon a motionless David. His energy as depleted as his soul. His mind the only part of him working and he wished it wasn't. The thoughts were trapping him in a helpless cocoon as if he was preparing to lay there forever and just wait to perish properly.

All of a sudden, a switch flicked inside his head like a lighter in an empty tunnel. A final flicker of hope and sanity. He may feel like a failure, but he could still do something, there is always something that can be done and he owed it to everyone to try. Failing is one thing, but quitting wasn't an option. *Whatever it takes,* he reminded himself, so with all his mental might, he pushed himself up off the floor. As he got his legs beneath him, the sky came back to life. A gigantic imperial red sun appearing up above. A flurry of flames flying out of it to light the world once again. He cast his eyes up to the sinister sight, feeling the sun's radiation immediately scorch his pupils like a devilish stare, making him turn away instantly. He crunched his eyes closed to squeeze out the demonic energy trying to penetrate him and when he opened them again, he couldn't believe what he was seeing. It looked like the aftermath of Armageddon. Rivers of slow moving lava bubbled across the vast baron wasteland of molten rock. Rapid bursts of steam shooting up from giant geysers in every direction. There was something else too, scattered across the entire land were tall shards of red rocks, like crystals. He gulped nervously as they reminded him a bit of tombstones in a graveyard. At first glimpse there must have been thousands of them, if not millions, and one was directly in front of him.

Keeping his eyes off the sky, he reached out an airy hand and stroked the pentagonal shard which glistened in a diluted shade of ruby. He stepped around the strange object, trying to work out what is was. *Bloody Hell!* he gasped. There was a young woman trapped inside the thick casing. Pure fear etched on her face. Her wide eyes staring back at him. *What happened to you?* he thought, looking around at the others nearby. *What happened to all of you?*

With so many questions in his mind he began to miss Grace even more. This was the first time he'd experienced the afterlife alone and it just so happened to be the worst place to be. As cliché as it sounded, it was like he'd fallen into a nightmare and he was scared. He put his fear to one side however, and took a deep breath. *Well, I'm not going to get home by standing still am I.* All there was to do now was to wander idly through the realm in the hope of finding a way out, and pray he didn't lose his mind trying.

After a few minutes of walking the sky went dark once again and this time, a strange noise followed, like clicking crickets. *What is that?* A ghostly chill crept over his arms. A warning that something was coming. Then, from nowhere a sharp pain stabbed David's lower back like a cattle prod and he started running. He sprinted blindly in the darkness. A crimson glow over his hands. The energy stung his palms and made his body jolt from side to side as if guiding him on a path away from the dangers, enabling him to dodge erupting geysers and lava pools like it was second nature to him. The clicking continued to grow louder and louder as if there were now bugs nestling in his ears, making him smack them violently while he ran to try and get the noises to stop. It wasn't working however, and with the daunting distraction it caused him to slip off the rocky path and he plunged a leg into a pool of lava. He screamed in agony as the feeling immediately came back to his limb, like the realm wanted him to endure the pain. The boiling liquid searing his skin up to his calf and caused him to collapse onto the floor. He went to clutch the wound, but it was far too tender to touch and the clicking was now right upon him. Bracing for the inevitable, he dragged himself away until his back smacked into something, making him feel claustrophobic as he was backed in a corner. His heart climbing out of his dry throat. The noise was now upon him and his chest tightened as he saw a dim red glow appear ahead. He cowered up in a ball to protect himself until suddenly, there was a flash of diamond-blue.

Someone was standing in front of him defensively. A blue flame flickering off their palms to reveal a pair of giant pincers coming at him. Whatever it was, the person protecting him quickly set it alight and David watched, gobsmacked, as a strange creature scampered away in a high pitched whine. The fluorescent flames racing across its body. The creature must have been the size of a large dog. There was a pair of oval wings on its back and it had six spiky legs. The antennae on its head looked more like antlers as its whole body looked to be made of bones. The creature eventually stopped whining and rolled onto its back. Its legs curling inwards as its body slowly disintegrated onto the rocks like coal dust and in the same moment, the sun and sky awoke once again.

David peered up at the strange, yet familiar figure who was yet to move and when they slowly turned round, he saw their diamond white eyes. 'You?' He pointed a finger at the boy. The same boy he had met in town on the day he died. Peculiarly, he was still wearing the same outfit of denim jeans, a light blue shirt and white diamond tie that matched his aura.

'You need to keep moving, David. It's not safe here,' the boy said.

'Who are you?' David quizzed.

'My name is Vinicius,' he said, kneeling down to cast his aura over David's injured leg to numb the pain.

'What are you?'

'It's not important,' Vinicius spoke abruptly as if angry.

'Yes it is,' David argued. 'I want to know.'

'All that matters is you getting out of here!' Vinicius glared at him. 'You shouldn't be here.'

Vinicius held out a hand to help David to his feet, but when David accepted it Vinicius instead tugged him over a diamond fence and transported them both somewhere else in the realm. David wanted to ask more questions, but Vinicius had already begun walking away towards a cliff edge and he quickly followed, hobbling behind him. His mouth never opened, though, as he sound of distant screaming took precedence as it echoed over the land. 'What is that?' he finally asked.

'That, is the sound of panic, desperation... and hope,' Vinicius answered. 'Something you are going to have to deal with.'

David gulped, his throat so dry now it was like he was swallowing sand.

'You shouldn't be here, David. How can you be so stupid?'

David snapped his head at Vinicius and double-blinked. 'Excuse me?'

'You heard me! And you know it, too. A heart and soul like yours should never have found itself here. This was not your path.'

'I thought my path was blank? I saw my file.'

'Your file?' Vinicius scoffed. 'A file is a log book for G.As to follow and record in. You are a mortal guardian who can't be influenced easily... of course your file is blank!'

'That's not how Diego put it.'

'I wonder why!' Vinicius raised his voice. 'What possible reason could he have for lying to you?'

David rubbed his shoulder and stared out over the scarlet wasteland.

'Why did you do it? Why did you let him clip you?'

'I didn't!' David shouted back. 'I was trying to save my dad! Protect him!'

'Protect him? Your father died for you!'

David's entire body crumpled up at the news.

'How do you think he feels now? Knowing his son, who he died for, got himself killed. Not once! But twice! It's insulting.'

'I...' David didn't know what to say. There was an uncontrollable anger raging inside of him, but there were no right words to express it. 'Diego said he could bring him back. Back alive. I did it for him. For mum.'

'Diego lied! And besides, what kind of parent would want their child to give their lives up for them? It's natural for parents to protect their young, not the other way around.'

'I... but, why? I don't understand why any of this had to happen in the first place. I...'

'Look,' Vinicius spoke softer. 'You are still young and I get you have found things tough-'

'Tough?' David interrupted him. 'What do you know about any of it? It has been a bloody nightmare!'

'I know more than you think! mortal guardian or not, you still had people looking over you.'

'Oh really? Well, they did a mighty fine job didn't they?'

'Don't blame others!' Vinicius thundered. His voice echoing out over the realm. 'I see everything! I watch everything! And I watched you the closest.' He shoved a finger at David. 'I may not have been able to influence you, but I watched your mother try. Your father try. Grace try. You're the one who didn't listen or see the bigger picture. Too 'always alright' with everything to make use of your life and challenge the status quo. Instead you squatted in your pit of misery and jumped.'

'I didn't jump!'

'You might as well have done! And here you are! You're lucky Grace was where she was at that moment.'

David frowned. 'Grace?'

'What? You think she was just there by coincidence when you jumped off that cliff? You may be a closed book, but it doesn't mean we can't influence people around you to help. To come to you.' David turned away. 'And it was a good job I did or you would never have fallen into the G.A.F as an M.G, but as a regular angel.' There was a short pause before Vinicius continued his lecture. 'Fate is a peculiar thing, David. It is never one person's. It is nature. It connects us. It intertwines with everything, everyone, everywhere, all at once. That's how paths cross and destinations get reached... and you've got one hell of a difficult detour ahead of you.'

'What do you mean?'

'Your journey isn't over. There is still a destiny to fulfil.'

'What if I don't want it? What if I'm tired of it all?'

'Then, you can watch the entire world burn.'

David scratched his forehead and looked away.

'You know what's about to happen. That was the one thing Diego didn't lie about and it's your destiny to stop it.'

'How? Where am I even going?'

'Hagitol,' Vinicius said bluntly, pointing over the fiery horizon. 'It is located in the centre of this realm and in the centre of Hagitol is a labyrinth. You must find your way through it to the gateway to escape. The souls who make it are given a second chance in the G.A.F. It was a deal we struck with Amb. Ermêl, but it is not going to be easy.'

'Is that how my dad got out?'

'Yes. Eventually. However, he wouldn't know it as the journey took its toll on his mind.'

'Yes, so I saw,' David said flatly.

'Yes. Well now it is your turn. Get out of here and keep your mind strong. That creature back there, it is a Déliánt. An Idle creature who preys on the weak minded souls here and puts them out of their misery.' Vinicius pointed at a ruby shard to the left which had an elderly man trapped inside of it. 'They clearly sensed your mind was weak enough to attack.'

David didn't reply as he pictured the ugly creature Vinicius had saved him from and shivered at the thought there were more waiting for him.

'Good luck, David. I'll be watching.'

'Wait! What? Aren't you going to help?'

But Vinicius had already disappeared in a flash of sky blue and David was left peering over the cliff by himself. The distant screams making his melting body shiver. Every single word Vinicius has said was niggling away on his eroding mind. For someone who always put others first it felt like a very harsh lesson to learn, but he understood it. Why didn't he listen? Why did it have to come to this before he acknowledged what they were trying to tell him? All those helping hands he had batted away because of this silly self-destructive path he put himself on. Well, now was the time to change. Arguably it was a little late, but better late than never and he owed it to everyone you had tried to help him.

David took a deep breath and removed his jacket. He threw it on the floor behind him as well as his tie and undid a couple of buttons of his shirt. It didn't make any difference, but it made him feel better. Less confined against an establishment he knew little about. He stared out over the volcanic landscape. 'Okay. Okay. Come on David. Let's get out of here.'

Chapter 30

While admiring the blade in his hand, Diego brought it to Limbo. Only wishing he could harness the power running through it for himself. The moment he came back, he could feel the buzz of excitement as if the unconscious bodies were emitting their own energy of anticipation, awaiting to finally be woken and put to use. He peered up at the energy on the ceiling and watched it speed up as though it was a Devilish pet eager to see its master again, shooting out bolts of crimson over the entire room. Up on the platform meanwhile, he noticed Cedric waiting. His hands cupped in front of him like a proud godfather.

Diego approached him. A crimson connection in their eyes as they put their egos to one side, knowing nothing else mattered now.

'Well done,' Cedric spoke. 'We'll make an Idler of you yet.'

Diego puffed out his chest. 'What now?'

'Now, throw it into the void.' Cedric waved a hand behind him.

Diego slowly approached the giant vortex. Gazing into its fiery beauty with a sinful smile. *So it begins.* He launched the blade into the whirling energy and the second it went through the vortex spun faster and faster. The colours from the blade splintering through it like veins in an eyeball. He could feel the force of it blowing him away. His feet skidding on the platform while his tie flapped behind him. The room shook from the sheer power. Clumps of rocks falling from the ceiling and bouncing onto the metal grates with a heavy clunk. He raised his hands to shield himself from the radiation, all the while not wanting to take his eyes off the magic occurring as the vortex began to change colour. One by one, the relevant light burst out of its nucleus like a torpedo.

Emerald. Citrine. Amethyst. Gold. Sapphire. All sparking out and lighting up the room like a flash bomb. The last one, crimson.

The vortex remained in its crimson state as it started to shrink, revealing a stone wall behind it as the energy swirled in a ball no larger than a fist, pulsating frequently as it floated outwards. A loud ping chimed through the room as the energy began to morph. Sparking strands shooting out of it like wild fungi, growing and growing until it was over seven feet tall and once it appeared to hit its peak, its centre ignited. A rush of crimson flames spread over the creation to construct the outline of a fully formed being.

Diego watched in awe as the flames slowly died down to reveal a boney body hidden beneath a skin-tight dress made of the crimson flames. The colours complementing their ruby shaded skin. 'Finally!' Amb. Ermêl said, her crimson eyes flaring up as she admired herself. 'I am whole again.'

'Amb. Ermêl.'

Diego turned to see Cedric bow his head and so he quickly copied and stared at the platform until he was instructed otherwise. The static buzzing of Amb. Ermêl's dress grew louder as she glided past him.

'Nice to finally see you again, Cedric,' she said. 'You did well.'

'Thank you,' he replied. 'It has been a long time coming.'

'Yes. It has. And you played your part well.' Amb. Ermêl approached Diego.

'Yes. Thank you,' he replied.

'I had my doubts, Diego. I had my doubts, but you came through.' He felt her cold hand pat his shoulder as she glided back to where the vortex had been. 'Now there is no time to waste. We must make the necessary changes quickly. Before they awake.'

He peered up to see Amb. Ermêl press her palm against the stone wall. A crimson glow taking over her hand and lighting up the stones to reveal a large archway. Then, without a word, she disappeared through it.

Diego turned back to Cedric to see if he was going to follow, but he was already halfway down the platform steps. Clearly there was something else he wanted to do, but not for Diego. He needed to know what was behind the wall. He quickly stood up straight to realign his jacket and tie and headed for the archway, stepping through it without a thought and into the darkness. The only light coming from Amb. Ermêl's flaming dress. His footsteps echoed out as he walked further in and suddenly Amb. Ermêl started to speak again. Almost like she had expected him to follow.

'Once upon a time,' she begun the story. 'This was where we would meet. All us realm guardians.'

Diego watched closely as he saw her study a glowing red orb embedded in the ground. It looked as though she was trying to remember how it worked, but then the room suddenly got brighter.

'Eden, Idle, Tavern and Yutopia.'

After each word, a new quadrant lit up in a dim ruby red until the circle was complete. Idle's quadrant was the only one with live flowing energy and with the room now visible, he spotted the strange stones in the floor and crouched down to inspect them, running his hands over the bumps and smiling as he pictured the other guardians all standing in their zones.

'We used to meet regularly, Amb. Ermêl continued the lecture. 'All of us appearing before Divinity to offer our services and ideas to help benefit the G.A.F and Earth. Those were the good times.'

'What happened?' Diego asked.

'They went dormant!' Amb. Ermêl answered like a bitter child. 'They believed Earth had grown to a point of sustainability. That our involvement was no longer needed and that we should allow the G.A.F to assist fate naturally and... what will be, will be... fools!' The room suddenly flared up, making Diego jump to his feet. Amb. Ermêl suddenly became animated. She started shouting at the walls as if there were angels there, clutching her crimson beaded necklace as she did. 'It was obvious Earth wasn't ready! Now look at it! Utter disaster. I knew the G.A.F wouldn't be capable of the task. That's why I tried to put more Idlers into the domain, but apparently that was an act of disregard. An act of rebellion. They tried shutting my operation down. Saying I was too unstable. Too unreliable to fulfill the needs of re-souling and then, when I protected it from them, they banished me! Imprisoned me in my own realm! Well, I'll show them! I'll show them what should have happened!'

All of a sudden another quadrant burst into life. The stones either side of it glistening like citrine gems through the amber light. Amb. Ermêl moved closer to it. Her mood going from hatred to love in a matter of seconds as she held her arms out wide to greet someone. 'I hoped you would come,' Amb. Ermêl said.

'As if I would miss this.'

The two ladies embraced one another and recognising the ginger afro, Diego pointed. 'You?' He smiled disbelievingly at the lady who had served him in the Tavern when fetching Stephen. 'Why are you here?'

'I am here to help,' she replied continuing to hold Amb. Ermêl's hands after their embrace.

'Help? Why?'

'Diego,' Amb. Ermêl spoke to him like a stern parent. 'Be nice. How do you think you got into the Tavern in the first place?' Diego double-blinked. 'I merely spoke to you about going through our Idle connection, but without Dr.

Bantère you wouldn't have been granted access. She has been more than helpful.' Amb. Ermêl stroked her cheek.

'But, why?' Diego scowled. 'Why are you a part of this?'

'Because Ermêl is right,' Dr. Bantère replied happily. 'The G.A.F is failing. Do you know how many weak souls enter the Tavern? How many times I have to stand there to help them reflect on their lives just to hear them whinge and moan about how unfair things are. How unfair the world is. How unfair it is that they didn't get to live a fulfilling life. How they feel misguided. Neglected. Blah blah blah.' She rolled her head. 'It's always someone else's fault and then, do you know what they do? They all decide to join the G.A.F. All these souls who arrive with bitterness in their hearts and minds, join the G.A.F. It's not right.'

'That's what I've been saying for years!' Diego held out his hands excitedly. 'These weak souls are poisoning the G.A.F.'

'Yes they are!' Dr. Bantère's afro bounced as she nodded. 'And the more it goes on, the worse it's going to get for the new generations. Something needs to change and as Divinity won't do it.'

'We will.' Amb. Ermêl turned away back to the orb. 'It's time for Idle to stamp its authority on the G.A.F. To take back control.'

Diego watched Amb. Ermêl wave her arms over the orb as if she was conjuring up a spell and seconds later a tall staff appeared in her hand. Four inverted talons at the top of it as if there should have been something sitting in the middle. She observed the staff closely, preciously running her hands along the black metal. 'Now, we can finally fix everything.' She slammed the staff down onto the stone floor. A crimson shockwave shaking the room.

'Dr Bantère,' Amb. Ermêl spoke over her buzzing energy.

'Yes.'

'Did you think I had forgotten?'

'Forgotten?'

'Forgotten what you did. What you did to me.'

'No, not at all,' Dr. Bantère replied. A smile still plastered on her face. 'I only hoped my recent actions would make them forgivable.'

'Forgivable?' Amb. Ermêl blasted.

Sensing conflict, Diego side-stepped away.

'You helped banish me!'

'You understand I had no choice,' Dr. Bantère pleaded. 'I cannot go against Divinity's orders.'

'Oh, I disagree. Look what you are doing now.'

'They are dormant now.'

'Irrelevant.' Before Dr. Bantère could speak again, Amb. Ermêl plunged her staff through Dr. Bantère's chest with both hands. Her eyes wide open as if she was savouring the moment. 'You betrayed me once,' Amb. Ermêl hissed quietly. 'You won't do it again.'

Like a poorly poured beer, Dr. Bantère's appearance turned foamy and she splashed down on to the stone floor. The liquid quickly soaking away as the quadrant faded back to a shade of ruby.

'Why did you do that?' Diego asked as Amb. Ermêl glided out of the room. 'She was on our side?'

'Was she?' Amb. Ermêl spun round to glare at him. 'If she was on my side she wouldn't have betrayed me in the first place and her energy would not have been a bar on my prison cell!'

'But, she helped us?'

'Yes. But that does not make her trustworthy. I have been tricked before by my so-called friends, I won't risk it happening again. Not this time.'

'But what about the Tavern? What will happen to the souls passing through?'

'It will sort itself out in due course. Right now we have bigger things to think about. We must act swiftly while Divinity remains dormant.'

Diego followed Amb. Ermêl and stood on the edge of the platform, unsure on what was his next move was. He watched Amb. Ermêl continue to glide over the room on crimson fences until she was directly beneath the bowl of energy. The power inside of it going berserk like a possessed spirit. Meanwhile, Cedric, was standing on the ground beneath her like an usher waiting to watch the show.

'Too long I have waited for this moment. Too long I have been out of touch with my own fate and the fate of Idle. Now. Now we make things right.'

Diego stared emotionless as Amb. Ermêl smashed the talons of her staff into the bowl. Limbo turned blood red in wayward lightning as the energy came gushing out; like a swarm of steaming souls howling around the room in search for their hosts.

One by one they possessed the corpses below. Crimson cloths dropped to the floor everywhere as the bodies slowly came to life, moving and twitching like zombies being raised from the dead. All of them bolting up right and standing to face Amb. Ermêl in the centre as if worshipping her. Men, women and children alike. All with black smoke wafting off their Idler suits.

With his heart in his mouth, Diego stared down at the cultish sight. There was a real sense of villainy in the air which unsettled him. Is this what he wanted? Were they going to do what he thought? He looked down at their stone-cold faces being indoctrinated by Amb. Ermêl and he didn't have a good feeling. It was like they were being programmed for something. Something far beyond what he was expecting. He just wanted the G.A.F to be organised better. For Idlers to do their jobs like they had done when he was still on Earth, but this... listening to

Amb. Ermêl's speech, he suddenly realised this was much more.

Diego loosened his tie as watched them all disappear over crimson fences of their own. No doubt entering the G.A.F to begin Idle's conquer. With the same energy running inside of him, he understood their motives. Agreed with them one hundred percent. However, now seeing it all unfold in front of him like this. Seeing an army be recruited. He wondered if this was the right way.

Chapter 31

Every time darkness fell, the screaming got worse. Each one that rang out felt like a chisel digging away into David's eardrums, trying to corrupt his mind into a state of panic. His brain pulsated madly as if it was trying to defend itself from the paranormal onslaught and all he wanted to do was cover his ears to block out the noises, but he was too reliant on his hands to navigate through the darkness. He trod carefully along the jagged rocks while following a narrow zig-zagging path down another small cliff. Occasionally skidding on the loose stones on his backside as his numb body made it difficult to keep his balance. The fear of falling still a major factor on his mind as he didn't fully understand the natural rules here, but not only that, he didn't want to injure himself further and be easy prey for any Déliánts lurking nearby.

Now back on level ground, David walked a bit easier. Rocks and stones crumbling off the ledges as he dragged his heels along. He pictured Vinicius's diamond eyes watching him from above somewhere and it made him wonder, had he really been watching him this whole time? David's mind was too tired to dissect the possibility, but it didn't stop Vinicius's words from whirling around in his head. Words which only motivated him to get to Hagitol and escape this horrible realm quicker. To make things right.

The imperial sun spontaneously burst open once again to ignite the sky and each time it did, David felt like he was getting a little bit of his senses back. It was as though he was slowly absorbing the rays that sizzled down upon him to reconstruct his nerves and he wasn't sure whether to be grateful or not because the heat was becoming unbearable. A hundred times worse than the tropics of Eden. Right now it felt like he was walking on the sun's surface and it was only getting hotter. His knees began to ache as he marched along the molten mountainous terrain. He passed another cluster of crystals and gazed at the glistening shards with sympathy, thinking about how the people inside must have lived their lives to end up like that. Did they all deserve it? Or were they just lost souls who'd been forgotten about? It was a question he didn't really want an answer to as it was easier to think they were all sinners, but the thought never left his mind. Then, with more crystals appearing up ahead it suddenly dawned on him. There was no one else here. He was yet to see another actual person. Someone who wasn't trapped in a crystal. Surely he couldn't be the only one in Idle?

There were many questions lingering on his burning mind, like Vinicius for example. Who was he really? What was he? And if he wanted to help why couldn't he have got David closer to Hagitol rather than leaving him where he did? It didn't make much sense, but then what did? He tried not to dwell on it too much as he knew he had bigger things to think about and he needed to keep his strength. Especially as he was approaching another sheer cliff edge he needed to navigate down and of course, the sky went dark once again.

Buckets of sweat dripped off his oily body as he cautiously made his way down. He weaved around the hazardous rocks, eager to get to the bottom and tried to stay as quiet as possible. Desperate to get back to more stable ground he picked up the pace, but in his eagerness his foot slipped. He tumbled over the ledge and quickly smacked face first onto something solid. His nose throbbing angrily. He laid there for a short while to catch his breath. His heart banging in his chest while his palms stung manically as if warning him there was danger from every direction. He was clearly stuck on something leaning over the cliff face, but before he could attempt to move, he heard a crack.

He held on tight as what ever he was on broke away and hurtled downwards. It fell at some velocity for what felt like ages until finally it smashed onto the molten ground. David hit his head as the object shattered on impact. Shards of rock splintered out everywhere, causing cracks in the ground which resulted in bursts of steam shooting up around him. Thankfully, he was unharmed. Merely a bit bashed and bruised, but he was shaken nonetheless. The sky suddenly ignited once again and as David lifted his head he saw a pair of large black eyes staring back at him. Crimson flames flickering in their pupils as they mirrored the sky. The horrific sight made him fall off the crystal and scamper away on all fours. A moment of weakness consumed him as his mind went weak and panicky, like an insomniac trying to get through a bad day. His head continued to pound as if it was still fighting for its sanity and the dense humidity was squeezing his skull like a vice. All he wanted to do was stay there until the horrors passed, but he knew that wasn't going to happen. He had to keep going. *Come on, David,* he urged himself. *Come on!* He got himself back to his feet and shuffled past the broken crystal. Ignoring the poor person sticking out of it and looked to regain his bearings. He raised a hand over his eyes to scout the land. Happy to see the terrain was flat from here on out as if he'd entered the belly of a crater. There were still some bubbling lava pools and creepy crystals, but there was something else. Something in the far distance. He took a large stride forward. His eyes fixated on it. A wall. 'Hagitol!'

With what looked like the end in sight, David forced himself to run. He swerved round all the glistening crystals and bounded across the molten rocks as if he was on an obstacle course. Soon, he was running parallel to a treacly river of lava which looked to be flowing directly to Hagitol. Finally, he felt as though he was getting somewhere. He jumped over a small puddle of lava when suddenly, there was a loud scream. The ear-piercing shriek was so loud it made him come to an abrupt stop. They hadn't fazed him for a while, but this time it was different. This time, it was close. Like a meerkat on sentry duty, he scanned the area around him, but there was nothing in sight. He waited a couple more seconds before moving forwards, but as soon as he did, the scream rang out again. He darted his head to the left and very slowly followed the sound, cautiously manoeuvring past the crystals until he stopped again. His body completely shutting down. It was a Déliánt.

His eyes got stuck staring at the creature. A man's head between its pincers. He watched helplessly as the man's body flailed about like a mouse being held by its tail. The Déliánt's antennae glowing crimson as it extracted the energy from its prey. Every instinct in David's body was wanting to help. To do something, but what was he supposed to do? Fight it? Lure it away and put himself at harm? It has been made very clear to him he shouldn't, but also... who was the man? Perhaps he deserved it? Perhaps this is the perfect ending to the life he lived? After all, he was in Idle.

He watched as the man's body eventually fell limp. The last of his energy clearly depleting and then, a thick red mucus drizzled out of the Déliánt's pincers, covering the man from head to toe. David held a hand over his mouth, completely hypnotised by the horror and within seconds the mucus had solidified. Glistening under the fiery sky and the Déliánt dropped the crystal down onto the rocks. David swiftly turned away, but didn't look where he was going. 'Argh!' He immediately jumped backwards to take his other foot out of the lava and stamped it on the ground as if trying to squash the pain. Luckily, he had reacted quickly enough and it hadn't burned him as bad as it had before. 'Come on, David. Focus!' he lectured himself.

His ears suddenly pricked up at the sound of clicking and he slowly turned back. The Déliánt was gone. A sudden twitch came over his shoulder as he got back up and slowly hobbled away while keeping an eye out for the creature. His heart quickening in his chest. The Déliánt was still nowhere to be seen, making him think he'd heard is scuttle away, but there was something wrong. His palms continued to tingle and then, there was a buzzing.

What's that? The noise got louder the more he looked around, but there was nothing in sight, until he looked up. A Déliánt was hovering a couple of metres above him. Its wings buzzing like a big bluebottle. Its pincers snapping together excitedly at the thought of more prey. The sight left David's body frozen on the spot by its presence and then, the Déliánt dived towards him. He broke out of his trance just in time as he dodged out of the way and ran. The demonic buzzing stayed close behind him. His anxiety was beginning to get the better of him as he felt vulnerable in the open space, but there was nowhere to hide and the wall of Hagitol was still some way off. He scanned the land for something to help him. Desperate to find some sort of cover, but there nothing.

The Déliánt made another dive for him and he quickly ducked down to avoid it, collapsing onto the rocks and scraping his body. He watched the creature swoop away to circle back around him and he hit his fist into the ground. 'Why is it even after me?' he grumbled. 'My mind isn't weak! I'm not gone!' He went to thrust himself up when the buzzing came back, growing louder like an incoming missile, but even with the added time pressure, David struggled to pick himself up. He half hoped Vinicius was going to re-appear, but he never did.

Snap!

A sharp pain stabbed through David's temples, triggering him to throw his hands up and try to pull the pincers away, but they were too strong and locked into place inside his head. He puffed his cheeks out frantically as he was lifted off the ground. Doing his upmost to stay calm and not join in the screaming match with the other souls in the realm. The sound of whirring energy soon overlapped the creepy clicking and he pictured the Déliánt's antennae glowing crimson, preparing to extract the energy out of him, just like it had done with the man previously. He remembered their face. Their panic. 'There's no way I'm going out like that. No way!'

Through gritted teeth, David gripped the Déliánt's pincers tighter. His eyes narrowing on the rocks below him as he focussed all his energy into his arms. His body absorbed the ferocious rays of the red sun above him, making him hit boiling point. He could feel the heat radiating over his skin and giving him the extra strength required as the pressure began to ease in his head. The Déliánt let out a loud screech, clearly upset with his efforts to break free and stamped its legs back and forth while swinging him from side to side, but David wasn't giving in. His biceps on the brink snapping.

Finally, his mind was free as he held the pincers away from his head with shaking outstretched arms. His feet dangling below him. Still using the tension in his arms, he slowly began to lift himself upwards until the pincers were level with his waist. He held his position for a few more seconds, enduring the pain as if it was giving him an extra boost and then, he dropped down. Still holding onto the creatures pincers he used his momentum of falling to drag the creature down with him and catapulted it over his head, slamming it down onto the ground. The heavy impact caused cracks to appear in the rock with large pockets of steam shooting up into the air. The Déliánt quickly rolled back onto its legs, stamping its feet and snapping its pincers in an act of aggression. David, meanwhile, stayed planted on his knees, waiting for the next inevitable attack to come again. The Déliánt made a dash for him, but the where the ground had been breaking apart a new stream of lava was created and its body was too heavy to retreat as its legs fell in. It tried to scatter away, but its panicky attempts only made it sink faster and soon, it disappeared in a few volcanic bubbles.

When the screeching stopped and the Déliánt was completely gone. David fell onto his backside to catch his breath. He knew full well he had gotten away with one. The imperial sun vanished from the sky, but David wasn't sat in darkness. He held out his hands in front of him. His eyes wide with wonder at the crimson now surrounding him. Idle's aura. Had it obtained it from the Déliánt? As he stared at it, he soon realised his body was back to normal. There was no pain or numbness, nor was his arms aching. In fact, he felt stronger than ever. Even the heat didn't seem to be a problem anymore. *Could have done with this a lot sooner,* he thought, trying to laugh, but when the screams returned he swiftly got back up to keep moving.

Chapter 32

The darkness stayed for a long time after his encounter with the Déliánt, but thankfully, this time, he had Idle's aura to help light the path ahead. He followed the river of lava for as long as possible, believing it would lead him to Hagitol, but it had stopped a while ago and now he was just wandering across the open molten plain. The number of crystals were forever increasing the longer he walked and now it was as if he was passing through a congested cemetery. The ruby shards were scattered randomly around him as if they had formed their own maze and he soon lost his bearings, like being stuck in a house of mirrors at a carnival. He did his best to ignore the people trapped inside the rock, but as his aura glistened on one in particular, he couldn't turn away from it. Most of the faces he'd seen preserved within the crystals showed expressions of sadness, anguish or fear, but this one, the woman inside of it had an expression of anger, like she was fighting. Her eyebrows narrowed over her eyes. Her mouth was open with her right arm raised above her head depicting a warrior roaring into battle. The sight made him curious and as he looked closer at the other crystals circling him, his suspicions became more evident. They were all at different heights and angles, some even laying horizontal on the floor, but all of them had a fighting look about them and all of them were facing the other way. Away from Hagitol. 'What happened here?' he said aloud, pressing his palm against the shard in front of him. 'Who were you fighting?'

All of a sudden, the ground began to tremble. Massive ash clouds began to form in the distance behind him and within them, were glowing antennae. A stampede of Déliánts was heading his way.

Without a second thought, David ran, weaving and ducking round the battlefield of crystals to try and get as far away as possible. 'Oh, come on!' he yelled as a swarm of Déliánt's also came from above. Fortunately the crystals were providing cover from an aerial onslaught, but it didn't stop them trying. Every so often he'd hear the buzzing attack his ears as they dived down after him and crash into the shards from behind and above. Their pincers snapping away angrily. For now, he felt somewhat safe, but as usual, his luck was bound to run out and stride after stride, the crystals began to deplete. The clicking and buzzing stayed within close pursuit. He tried not to turn around in fear of how the sight might affect him, but as he focussed forward, he knew he didn't need to. There was a subtle glow in the distance. At first he thought it was just another lava pool reflecting beneath the sky, but beyond it, he could see Hagitol. Crimson lights, like demon eyes, glaring out at him from its wall. *Come on!*

He continued to run as fast as he could. The Déliánt's now nipping at his heels. The closer he got, the quicker he realised that it wasn't a pool of lava ahead, it was a moat. The bubbling scarlet liquid flowing anti-clockwise around Hagitol. How was he supposed to get over that? More cracks began to appear among the rocks ahead of him, symbolising he was quickly approaching the edge. Rapid bursts of steam shot up like warning signals, but he couldn't let up. Not with the Déliánts right on his tail. His toes approached the edge of the rock and his instinct was to jump. He launched himself over the moat, hoping and praying he'd done the right thing, but what would he have done instead? He let out a loud cry as he fell towards the bubbling lava. His hands out in front of him with his eyes closed to prepare for the pain that was bound to follow, but his aura suddenly flared and he landed on something solid. He slowly opened his eyes and fell backwards as his face was only a few centimetres away from the bubbling liquid, but to his relief, he was on a fence. A crimson fence.

'Yes!' He smacked his hands together, watching the fences continue to appear as he carried on running towards Hagitol. A screeching shockwave carried him a couple of metres as he saw the Déliánts stationary on the outskirts of the moat. Even the ones in the air had circled back as if they weren't permitted to cross over. He continued along his fences until he reached the other side of the moat and stepped over the wall of burning igneous rock, covering his nose at the sulphuric stench rising off it. The screaming inside was so loud that even his hands couldn't stop the noise from attacking his ears. He peered down to see masses of people deliriously running around like escaped lunatics from an asylum. Most of them screaming obsessively while clutching their heads. Hagitol itself looked like the ruins of an old bailey. There was molten debris everywhere, some of it still on fire, and further out beyond the immediate remains and past the large broken gates, was the dark shadows of the labyrinth Vinicius had spoke about. He could see the maze-like molten walls stretch out far into the distance. 'That's my next step.'

All of a sudden, David's fence disintegrated from beneath him and he thumped down into the rocky courtyard. His aura still intact, but before he could get up, he was immediately mobbed by a horde of frenzied people. All of them screaming and shouting while flailing their fists as if trying to grab ahold of him, targeting him as if they believed he'd arrived to save their deluded souls.

'It wasn't my fault! It wasn't!'

'Please! Help me!'

'My head is burning!'

'Déliánts are everywhere!'

'Save me!'

221

Through overwhelming fear, David fought back, shoving and punching the decrepit bodies to break away. 'No! I'm not here to help!' he yelled at them. 'Getaway! Getaway!' He threw fist after fist until they all got the message and ran off in random directions, finally leaving him alone to venture through the rubbly courtyard.

He panned his eyes around at all the lost souls and amidst the mayhem, there were some who appeared much calmer. Some even hospitable as they smiled and nodded at him on his way past. Others were walking about with their arms folded completely oblivious to their surroundings and some were even huddled up on the floor. Almost like they'd accepted their fate and was just waiting for the nightmare to end. It was strange to think not everyone here was evil. Some were just unlucky, and also there were angels here. How did that work? Could they escape too? Was there any justice in a place like this?

He continued to push his way through the crowds when he spotted something odd. Through the masses of bodies, he could see another glow. An amber glow, like a moon reflecting the Earths sunlight and it was moving. It was an aura. Although it was a different colour to what he had experienced before, in his mind an aura generally meant it was someone who could help or at least know something important.

'Hey!' David called out, diverting his route towards them. 'Hey, wait!' He bustled through everyone in front of him. Sometimes literally having to grab their jackets to pull them out of the way and threw them to the floor. Anything he had to do to get through and after a few more shoves, he could see the aura shining over a small woman. She was wearing the most bizarre orange tuxedo and her ginger afro was bouncing with every step she took.

'Hey!' David called out again, waving his hand in the air to try and get her attention. 'Hey!'

The woman soon stopped and turned round. A sad, defeated expression on her face.

'Hi!' David said a little out of breath as he caught up to her. 'Something tells me you can help?'

The woman just frowned at him. Still not saying a word.

'Your aura,' David urged her to figure it out. 'Orange isn't the colour of Idle and you're the only one here who even has one!'

Rather than replying, the woman held out her hand as if inviting him to shake it.

'Really?' David questioned. 'Okay.' He gripped hold of her smooth foamy hand and saw orange sparks flare up in her eyes and after a few seconds, she finally spoke to him. 'David!' A smile now appearing on her face. 'You're, David!'

'Y-Yes.'

'Thank goodness!' The woman put her free hand against her chest before giving him the biggest hug. 'I knew you'd get here!' She said in his ear before stepping away. 'Quick, the labyrinth is this way,' she said, still holding his hand to pull him through the crowd.

'Who you are?' David called out.

'Dr. Bantère,' the woman replied without stopping. 'I was the realm guardian of the Tavern.'

Realm guardian? 'Like Rev. Li?'

'Yes! Of sorts!'

Rev. Li turned out to be a great ally so surely Dr. Bantère would prove to be one, too? 'What are you doing in Idle if you are a realm guardian?' he asked.

'I was a realm guardian. Right now I am just an angel needing to help.'

'Help with what? Help me?'

'Help make amends.'

Dr. Bantère let go of David's hand as they entered a clearing and David jogged up to walk beside her. 'What do you mean?'

'Fate has been on a course of destruction ever since I opened the Tavern doors to Diego. I thought he would help, but... I was wrong. It was the wrong person.'

David frowned. 'I don't understand. What do you mean?'

'Your father.' Dr. Bantère turned to face him. 'When he entered the Tavern I couldn't read him like I could the others. Therefore, like everyone else, I thought he was the mortal guardian. After all, there was so much chatter about it. Anyway, Diego's path to Idle was obvious and so I thought by putting the two together I could change Diego's fate. Even perhaps use him against Amb. Ermêl.'

'But it didn't work...' David said quietly.

'No because he wasn't the M.G and now Amb. Ermêl is free and we have very limited time.'

David remained quiet as he looked around at the ruins thinking he was at fault for that too, and soon he realised, they were more or less alone. The herds of people seemed to have been left behind and there were only a handful of rogue souls limping around now. Up ahead he could see another wall with crimson energy bleeding through it like arteries, only this one had an archway. A crimson glow filling the entrance.

'We're here.' Dr. Bantère stopped. 'This is the entrance to the labyrinth. You must get to the centre.'

'That's where the gateway is?'

'Yes.'

David took a hesitant step forward until he heard muffled screams. 'How many have made it?' he gulped.

'A few.'

'A few?' David raised his eyebrows.

'In the last few centuries.'

'I see, well, that fills me with confidence.'

'It is a test of character and strength. It won't be easy, even for someone like you, but there is always a chance. And it is a chance we all need you to take.'

'Whose we?'

'To err isn't just human.' Dr. Bantère stared at him. 'We all make mistakes, but we aren't all gifted with the chance of fixing them, like you are.'

David didn't know how to respond to that and simply looked away.

'Being a mortal guardian is a gift, David. At times it will feel like a burden. Perhaps more often than not, but it is a gift nonetheless and you need to see it through.'

'But, I was clipped... I'm not a mortal guardian anymore...'

'Then, just be a blimen' good guardian. You still have the power, even if you haven't got your mortality.'

David nodded at the empowering lecture. 'Are you not coming?'

'No.' Dr. Bantère smiled. 'My fate lies with Divinity. Yours however, lies with you. Now, off you go.' Dr Bantère waved a hand to see him off.

David turned back to the crimson energy and slowly approached it. He reached out a steady hand and wondered what horrors awaited him on the other side.

Chapter 33

Crimson. That was all Diego could see. The new Idlers had quickly got to work with their instructions and obeyed Amb. Ermêl's every command while she continued to play about in Limbo with Cedric's aid. He, meanwhile, was on supervisory duty. Supervising what exactly, he didn't know. For the Idlers were an uncontrollable force running amok. They attacked every G.A they saw like a plague of locusts on crops. Many G.As had already fled as if sensing they were coming and some even disappeared in Eden's energy.

All the while this was going on, Diego just slowly strolled down the crimson carpet. His hands cupped behind his back. He'd never known the library to be so empty and quiet. He thought he'd be enjoying it a lot more, but the truth was, he was conflicted. Was this really what he wanted? In some ways it was. The G.A.F was being cleansed. Weak G.As were being clipped and the Idlers were fulfilling their roles better, but did they have to be so harsh? Whereas the first four Idlers were too lenient, these ones had no conscious, hunting every G.A they could find as if they were the enemy in a war. Every now and again he would he a faint scream or holler, followed by a pop, but that was all he did hear. Other than the consistent buzzing, which got louder as he passed a couple of Idlers clipping a G.A to his right. No words spoken. No warning. Just blades in their hands which ended up in the G.As stomach and he had to turn way.

Was that me? he questioned himself, remembering the G.As he'd clipped and showing them no mercy as if they had somehow betrayed him. It was becoming clear just how badly Idle's energy could affect them. How a little bit of anger could amount to such brutality and now it was unleashed on the G.A.F and it made him wonder... what would happen to Earth?

He suddenly picked his eyes off the floor and stared directly ahead. He listened intently as he thought he could hear someone crying and tried to pinpoint where it was coming from. It was coming from behind some scarlet bookcases and eventually, after turning a corner, he could see a young girl huddled up on the floor. Her head buried in her tanned arms. The image hit him hard in the stomach as he pictured her weeping on the deck of a ship just like the girl he abandoned. Well, he wasn't going to abandon this one.

'Little one,' Diego spoke heading towards her, but the second she saw him she began crying more and pushed herself against the bookcase. 'It's okay, I'm not going to hurt you.' He knelt down, staring at his crimson hands. 'It is no wonder you are so frightened. This energy has evolved into a disease.' He clenched his fists. 'We need to get you somewhere safe.' He reached out a hand towards the girl, but she was still reluctant to take it. 'Come now, child,' Diego's voice softened. 'I'm not going to hurt you, but you shouldn't be here. We need to get you away to Yutopia. It's much more real than you think and you'll be safe there. You can be whoever you want. See whoever you want. Does that sound good? Shall we get you there?'

The girl stopped crying and wiped the tears from her eyes. 'Okay,' she gurgled. 'Just not Idle. Please.'

'No,' Diego sighed. 'You don't belong in Idle. I don't think anyone here does to be honest. I've made a terrible mistake.'

'Can you correct it? Your mistake. Can you bring everyone back?'

'I can't bring them back, no. It's too late now.' Diego scratched his chinned. His aura fading as he thought. 'But, I can try to help those left. Starting with you, come on.' He held out a hand again. 'Let's get you to Yutopia.'

The girl apprehensively reached out for him and he pulled her to her feet. Her watery eyes still nervous and he didn't blame her. He stared at her yellow aura, not believing how out of place she looked in the one place designed for her. 'Ready?' he asked.

The girl nodded and Diego created a golden fence, preparing to lead the girl over it, but before he could take a step, he heard buzzing. The fence quickly dissolved away and he tucked her behind him as three Idlers came into view. All appearing from different paths, two women and one male teen. They stared at him like confused zombies. Their heads twitching from side to side with blades clutched in their hands.

'Leave her be,' Diego demanded taking a step forward, but they didn't reply, nor did they leave. 'Leave her be!' he shouted louder, but again, the Idlers remained still and left a horrible feeling burn away in his chest. *Their not going anywhere.* In one swift movement, Diego lunged forward, summoning his own blade and stabbed the woman standing in the middle. Her aura immediately imploding into flames and triggering the other Idlers to attack, but Diego was too quick for their robotic minds and clipped them both with only a couple of movements. Both their auras bursting into flames, too. Afterwards, he stood still, breathing deeply while waiting for a consequence of his actions to happen, but it seemed as though he'd gotten away with it. Perhaps because of the number of Idlers running around it didn't matter if a couple were clipped. 'Right, ready?' Diego spoke turning back round. 'No!'

Another Idler had appeared without him knowing and all he could do was watch as they thrusted a blade into the girls chest. Diego ran back over, but by the time he got there, the girl had already disintegrated into crimson. He watched the last specks of her light disappear into the imperial red sky.

A new found rage took over his body. His crimson aura coming back to life with steam floating off his shoulders. He flashed his wrist at the Idler and sliced his blade across their throat. His actions causing more and more Idlers to appear around him, circling him with blades in their twitching hands. 'Come on!' Diego bellowed. 'Give it your best try!' He rocked back and forth preparing to fight, but they never advanced. Instead, one by one, they disappeared over their crimson fences and left him alone.

Diego threw his blade into the ground and gripped his head tightly. *What am I doing? What am I doing!?'*

'Diego!' Amb. Ermêl's voice screeched in his ear. 'Island. Now!'

'On my way,' Diego replied quietly, staring at his blade. 'On my way.'

Chapter 34

Idle fell into darkness. The smell of sulphur continuing to pour into David's lungs from the labyrinths ten foot walls. Its flowing arteries and his crimson aura the only things guiding him along, but where to, he didn't know. How was he supposed to know where he was going? It felt like he had been wandering around aimlessly for hours. Second guessing every turn he took as he hoped the energy in his palms would tell him something, but it seemed even Idle's energy was useless in here. It made him wonder what would happen first. Either he'd run out of time, choke to death or lose his mind, and right now, all three were in contention.

The labyrinth was certainly living up to its reputation. Its hot claustrophobic conditions was already taking its toll on him. The alleys were only just wide enough for him to turn round in if needed and he was constantly grazing his shoulders against the rocks. He even tried to use fences to walk over the top, but as expected the energy dissolved quicker than he could create them. He approached another junction and sighed at the three possible routes. One left, one right and one straight ahead. He waved his hand ahead of him, still hoping it would trigger something, but he quickly dropped it in a huff. It was obviously down to pot luck whether or not he'd make the right choice and whenever luck was involved, he normally lost. 'I'm never getting out of here,' he sighed, opting to turn right. Again, questioning whether he made the right choice after a few paces.

'Nope. Wrong way.'

'Who said that?' David spun round, accidentally smacking his head.

'Who do you think?'

David froze on the spot. The voice was familiar... too familiar. 'Nah, this isn't real! I can't have gone insane yet.'

'Not yet!' the voice giggled inside his head. *'But you're not far from it.'*

'Seriously! Who are you? What is this?' David asked, slowly walking on.

'Remember that numbness? As if your soul had left your body?'

'What?' David frowned.

'Ta da!'

'Wait, wait, wait! My soul?' he laughed. 'You're trying to tell me I'm talking to my soul? Ha! I really have gone insane! Man I'm in trouble.'

'Can't be in any more trouble than you already are. You're still walking the wrong way fyi.'

David halted in his tracks and stared at the walls, trying to find a face or anything resembling another person. 'Look, this must just be some sort of Idle trick! A challenge. Talking to my soul!' he laughed again. 'As if.'

'Why is it so hard to believe? You talk to yourself all the time. Only now you're getting a proper reply.'

'What do you mean by that?'

'Well, I'm the real you. Might as well give you the real answers.'

'The real me?' David raised his eyebrows, still walking onwards as he chatted away. 'And what is that suppose to mean. The real me... I'm the one walking and talking and has a physical presence.'

'Meh, maybe, but maybe you're just a vessel.'

'A vessel?'

'Well, technically you are an empty vessel right now and let's face it. Even before the G.A.F you were pretty much like this. Just an empty vessel.'

'And what makes you say that?'

'When was the last time you said what you wanted? Did what you wanted? And don't say when you died because that's just depressing.'

David's comical smile fell from his face. 'This isn't funny anymore. Whoever you are get out of my head!'

'I can't... because I'm you!'

David clenched his fist. He wanted to smack himself across the head so badly to try and thump the voice out. 'Well, what would you say then?'

'Our last moment with Jess.'

'What?'

'Come on... you know, because I know. The last time we did something we honestly wanted to, was when we were last with Jess. Since then it has been blockade, after blockade, after blockade, after blockade... you lost me long before you ended up here. I mean, we didn't even fight for her.'

'It wasn't our fight! If it was meant to happen for us then...'

'Oh, pish posh! Yeah, yeah, we took the moral high ground because it was what she supposedly wanted, but look where it left us. Living by that silly letter.'

'It put us on this path did it not? Look at what we are doing now. Where we've been.'

'Now? We are dead right now. Twice technically, and you are still walking the wrong way!'

'Oh shut it! What is even happening right now?'

'Well, from what I understand, Idle literally tears your soul from your body and luckily for you, it is working in your favour.'

'In my favour! How did you come to that conclusion.'

'Because I've been gone for so long... it's nice to finally be on the surface again! Come on, David, you can't say you haven't missed me. I am your soul. Your identity. Why did it have to take you dying for you to find me again?'

David remained silent as he turned another corner and immediately hit his palm into the dead end.

'I told you this was the wrong way.'

Ignoring his so called 'soul', David turned round and headed back down the alley towards the previous junction. Surely this was just a trick and the longer he ignored the voice, the sooner it would disappear? It had to. Maybe it was a sign he was nearly there? He'd passed some sort of checkpoint which triggered this nonsense? He hoped he was nearly there anyway because his energy was running low and there was no way he'd be able to put up with this the entire way.

'Deciding to ignore me, hey. I should have seen this coming. What if I changed to this voice?' All of sudden it was his mum's voice in his head. *'I worry about you, David. Don't abandon me like your father. Are you ever coming home? You promised to look after me.'*

David bit the inside of his lip as he pictured his mum waiting for him on the sofa, just like she'd been doing with dad for all those years.

'Oh, my mistake. I forgot, you don't talk to me because of some silly righteous reason. Will you talk to me now?' His dad's voice suddenly took over. *'Come on, son. What are you doing. Everything I've ever done, I've done for you and you go and do something as silly as this. If I'd known I would have let the Idler take you the first time round.'*

Idle's aura around David began to pulsate the more this voice persevered, making his tired arms throb as they dangled from his shoulders. He approached the junction again and this time he opted to go straight on.

'I don't think its this way either son.'

'What if it is, though?'

'No this isn't the way. We were better off taking a left there. That was the correct route.'

'And how do you know that... Dad!'

'No, I'm still you, silly. I was just impersonating dad...'

David closed his eyes and took a deep breath. 'At this rate I'd happily die for a third time!'

'Seriously, though, you are going the wrong way again.'

'Oh really!' David shouted. 'Give me one good reason why I should believe you. Tell me why I should believe anything you're saying!'

'Because I am you and believe it or not, your instincts are on point. We always know the right thing, but unfortunately we're addicted to losing. That's why we make the wrong decisions. Thank goodness I can see things clearer from this angle. I can be much more helpful from here rather than buried in your mind.'

Again, David fell silent. This really was a cruel joke and he wasn't prepared for it. Was he really meant to tolerate this? Zombies and Déliánts were one thing, but this... at least he could try to fight or out run the others, but there was nothing he could do about this psychological torture. Nevertheless, he did turn back to take the suggested route. After all, his 'soul' was right the first time.

He continued along the narrow passage, now enjoying the silence as his 'soul' appeared to be giving him a break. Instead he heard more screams echo out as their sound waves bounced off the molten walls, making his body shudder. He was somewhat surprised that he hadn't met anyone else yet or anything else for that matter. Perhaps the dark labyrinth and the mind games were enough? Perhaps this was all there was to it. Just a difficult maze with a delusional voice in their heads... but then, why was there still screaming?

After a few more junctions, his 'soul' returned. This time impersonating Jess's voice. *'You know I still love you right? I was just confused with everything that was happening. If you'd have stayed a couple more days or even a couple more hours, I'm sure we could have figured it out. After everything we went through together. Everything you did for me. Part of me thinks we were destined for one another.'*

'Well, obviously not.'

'What do you mean obviously?' his own voice responded. *'Man your worse than I thought. And take a left here.'*

'What now?' David replied, taking the new direction.

'Well, how can you use the word 'obviously'. Nothing is obvious. The only reason you say that is because you gave up on the first hurdle.'

'The first hurdle? I could have given up long before that moment occurred, but I didn't because I had the same thoughts as you're telling me now. Sometimes you just have to read the signs.'

'But the signs are open to interpretation.'

'Yes... and I interpreted them for what was best for me.'

'Really? You're going to stand by that, in spite of how everything turned out for us?'

'I... Oh, shut up!' David coughed. The toxic fumes finally getting the better of him and causing him to pause.

'You giving up on this, too?'

'I'm tired, alright!' David replied breathlessly, leaning against the wall. 'I've been walking for ages.'

'Well it's your own fault you're here.'

'Yes! Alright! I'm well aware of how I got here. It doesn't make getting out any easier.'

'How much easier do you want it? I'm guiding you the way.'

'Perhaps a little silence. You're so draining!'

'I'm only draining because you're draining.'

'What's that supposed to mean?' David queried, sliding down the wall to sit on the floor.

'Everyone finds you draining. Especially those who know you. How many hands have you batted away from those trying to help. You're lucky they haven't all given up on you otherwise you truly would be alone.'

'I don't know what you mean.' David squeezed his head.

'How about me?' Laura's voice sounded making him picture her leaning on the café counter. 'I ask you every day how you are and you never answer me honestly.'

'Give it a rest!'

'Or how about me? You can't say no to me. You love me.'

'I said enough! Get out of my head!'

David exhaled slowly as the voice seemed to finally vanish. Of a matter of fact, there was no noises at all now. No screaming. No clicking. No buzzing. Was it all in his head? Had he overcome it? Hearing all those people speak to him was too much and when it decided to mimic Grace... that was the last straw. That was still raw. He exhaled again and closed his eyes. Whatever was happening, the voice caused a lot of things to resurface. Things he'd hoped he would have gotten over by now. Thankfully, a cool mist, like air conditioning, began to wash over him and calm his mind. 'That's better.'

'Glad you think so.'

David peeped an eye open and saw a glistening white cloud, the size of his head, hover in front of him. 'What now?' He closed his eyes again. 'Just give me a few seconds to rest and I'll get going again.'

'You haven't got a few seconds. Come on, time is running out.'

Suddenly, he could hear the energy whirring as if it was doing something and when he opened his eyes again, he could see it expanding. The cloud grew as big as him. Taking the shape of something. Something like... 'You're joking right?' David glared at the mirrored image of

236

himself which was glowing a ghostly white. 'What, now you've got me hallucinating, too?'

'Does it make it more believable?'

'Nope, just more annoying!' David looked away.

'Come on. Get up, you need to keep moving.' His soul started jogging on the spot. *'Come on.'*

'I told you. I just need a few seconds.'

'Well, its been a few seconds. Any more seconds and you might as well not get up at all.'

'I don't get it.' David stared back at himself. 'If this is an Idle trick, why are you trying to help? Surely you should be telling me to quit or give up?'

'That's probably how this is supposed to go, but we're better than that. You're stronger than that. Besides, you've got all the negativity inside of you already. There's not a lot else I can add.'

'I see.' David rubbed his shoulder.

'You know what I think. I think a soul is the most honest image of ourselves. It's us at our core. If you think about who Idle was designed for... imagine what their souls would look like, of course they'd never make it out of here. They'd go insane within milliseconds. But not us. Not you. Our core is too good. Too pure, and deep down you know it, because I know it.'

David peered back into his sparkly white eyes and you know what, he did recognise them. This was him or rather who he used to be. This warm, friendly, happy person who was, ironically, full of life. It really had become lost. A buzzing sound came from above and David glanced up at the sky to see some Déliánts fly overhead. Ruby crystals attached to their feet. Now it made sense why he hadn't seen any crystals in the courtyard. They obviously transported all their prey from Hagitol into the wasteland beyond the walls.

'Time to get going.' His soul held out a hand. *'Come on.'*

David stared at it for a short while before reaching out, but he didn't get ahold of anything as his hand just swished straight through the energy. 'Really?'

'Hey, it's your sense of humour.'

The two of them laughed like bonding brothers and David's crimson aura had completely faded away. They continued to laugh for a good few seconds before the ground quaked. A very faint crimson light appeared down the alley. So faint, he wasn't sure if it was just a part of the wall, but within seconds it got brighter and brighter and suddenly, he heard the screech which turned his body cold.

'Time to go!'

'Yep!'

David hoisted is body off the floor and sprinted down the alleyway just as the Déliánt's antennae came into view. Its legs scuffing along the walls as it squeezed itself down. 'I hope you still know where your going!' David shouted at his soul, who was leading the way, taking a left, then a right, then another right and a left again.

'Well, I'm going where I think and I did it better than you earlier. Any doubts just shout!'

'No, I trust you. Just, hurry!'

They must have run a good four hundred metres and had taken so many turns David was beginning to go dizzy. He also hoped it meant the creature would get lost behind them, but the clicking and screeching continued to crawl over his skin and that wasn't all. He could now hear bubbling. As he raced round one more left-hand turn he came to halt. There was another miniature moat of scarlet lava in front him. A castle's dark turret in the centre. 'Have we made it!' he shouted out. 'It looks right!'

'Not yet!'

He turned to see his soul still running around the lava's edge. There was a drawbridge down about a third of the way round and he quickly headed for it, catching up with his soul in no time. 'Can't believe we're nearly there!'

Suddenly, another Déliánt rushed out of an alley snapping its pincers. Then another one. It seemed every entrance they ran past, another Déliánt appeared. All of them rushing out like rats from a sewer one after the other. Their pincers snapping. Their wings clicking. There must have been at least twenty now in close pursuit. Some climbing over and along the walls like ants on a carcass. Some even barging others into the moat with a mighty splash and shriek.

The drawbridge was close. So close that David could even see a glistening archway on the turret. 'We got this. We got this,' he panted, pumping his legs as hard as he could. He leapt onto the molten drawbridge. Thousands of rubies embedded in the construction. Each one lighting up as his soul ran over them. He looked back over his shoulder to see the Déliánts also on the drawbridge. Their heavy bodies causing it to crumble and crack. Lumps of rock splashed into the hissing lava. More Déliánts came flying in and landed on the other side to create a barricade. It was no wonder hardly anyone made it. How was anyone meant to get through this? He couldn't fight all of them. 'What now?' he called out desperately to his soul.

'What do you think? What do you want to do?'

David looked at the energy surrounding his soul and he got an idea. His soul smiling back at him as he clearly read his mind. *'I like the sound of that. Just promise me one thing.'*

'What?'

'Don't lose me again.'

'I won't.'

As they approached the other side, David could see the Déliánts waiting for them with menacing excitement in their six crimson eyes. Battling each other for the prime position as they all wanted to reap the rewards of turning him into a crystal. They were only a few metres away now, as were the army of Déliánts behind him and now felt like the right time.

'Go!'

Without slowing down David and his soul collided against each other side by side. Their bodies conjoining into one as David slowly absorbed the white energy. The two of them glowing brighter and brighter the more they merged until it was just David, beaming out like an illuminating full moon. He could feel the energy swish around his empty vessel and revitalise him, bringing a new lease of life he hadn't felt in so long. With his fists clenched together, he focussed heavily on his new aura and just as a whole load of pincers made a dive for him. It exploded. His white light burst out over the moat and through the labyrinth. Briefly brightening the entire dark domain for a few seconds. Dead Déliánt bodies flew off the drawbridge and into the lava, others disintegrated on impact. Then, as the light faded, David arose from the centre. His white aura still glowing over him and with a smile on his face, he casually walked through the turret's crimson archway. His heart beating loudly like someone waiting to be rewarded. He carefully stepped into the dark oval room. Ripples of lava flowing down the molten architecture as if he'd entered a tiny volcano. 'Hello?' he called out. 'Hello?' But there was no one here.

'Strange. What do I do now?' he asked himself, walking past four columns in the centre of the room. There was something at the other end which caught his eye. It was very dimly lit, but whatever it was looked to be made out more molten rock as it blended in with the walls. The only difference was the rubies embedded in it, which were evenly dotted along the object. One large ruby glistening at the very top. *It's a throne!*

For a brief moment, he contemplated sitting on it, wondering whether it would trigger anything, but he wasn't comfortable with that idea. Just incase its owner came back to protect it. What he did notice, though, was an old medieval torch laying on the floor next to it. He picked the item up, coughing at the familiar stink of sulphur soaked on its end. Although, the smell didn't last long as within seconds of him picking it up, the torch flickered to life in a white flame as if it was ignited by his aura. He waved it about to try and find something significant and as he stepped back down towards the centre, he noticed more torches sitting in steel brackets against the four pillars now surrounding him. 'A little more light would be good,' he said, raising the torch above his head.

Once the next torch was ignited, the flame went green, even though the one he was holding remained white. 'Okay.' He moved on to the next one, walking anti-clockwise. The next torch flickered crimson. The next purple and finally, amber. The room was now completely lit and it reminded him of something. Not the throne, which was now lit up in an eerie crimson spotlight, but the colours, the quadrants. It was like the room he and Grace had entered after escaping the inferno, only on a much smaller scale. Rather than the quadrants being separated by gems. Each pillar had just the one gem in its centre, now glistening beneath their corresponding flame.

'There must be something I'm missing...' He stepped back, nearly tripping over as he knocked an object onto to the floor with a loud clatter. It was a tall ivory candelabra. He quickly picked it up and placed it back in the centre of the pillars and once it was in place, he spotted the wick at the top and got an idea. He raised his torch towards it and watched with fascination as the white flame took ahold. The whole object now glowing. 'Cool,' he whispered, but the magic didn't stop there. All four pillars became transparent to reveal strange items levitating in colourful air that matched the gems.

Firstly, he approached Eden's pillar. Where there was a small branch glowing within the emerald light, slowly spinning around as if it was an exhibition. It was roughly the size of his forearm and it had five bright leaves grown on its end to depict a small hand. He quickly moved on to the amber pillar to see an umbrella spinning with a bright citrine handle. Then there was an eccentric purple telescope twirling in the amethyst light. The crimson pillar however, Idle's pillar, was empty.

As spectacular as the whole thing was, he still needed to find a way out. Why was he still here? What did he need to do? He continued to stare round at the colourful room which now looked like the sun was shining through a stained-glass floor and suddenly, the citrine gem began to spark. The sound of pouring champagne filled his ears as he watched the energy spill on to the floor and rise up to form... 'A fence!'

He quickly ran over to the twinkling rails and stared at it, remembering Dr. Bantère aura. 'The Tavern.' David took one last look around the cosmic room and then jumped over.

Chapter 35

Specks of blazing amber glistened around David as he entered the Tavern. The little balls of light beating like baby heartbeats in his ears. He reached out to touch one, curious to see what the energy would feel like and found his arms being restricted by sleeves, but when he looked it wasn't the same suit as before. It was white. His tie, his shirt, his jacket, even his shoes. 'Cool,' he said, running his hands down his smooth silky jacket.

Up ahead he could see the amber specks merging to a certain point and he headed straight for it, admiring the simple clean-looking realm on the way. No wasteland. No habitats to trek through. Just a vast white canvas which matched his new suit and when he approached the twinkling glow, he stepped through the light. He immediately saw the amber bar ahead and walked straight for it, glancing at the gold and amethyst fences either side of him. *First time I've seen one that colour,* he thought, sitting on the one barstool available. 'This is my kind of realm.'

'Right, right, right, I'm sensing you want... nothing. I'm sensing nothing... Young man?'

David looked up at Rev. Li. 'Hi.'

'My goodness!' Rev. Li exclaimed. 'You're back! You did it!'

'Yup.' David shrugged.

'You shouldn't have gone in the first place mind you!' Rev. Li turned sour, collecting a bottle of Chenin from beneath the counter. 'Do you have any idea what's been happening!'

'A little...' David was about to explain, but Rev. Li was quick to speak over him while unscrewing the lid of the wine.

'It's exactly as we predicted. Amb. Ermêl didn't hesitate to get things going once she was released, thanks to your little doo-whoops!'

'Hmm.'

'Hmm, indeed!' Rev. Li took a few gulps of wine straight from the bottle. 'There's an army of Idlers in the G.A.F right now, 'clearing it up'. They're nearly done you know. They'll be making roads into messing about with Earth soon. I can't believe how quick things are falling apart.' She drank some more.

'Has... anyone...'

'Your father is fine!' Rev. Li answered reading between the lines. 'He came to me the second you sent him to Eden. It's everyone else I'm having trouble with.'

'Everyone else?'

'Yes, with everything that's been happening a few more have entered Eden since you were last there, young man. I'm practically running a second world there now.'

'How many more people have you had?'

Rev. Li continued to drink a bit more before answering. 'A few thousand! Have you ever tried to re-home a few thousand people in a matter of minutes? It's tough!' She drank some more. 'And it doesn't help Dr. Bantère got herself clipped in this mess!'

'She was clipped?'

'Yes. The silly woman tried changing a fate that couldn't be changed.' Rev. Li shook her head sadly. 'I admire her effort, but she shouldn't have got involved. Now I'm running this place too.'

'Is there no one else?' David asked.

'Young man.' Rev. Li hit the bottle on the table. 'Out of all the realms, Divinity is dormant, the Captain is still at sea and Ermêl is evil... of course it's going to be me! So, yeah its all gone pretty peak-tong!' She drank some more, getting to the bottom of the bottle now as she had to hold her headdress on while leaning back.

'Sorry about all this.' David winced.

'You can't take all the credit. From what I've heard I think this was the most likely circumstance, but it doesn't mean we were prepared for it. We really ought to have... wait.' She put the bottle back down. 'You're wearing a white suit.' She pointed, patting his shoulders.

'Y-yeah.'

'Boy, you really are the mortal guardian.'

'Minus the mortal part remember.'

'Shush, shush.' Rev. Li waved a hand at him. 'I can't believe you got to the armoury.'

'The armoury?'

'Yes, that is what I said. The turret. The crimson portal you went through. Those who make it through get taken to Amb. Ermêl's Limbo for re-souling, but you obviously skipped that part and managed to go all the way in. Into the armoury.'

'Strange to call it an armoury. There didn't appear to be any weapons in there.'

'Well, they wouldn't be to you, but to us they...' Rev. Li stopped talking and downed the very last drops from the bottle before chucking it out of the apricot light so it smashed in the whiteness. 'Why are we talking? Go sort this mess out. Go!'

'Where?'

'Over there!'

David jumped off the stool and quickly walked away, feeling Rev. Li's awkward glare on his back.

'They won't be expecting you. As far as the Idlers are concerned you're gone. History. That is until you show your face of course.'

'And what is it I'm doing? Fighting Idlers?'

'Young man, you're clipping them. Send those demonic idiots back to where they came from. Amb. Ermêl included! You're the only one who can and seeing you here, now, in that suit. I believe you will.'

245

'Okay. Okay.' David stared at the amber wall puffing out his cheeks, preparing himself for what he could be facing. 'Time to-'

'Young man!' Rev. Li shouted out. 'I know you were quite fond of Grace, but it's a bit too soon to be seeing her again yet don't you think?'

'What?' he called back, but then he quickly realised his hand was holding onto the amethyst fence rail. 'Ah, I see.'

'Yes. You want the gold one.' Rev. Li pulled out another bottle of wine and opened the lid. 'Let's hope fate's still on your side,' she muttered as David corrected his course towards the right fence and without breaking a stride, he jumped over it. His knee planted down on a crimson carpet and he stared around at the haunting library. It was like something out of a horror movie. Everywhere he looked was a shade of red depicting blood. The carpet. The sky. The bookcases and even the files sitting on them. He may have only been here once before, but even he knew it wasn't supposed to look like this.

Slowly, he made his way down the aisle and scanned the neighbouring bookcases, expecting to come across an Idler at any moment. If it wasn't obvious enough from the colours, he could tell Idle's energy was here from the volcanic ash settling in the air, making his dry throat tingle. 'Hoped to have left this feeling behind!' he muttered.

Suddenly, he stopped. He could hear something. With the sound getting closer, he instinctively spun round. His fists at the ready, but it wasn't an Idler, it was a G.A. A young boy in distress. 'Are you alright?' David asked, lowering his hands.

'Can you help?' the young G.A asked. 'You look like you can help?'

'Umm, yes,' David replied. 'Are you okay?'

246

'I am at the moment, but they will be here soon. They are after everyone... they clipped my friends,' the G.A cried.

'Ssh.' David put a hand on the on the boy's shoulder. 'It's okay. Do you know where Amb. Ermêl is?'

'N-no... I don't know who that is. The only name I've heard is a Diego.'

'Diego?' David's aura flickered. 'And where is he?'

'An island? That's all that was said. It echoed out angrily.'

'Island? I wonder if it's the same one as before.'

'Whoever it was. They sounded scary.'

'I'm sure they did.' David rustled the boys hair.

'Hey, was that you?' The little G.A asked excitedly.

David broke out of his trance to see the boy pointing at yellow footprints on the carpet behind them. He lifted his right foot and saw that they were coming from his shoes. 'Looks like it,' he said, kneeling down to sweep the carpet and like brushing away dust, the crimson colour washed away to reveal its original lemon.

'How did you do that?' the G.A asked. 'Who are you?'

'I'm-'

A flurry of crimson fences suddenly circled them. Twenty Idlers plus, staring at him. Men, women and teenagers, all with buzzing blades in their hands. The G.A quickly hid behind his back and David tucked him up as close as possible. He waited for one of the Idlers to speak, but all they did was stand there studying him. 'Amb. Ermêl?' David called out, but he was met by silence. 'They're not very talkative are they.' The G.A didn't reply either, though, obviously too scared as he could feel him tugging at his sleeve. The Idlers slowly began to advance, glaring at them like vultures on dead meat.

'Stay behind me, okay.' David put a hand on the boy's head while slowly backing away. 'We'll be fine. We...'

Without warning, one of the Idlers made a dart for him. Her limbs flailing about as if they were separate from her body. Her blade swishing around wildly and forcing David backwards as he dodged every attack while keeping the young G.A behind him and ended up against a bookcase. His back squishing the boy against it as the other Idlers congregated around them. The Idler's blade swung at him once more, grazing his neck as he leaned to one side and it smacked into the bookcase. Now would have been the opportune moment to strike back, but without Idle's energy influencing him, retaliating didn't feel natural.

While the blade was stuck in the wood, he shoved the Idler backwards, getting a reaction from the other Idlers as they all took a couple of steps closer. Still it was the same Idler who fought him. The blade reappearing in her hand with a flick of the wrist and again, she swung it around without any purpose. It was as though she didn't care where it ended up as long as he was injured and this time the blade came incoming at shoulder height, but David managed to grab hold of her arm and locked it with his so she couldn't move. For a brief moment he thought he was winning, but then she tried to snatch the G.A from behind him. He watched her grotesque hand grab the boy's shoulder and he couldn't allow that. In a flash, he struck the woman around the face. The impact causing her to let the G.A go and stumble a few paces back. 'Don't touch him!'

The Idler continued to glare at him, unblinking. Her head twitching from side to side until she suddenly ran at him again. This time, David wasn't so passive. As she swung the blade he instinctively grabbed ahold of her wrist and thrusted her backwards. A stern look on his face as he took off his new jacket and rolled up his sleeves. No one was getting to this boy.

The Idler came charging yet again with the blade raised, but rather than waiting, David lunged forward and smacked a fist into her midriff with all his might. He could feel Idle's energy try to contaminate him as he made contact, but this time it wasn't going to get to him. He had blocked out the cruel energy with this newfound strength and then something unbelievable happened. In a burst of white light, the Idler disintegrated and disappeared like steam in the atmosphere.

Other than the sound of David's breathing, the library fell quiet. The Idlers as still as statues. He looked down at his hand to see a blade in his grasp. Exactly like an Idlers, only white. He raised it up to his face to get a better look. A soft tune, like an angel's hum, emitted a calm energy into his mind. The soft voice giving him a confidence as if being blessed by a higher power. He slowly held the blade out like an experienced soldier with a sword and waited for the next attack, daring the Idlers with his eyes to try and they obliged.

Two more Idlers ran at him. Their blades whizzing erratically. The energies chiming together at two different tones as David parried each one. Left. Right. Left. The ferocity in their attacks were powerless against his energy as he easily countered them, defending wave after wave. Doing his best to move them away from the G.A, but every time he steered them away, the other Idlers moved in closer towards the boy and so he had to return. He ducked beneath an incoming blade and thrusted his up into the Idler's abdomen, immediately pulling it out to swipe it across the other's chest and one by one they both burst into white steam. Despite his new winning mentality, he knew he needed to get to Diego and Amb. Ermêl quickly. This was like breaking down the barrier of pawns in a game of chess to get to the king.

David gulped heavily as more Idlers suddenly appeared. The conflict obviously attracting them all here and maybe that was exactly what he needed to do. Once they were gone, it would take an age for them to come back surely? They can't just be respawned.

This time, it was three Idlers who stepped forward. All of them in their teens, looking like a goth club from a school playground. David started to brace himself for the third round and turned to the G.A who was still hiding behind him. 'You've got to get out of here,' he urged him. 'They shouldn't be chasing you anymore. It looks like it's me they want.'

'That's because you're kicking their asses!' The G.A replied. 'Being near you is the safest place to be. Seriously, who are you?'

'I'm the mortal guardian.' David's eyes narrowed as he prepared himself.

Chapter 36

With his arms folded, Diego gazed out over the ocean. He was on the edge of the island pretending to breathe in the salty sea air. It had been a while now since he was summoned, but he was yet to see Amb. Ermêl. She was probably too busy with end of the afterlife stuff to see him yet. He knew if he was to leave she would find out so he didn't risk it and waited, wondering where it all went wrong. It seemed like only yesterday he was feeling like the luckiest angel around who had unlocked a power of great proportion. Finally fulfilling a fate he believed was a long time coming and being recognised by a higher power. Now it all seemed... wrong.

I don't understand, Diego thought, staring out over the horizon. *It all seemed, perfect. So right. The power of Idle at my fingertips. Accomplishing an Idler's role as it should have been done.* He winced as he pictured the G.As he'd clipped. The mortals he'd affected. The little girl. *Was I wrong? Was I not fulfilling a guardian's duty? These rules... they stopped me from being helped, shouldn't they prevent others from being helped too? Or was I... maybe I couldn't be helped. All this resentment inside of me. All this anger.* He stroked the scar on his neck where his father had cut him. *Maybe I couldn't be helped.* 'I should have just gone straight to Idle. Been a lost soul.'

'Do you even remember Idle?'

Diego turned to see Cedric standing on a crimson fence above the island.

'Of course you don't, because you weren't there long enough. You were hand selected, just like that.' Cedric clicked his fingers as he strolled over. 'I remember scouting you you know.'

'Scouting me?'

'Of course. No random soul can become an Idler Diego. We get hand selected by our predecessors.'

'Well whoever chose the four before me was pretty incompetent.'

Cedric chuckled. 'They were not Idler material that's for sure, but they had a different purpose.'

'How so?'

'The mortal guardian. They changed everything. Even when Amb. Ermêl was locked away in her realm, she knew what was coming. After being banished by her fellow realm guardians, she knew there was only one way to be free. To harness the power of a mortal guardian. One who held the power of all the realms. We missed an opportunity once... a long, long time ago. Amb. Ermêl did not take it well.' Cedric scratched his stubble. 'After that, she vowed to make sure it didn't happen again, but... it did. A trick was played. Played by Linus. The G.A you clipped.' Diego gulped as Cedric pointed at him without making eye contact. 'So while I went undercover in Eden, hoping to hear something or feel something. She dedicated her time to finding the real one and that's what she programmed her Idlers for.'

'So that's why they weren't policing the G.A.F properly?'

'Who cares about the G.A.F?' Cedric chuckled again. 'It's an organisation that was always doomed to fail. Mortals... they should be able to look after themselves. You know this... you've preached it enough times.'

'I do agree.'

'Then why is your mind tainted!' Cedric's mood suddenly changed to anger. 'You have clipped three Idlers!' he thundered, holding up the relevant number of fingers. 'Why?'

'They were attacking innocence...' Diego shouted back. 'I was taking them to Yutopia.'

'Yutopia...' Cedric scoffed. 'A pitiful realm of make belief. You think mortals have it easy.'

'That is what Yutopia is designed for. A realm to let souls rest in peace. Their peace. '

'But why?' Cedric shrugged, pacing around him. 'Why is the afterlife so complicated? Do you not think that when you die, that should be it? Pff gone. Finished. Idle is the only realm with purpose. Disposing of the waste. With only a selected few being granted entrance through the gates to watch over.'

'And how would you watch over?' Diego scowled.

'With the same care I have now. Rather than lifting mortals to limelight, perhaps they need taking down a peg instead.'

'Why? Why not just let fate run its course? That's all I wanted.'

'Where's the fun in that? Might as well put Idle's power to some use. Dictate and conquer. Don't liaise and share. The more that try, the more that fail.'

Diego rubbed his face with both hands. Total confusion fuzzed around his mind. What Cedric was saying sounded exactly like the kind of thing he would have said a day or so ago, but now... now it just sounded wrong. 'I, disagree.'

'What?' Cedric stopped to stare at him.

'I disagree. I think everything is as it should be.'

'How can you say that?' Cedric spat. 'Were Idlers!'

'Maybe that's where I came from,' Diego answered, looking down at the now golden fence beneath his feet. 'But it doesn't define me. I've been misguided. I see that now.'

'No... no! You were chosen! I chose you! How have you been influenced?'

'I don't know. But I know there is a place for the G.A.F. It has its issues, but nothing that can't be resolved.'

All of a sudden, Diego had a crimson blade buzzing under his chin. 'I chose you!' Cedric's face shook as he spoke. 'I have already embarrassed myself once to Amb. Ermêl with my failure. I do not expect to do it again!'

'You see me as a failure?'

'Yes. Just like your own father saw you.'

Diego's aura flickered.

'Yes, your father... now there was a man to admire.'

'What do you know of it?' Diego growled.

'I told you! I scouted you. I saw your upbringing. Who you were before a sorry Idle soul. Before a stupid G.A.'

'You know nothing!' Diego smacked the blade away from his neck. Not fussed by the sting of the energy. 'You have no idea!'

'Oh, but I do.' Cedric sniggered. 'Quite tough wasn't it... living with no mother. You see, the moment you entered the world you wreaked havoc. Wasn't long before it was just you and daddy sailing the seas as if you owned it. Living, breathing Gods of the ocean!' Cedric smiled. 'I loved watching the two of you. Taking what you wanted. No mercy. No care. Just two souls trying to survive... proper Idler spirits... then what happened? What did you do, Diego?'

Diego put a hand round his neck.

'Don't remember? I remember... because I was there.'

Diego's eyes sizzled from his rising energy.

'Oh, yes.' Cedric sneered. 'I watched you murder your father. Murder that girl. It is one of my most cherished memories.'

Diego couldn't believe it. After all this time. There was someone there. There was someone looking over him in his moment of need. And they did nothing! The hatred inside of him rose like a monster from a pit. His body electrifying in crimson energy. Sparks flying off his fingertips. *This is all his fault.* That's all he could think as he stared into Cedric's cold garnets. With a flick of his wrist he summoned his blade and saw a twitch in Cedric's eyes, like that was what he expected him to do. Did he risk it? Would he win? Was it too late?

The blade shook in his hands as it took all his might to hold back and through gritted teeth he said, 'Are we close?'

Cedric smiled. 'All the Idlers are in the library. There's only one G.A left in the G.A.F. The others have either fled or have been clipped. Once the last guardian light is vacant Amb. Ermêl will turn to the next phase.'

'Which is.'

'You know what's next.'

Cedric put a hand on Diego's shoulder. An unwelcoming touch that disturbed Diego's crimson aura. *Yes I do.*

Chapter 37

Burst after burst, the white vapour popped up around David. Each one restoring some colour to the library as his white energy began to dominate. Even the cream sky was coming back in pockets of light. The Idlers meanwhile, they just kept coming. Every time one of them was clipped, more turned up as if being summoned to avenge their fallen comrade. Right now, it was as if they were queuing up to have a go at him. Their blades pinging and dinging, blow after blow. The young G.A was still huddled behind him, enjoying the show freely as the Idlers were being to drawn to David instead. At some points he even cheered as the Idlers were clipped. Fighting was becoming second nature to David now as he could read the Idlers predictable and brainless attacks with ease. Left, right, up, down, whichever angle they came at him, he was ready. Even sensing their energy as some tried getting behind him and eventually, he was down to the last one. The largest of them all. They ran towards him like a crazy caveman. Hollering out gibberish while swinging the blade from side to side. David didn't bother engaging, though. Instead, he threw his blade at them and saw it shoot through their chest point first and hurtle down the library, lighting up the carpet the entire way. The Idler burst instantly in a bright flash of white which washed away all the crimson stains in a mile's radius. The library finally looked normal once again.

With the Idlers gone, David looked around proudly. Happy to see the oak bookcases, the lemon carpet and the cream sky back to how he remembered, at least from where he stood.

'Wow. A mortal guardian!' He heard the young G.A say as he picked up his jacket from the floor. 'You are so cool!'

'I'm just a guardian,' David replied, putting his jacket back on. 'I'm sure if you stay good and true you may even have this power one day.'

The G.A looked at his hands with a broad smile. 'Cool!' he said, waving them about as if pretend fighting.

'Alright, now I need you to go to Eden. I'm sure one more soul won't annoy the Reverend.'

'What? But I want to stay with you!'

'No can do I'm afraid. You saw these Idlers, they had no brains,' he joked with the G.A. 'But where I'm going now. Who I'm going up against. It wont be the same so I need you to go where I know you'll be safe.'

'Alright,' the G.A sighed. 'How do I get there?'

'I think you just ask.' David shrugged. 'Put your hands together and ask for Eden and...' An emerald fence suddenly appeared to their right hand side. 'There you go.'

The G.A walked over to it and was about to go over the rail when David called out. 'If you see Rev. Li, tell her what you saw and that I'm okay... and ask her to pass it on to my dad. He may still not remember, but I hope...'

'Okay. Will do.' The boy jumped over the railing before he could finish and disappeared along with the fence. David, meanwhile, took a deep inhale and flicked his wrist to summon back his blade. His hands now beginning to shake for he knew what was next. What was waiting for him on the island.

'That's it!' Cedric slapped his hands together. 'That's the last one gone! Now there is no trace of the G.A.F's original energy, Amb. Ermêl can create the new one. A crimson one. The Idlers shall return here soon and she will open the portal to bring the Idle realm here.'

'What about the G.A.F?'

'When I say we're creating a new one. I mean we're eliminating the old. Idle will be the new G.A.F and Amb. Ermêl will be its ruler.'

Diego stared out at the setting sun. 'You entrust sinners and villains to influence Earth?'

'Yes. Can you imagine it. With Amb. Ermêl's teachings they will correct the world and guide it as it should be and we will all be free from the realm's enclosed tortures.'

The two stood in silence as Diego pictured the world crimson and shook his head. He discreetly put his blade in the hand away from Cedric.

'They should be here by now,' Cedric muttered. 'The last G.A's energy has been gone long enough. The Idlers should be here.'

Diego prepared to make a swing at Cedric when he saw something. There was a distant glow, like a single star in the pastel dusk sky. 'What is that?'

'Let's find out,' Cedric replied.

Cedric stepped over his fence and Diego joined him. Both of them standing over the ocean fifty metres or so away from the island and watched the weird white glow approach them. 'Is that?'

'It's a fence.' Cedric scratched his chin, summoning his blade instantly.

Diego stared at Cedric, sniggering as his body twitched with nerves as if he was going back into a senile state.

'Who is it?' Diego asked.

'Just get your blade and be prepared.'

Should have gotten a bit closer, David thought as he slowly walked on his white fences. Not wanting to look down at the sea as it made him feel uncomfortable. He squinted up ahead to see two crimson fences teleport closer. One of them he quickly recognised to be Diego and he gripped his blade tighter, then he saw Cedric. 'What are you doing here?' he called out. 'I thought you'd been clipped?'

'David,' Cedric replied hoarsely. 'Good, you're here, have you come to help us?'

'Help you?' David asked, still walking towards them.

'Don't be fooled by our fences,' Cedric answered. 'We're here to stop Amb. Ermêl. Hoping our Idle energies would be more of a match for her.'

Diego looked at Cedric's dirty, wrinkled lying face.

David flicked his white blade at the pair of them. 'After what you've done how am I supposed to trust you?'

'We were only following orders, David,' Cedric spoke. 'This Idle energy inside of us is a curse. It binds us to Amb. Ermêl's needs, we had no choice. But now she's free.' Cedric waved his arms ahead of him. 'So are we and we can take revenge.'

'Huh.' David glared at Diego, wondering if it wasn't for this pure energy inside of him whether he'd have already sunk his blade into his skull. 'You're being awfully quiet.' Diego didn't reply. 'Tell me, if you're both here to stop Amb. Ermêl because you are now 'free', why is it I've just come from fighting all the other Idlers alone?'

'Other Idlers?' Cedric questioned.

'Yeah, the ones I've just clipped in the library. They didn't seem free from Idle's influence.'

Both Diego and Cedric shared a look which didn't sit well with him. Part of him wondered why he was even talking to the pair of them. One of them killed his dad and the other had clipped Grace and banished him to Idle. He should have clipped them both the moment he arrived, but there was something strange happening, especially with Diego. He didn't seem so... evil. So he decided to play along. 'So what's the plan? Where is Amb. Ermêl?' David asked.

'She's in the island,' Cedric replied.

'In the island?' David nodded slowly, motivating his anxious energy to remain strong. The Idlers were one thing, but what lies ahead was their boss. The guardian of the Idle realm and the very thought brought a chill to his bones.

'Once the last G.A has left the G.A.F,' Cedric began to explain. 'She will look to start a new one. That time has come. Any minute now she'll be rising to the surface with the orb.'

'Well, we'd better get moving then.' David pointed his blade forward.

'Yes. We should,' Cedric said.

The three of them started heading towards the island in complete silence. David's white fence in the middle while staying a couple of paces behind. The whole thing felt wrong and when he saw they were both holding their crimson blades it didn't help. He peered at their stone cold faces and a slight tingling zipped over his shoulders. Was he nervous because of what was about to happen or was he nervous because he was technically following two murderers. Either way, he didn't like it and he especially didn't like the fact Diego wasn't talking.

They approached the edge of the small, isolated island with waves crashing against its rocky base a good fifty feet below. Still no one spoke and it suddenly dawned on David. Neither of them questioned his escape from Idle. His white aura or even his white suit. Did they not care? Surely it should have prompted some sort of response? The uncertainty made him drop another couple of paces back. Adamant Diego had influenced Cedric back to his Idle ways and was leading him to a trap.

'She should be here at any minute,' Cedric spoke again.

'You seem to know a lot about what's happening.'

'Yes, well... I-' All of sudden Cedric unleashed a furious strike that slashed across David's shoulder. Idle's energy severely burning his skin, but there was no time to rest as another strike was incoming. This time he managed to block it. Their blades locking together as

David stared into Cedric's ghostly garnets which flared up like a coal fire.

'You shouldn't be here!' Cedric snarled. 'How did you get out of Idle?'

'Because I am meant to be here.' David thrusted Cedric back a few paces before engaging in another bout. Their blades clanging and ringing through the electric atmosphere. Cedric's strength was much more powerful than the other Idlers he'd faced, but he was determined not to give in. He tried to lunge at him, but Cedric was quick to evade and quickly came back, managing to slice his blade across David's side and cause him to fall to his knees. The energy scorched him like the lava pools of Idle and he swung his blade out in response, but Cedric avoided them too. 'Time for you to go. You won't survive Idle a second time.'

David threw his blade up in a desperate attempt to block Cedric's fateful attack when suddenly, Cedric's fence ignited into crimson flames. The fire quickly consumed him from head to toe and then, he exploded like a firecracker. Diego in his place. 'That's for my father!' he hissed.

David cautiously got to his feet. Steadily holding his blade out, awaiting for the inevitable attack, but then he saw the hurt in Diego's eyes. A side to him he hadn't seen before and astonishingly, Diego's aura faded and his fence turned golden. Then, he said something David really didn't expect to hear.

'I'm sorry.'

David double-blinked as he lowered his blade.

'I'm sorry for what I did. For what I've done. This anger I've developed. This blind rage.' Diego stared at his hands. 'It's no excuse, I know. Not for what I've done. What I've done to you, but with Idle running through me...'

David hobbled over to Diego, exhaling as he put a hand on his back. 'People aren't themselves when they're wrongly influenced.'

'It took me so long to realise.' Diego sounded almost tearful.

'Well, now is a good time to make amends. Help me.'

David waited anxiously for Diego's reply. His arms shaking nervously as he could tell Diego's mind was still split from his shifting eyes, but eventually, he nodded. 'Okay.'

An enormous explosion suddenly shook the worlds with a mighty bang. A giant crimson cloud erupted from the island, buzzing and sparking like a demonic cyclone as it gushed out into the atmosphere and blanketed the night sky in Idle's glow. Both David and Diego gripped their blades while standing side by side.

'Looks like she's here,' David gulped.

'Yes,' Diego replied, both of them now stepping towards the island.

'Is there a plan?'

'Fight.'

'Fight? Is that it?' David asked. 'I fought the other Idlers, but surely she'll be different?'

'Yes. She is much more powerful.'

'More powerful. Great. Thanks, I'll note that down!' David scowled. 'Anything else?'

'You are definitely Stephen's son aren't you,' Diego scoffed. 'Stop asking questions and just act. You can't prepare for the unknown!'

'Alright,' David sighed. 'Alright. Let's wing it!'

They were nearing the island's border when Diego said, 'can you hear that? What is that?'

'Get down!' David yelled, pulling Diego's shoulders towards his fence just as a Déliánt flew inches above their heads. The creature buzzing ballistically into the smoky sky.

'What was that thing?' Diego asked.

'That's the least of our worries.' David stared at the island as a tall, lean figure appeared through the crimson smoke. A staff in their hand with what looked like a crimson orb sitting on the top.

'Diego!' Amb. Ermêl's voice thundered out. 'You dare betray me!'

A couple more Déliánts appeared above them and immediately dived down at Diego. Their pincers snapping away at his limbs as he helplessly tried batting them away, but without Idle's aura he was left defenceless. 'I gave you a second chance at this life and you have wasted it!'

A pair of pincers snapped around Diego's head. He tried his best to fight it off, but he wasn't strong enough. His eyes widened at the sight of mucus forming in the creatures mouth, but he refused to show weakness. He scrunched his face up in determination to not go without a fight and suddenly, the creature burst into white energy. He fell back down onto his golden fence with David by his side.

'I got you!' David said.

'So! You've gone from mortal guardian to Saint!' Amb. Ermêl spoke strutting off the island over the raging ocean. 'You may have clipped my Idlers, but once the Idle realm takes over this world more will come and they will correct Earth just as the G.A.F should have been a long time ago! And this time, no one will stop me!'

Amb. Ermêl raised her staff into the air, causing lightning to strike down upon the island and through the crimson smoke, thousands of buzzing black dots flooded into view. David's body trembled as a swarm of Déliánts flew towards them. He shifted his body into a protective stance and held his blade at the ready, but this time he had little hope. The sheer velocity of the flying bugs powered towards him like a hurricane, carrying him and Diego high up into the crimson sky. Amb. Ermêl's cruel cackling echoed through the electrifying clouds. David swung his blade left to right, cutting through some of the Déliánts, but there were too many of them.

'David!'

He turned to see Diego. His limp body surrounded by the snapping creatures. His head again in pincers. 'The orb. On her staff.' Sparkling mucus began drooling down Diego's head.

'No! No!' David shouted helplessly, trying to bat the Déliánts out of his way.

'I'm sorry,' Diego whispered.

Fear turned to anger as David channeled his emotions and his body imploded in white light. Incinerating all the nearby Déliánts instantly. He was suddenly tumbling down the sky before smacking on to a fence just above the ocean. The water splashing about in a deep shade of purple. He peered back up at the crimson sky. Déliánts still buzzing about like Hellish predators. Lightning continued to strike the island as the crimson clouds expanded outwards, but there was no sign of Diego.

'I've got to stop this.' He took a couple of steps forward when he spotted something else falling from the sky. A ruby crystal. He watched it disappear into the waves without a splash, feeling some sort of pity towards the angel who had killed him, but that was all in the past now.

Keeping low, David stepped over his fence to appear at the foot of the island from the rear. He climbed his fences as if they were a steep white staircase towards the villainous peak. Idle's energy zapping away at him the closer he got to the electrical storm. Once he was at the top, he peered over the ledge to see Amb. Ermêl still gazing out in the other direction and so he slowly crept towards her, carefully observing the Déliánts cluelessly buzzing overhead. Lightning continued to strike down around him, making him zig-zag his way over, but remaining composed. He was now close enough to hear the fire crackling from Amb. Ermêl's dress and he reached out a hand towards the staff, straining his arm to keep as much of a distance from her as possible. His finger tips brushed over the iron-like metal when the staff suddenly swung at him and smacked him across the face, causing him to roll across the island. His body burning and spasming while laying on his fence.

'I can see why you were chosen,' Amb. Ermêl said strutting towards him. 'There is a lot of power in you, but you were never going to be a match for me.' A crimson bolt shot out of the staff and crashed into his chest, intensifying the energy already attacking him. 'It's almost cruel what they had you believe because, you see, the thing about goodness, is that it loses. Every single time. In order to get what you want. In order to achieve. You've got to be bad. Be selfish. That's how the world works and it's how this world works. Fate always works in the favour of sin. It's more exciting this way. The strongest minds are those who aren't afraid to do what is necessary and that is why I was always destined to return. To restore Earth's nature to how it should be.'

'I... disagree,' David managed to grumble, but he was instantly hit by another blast. Crimson holes now appearing in his white suit and eating away at his aura.

'Tell me. If what I am doing is so wrong... then why are you the only one here to stop me?'

David stayed silent.

'Exactly! They want this to happen as much as I do. Even the almighty Divinity. It's time the worlds abide by Idle reign.' Amb. Ermêl raised her staff over his head. 'I will paint all the realms crimson, starting with Eden and don't worry. Once I have conquered it I'll be sure to recruit your father! May even use him to influence your mother... to help her cope,' she laughed hysterically. 'You did want them together again, didn't you!'

David's body heated up with rage. His aura now absorbing the energy restricting him and turned crimson. His eyes burned. Steam poured off his skin and just as Amb. Ermêl plunged her illuminating staff at him, he grabbed ahold of it with both hands, pushing back to keep it away from his face. His arms shaking as he narrowed his eyes at Amb. Ermêl. The evil in her small ruby eyes giving him the desire to keep fighting. Slowly, he elevated to his feet. Déliánts now circling them as if they didn't know who to attack. Amb. Ermêl fought back, the tension between them causing the staff to bend and all of a sudden... crack!

The staff snapped in two. All the power surging through it exploded out like a radiation pulse. Barrels of lightning struck the islands surface and the ground cracked and crumbled beneath their very feet. Even his fence was affected and before he knew it, he was being sucked down into the island's centre. Rubble collapsing down on top of him as he slapped down on to the slate floor. The storm still raged on from above and echoed around the stone walls.

Coughing and spluttering, David pried himself away from under the rubble and groggily got to his feet to stare at the misty room. 'I know this place,' he whispered limping to the centre while staring at the four shady quadrants. He cast his eyes to the only one illuminating. A bright image of a castle's turret shining back him. 'No way.'

His feet slipped into a groove on the floor and he looked down. *The orb!* It suddenly clicked why he needed to get it and he quickly rummaged through the debris, throwing random clumps of rock about in search for it. 'Come on! Come on!' He hurried, feeling the pressure of time against him. A few more erratic seconds passed and suddenly, David felt a strange calmness wash over him as if time itself had slowed down. Breathing slowly, he followed the feeling and when he lifted up a large rock, there was the orb glowing brightly in its crimson glow. He picked it up. Entranced by the energy swirling inside of it as it turned white once again with his touch. He headed back to the centre of the room and following his instincts, he crouched over the groove to place the orb in.

'Stop!' Amb. Ermêl's voice screeched across the room. 'mortal guardian or not, you know what I'm proposing is right. You know these world's are broken... and there is a place for an entity as strong as yourself to thrive...'

'Save yourself the speech,' David said abruptly. 'Diego has already giving me the lecture and eventually, he realised he was wrong. Just as you are now.'

'The Earth is doomed. You think you are stopping me? I will succeed. It's my destiny! Things will be corrected and Idle will reign supreme... one way or another.'

'Maybe so, but not in my life times. Not while I'm still here.'

Amb. Ermêl blasted her crimson aura at David in an attempt to stop him, but he was too wise to it. He dropped the orb just as the energy crashed against him and propelled him against the wall. The orb slotted into its groove and immediately shone a bright sapphire. Its light shooting and sparking straight into the sky. Inside the room all four quadrants came to life in their vivid colours. The gems on the ground now glistening brightly.

'No! No!' Amb. Ermêl screamed as a technicolour prism of amber, amethyst, emerald and sapphire shot into her from the gems. The whirling light completely engulfing her in the Idle quadrant. The light getting brighter and brighter, like a resurrecting star until it reached its peak and then, it faded. Amb. Ermêl was gone. The Idle quadrant burned out back to solid stone. The orb meanwhile, continued to shine brightly. Lighting the entire room in a subtle sky blue.

With it now over, David finally rested. He laid on a giant slab of broken rock. His eyes closed while he took deep slow breaths and wondering if there was anyone out there who was watching over him right now. Like an afterlife to an afterlife. The very thought made him smile and elevated his soul and when he reopened his eyes, he found himself floating. A blue glow was circling the rock he was on. He immediately sat up to look around and see he was he was surrounded by floating rubble in the same glow. *What the?* He peered down to see the room below now free of debris. It was as if the island was reconstructing itself. The slab he was on being the last piece and the moment it slotted into place an enormous explosion of sapphire energy shot out across the sky like a supernova. Evaporating all the remaining Déliánts and cleansing the sky from Idle energy. The sapphire light staid lit for a few more seconds before slowly fading away to reveal a beautiful starry sky. The night now silent, with David now on the island's summit, sitting on his glowing white fence.

Chapter 38

Thirty minutes or so had passed and David was still sat over the island on his fence, gazing out over the vast calm ocean. He was smiling wide as if he'd never seen the world looking so beautiful and he was eager to explore it properly as soon as he could, but not yet. He half-expected someone to have turned up by now to speak to him about it all. Rev. Li, Vinicius... but no one seemed to be coming and that was fine because he wanted to savour the moment a little longer.

'So... I guess that's it, then?' he said aloud, as if talking to the moon hovering above. 'That's me done, right? Purpose fulfilled?' He waited patiently as if expecting a reply. 'So... what now?'

'What do you want to happen now?'

An unnerving chill trickled down David's back. His heart quickening as someone came to sit beside him. 'Hi,' he said.

'Hello, son.'

David's eyes widened. 'You remember!'

'I remember.' Stephen put a hand on his shoulder. 'I remember.'

With his eyes tearing up, David went to hug him. His arms open wide, but was left shocked when his dad punched him hard in the shoulder.

'Ow! What was that for?' David scowled, rubbing it better.

'That's for what you did for me... you stupid boy.'

'Oh, Come on, I...'

His dad then embraced him. One of the warmest hugs he'd ever experienced as he wrapped his holy arms completely around him. 'And this is for being you.'

'For being me?' David hugged back.

'I may have missed a few years, David, and for that, I am sorry. But, now you know why.'

'It still doesn't feel real,' David croaked, tearing up again. 'As you can tell its been quite emotional,' he tried to joke, making his dad chuckle.

'Yes, I'm sure it has been, but look what you've accomplished. You always wondered what was in store for you and now you know.'

'This wasn't exactly what I had in mind, though.'

'No, perhaps not.'

'So, now what?' David leaned away to wipe his face. 'Are we going to be G.As together? Is it still a thing? What will happen to Earth?'

'Calm down.' His dad smiled. 'Plans are already in place. As I came here, a lot of other G.As have been returning to the G.A.F to try and pick up where they left off. You're the talk of the sky at the moment.' His dad jabbed him playfully in the chest. 'Rev. Li has called a meeting with the other realm guardians and I think I heard her say they were going to wake someone up... or something like that. Anyway, it'll be alright. I'll be alright.'

'We...' David corrected him. 'We will be alright.'

'Hmm.'

There was a slight pause as David looked at his dad's mischievous face. 'What?'

'Fancy a walk?'

'Sure?' David frowned.

He watched as his dad got up to step over the fence and with their energies linked, he followed him over. Now they were standing over a small reservoir and David immediately fell silent as he remembered what had happened the last time he was here. He could still feel a hint of energy lingering around the water.

'I heard about what happened,' his dad spoke. 'After the fire. I can't imagine how you felt.' David remained silent as he stared at the ripples. 'Grace protected you, just as Linus protected me. They'd be so proud of you David, as am I. Not for what you've done, but for what you've overcome.' David looked into his dad's serious proud eyes. 'I remember our chats. I know how messed up you can get,' he teased, making David smile. 'There's no doubt you've found it hard, but you came through. Just like I knew you would when Linus first told me of your fate.'

'Thanks to her, too, protecting me is one thing, but you could say she saved me. Twice.'

'You could, yes. And I am sure you will see her again one day.'

'Man I've missed you,' David cried again. 'Ugh, I hate this,' he said, wiping his eyes.

'At least you've learned to show your emotions now.'

'There's so much I need to speak to you about! There's so much I need...'

His dad held up a hand. 'Ssh, calm down and follow me.'

They stepped back over another fence. The pair of them appearing outside their house and David stared at in shock. 'It's fixed?' He pointed.

'Yes.'

'I don't understand...'

'When Linus first contacted me about what was going to happen. I didn't hesitate to protect my family.' His dad raised his eyebrows. 'An aura was cast over this house to protect it and if anything were to happen, the energy would make it so it never did.'

'So...' David ran over to the living room window to see his mum curled up on the sofa with Buddy on the floor beside her. A wave of relief flowing off him. 'Hi Mum,' he whispered.

'Grace may have been there for you when you were in the G.A.F. But you're mum has always been there for you. Even when you thought you were lost, she knew where

you were. Even now, she waits. And our little chats...
where do you think I got my wisdom from?'

David watched over his mum as he remembered how
hard she had tried to talk to him all those days ago.

'I'm not the smartest man, David. I'm not the most
understanding man, but your mum... she's more of a
guardian angel than I'll ever be. Than anyone will ever be.'

'We'll be sure to look over her,' David whispered.

'I will, yes.'

'Huh? That's twice you've done that. What's going on?'
As he turned round his dad pulled something out of his
pocket. 'Grace's necklace?'

'Hmm? Oh, yes right. Well, turns out Grace was just
keeping it safe for me. As did Linus before her. She
managed to sneak it into my pocket before Diego and
Cedric took me from Eden.'

'What is it?'

'If I remember correctly, it's called an Arvon.'

'An Arvon?'

'Yes, David.' His dad tutted.

'Sorry.' David smiled a little as it felt like old times.

'You see, the thing about a mortal being clipped is that
it's not just your energy you lose, but your mortality, too.
That's what Linus said anyway and me knowing you, I
knew you'd inevitably do something loyal and reckless,
with good intentions I know, but stupid nonetheless, so
this was a back up.'

'Wait...' David tried piecing together what he was
saying.

'When the Idler, Cedric, clipped me. Killed me.
Instead of getting the essence of the mortal guardian. He
got my essence, my mortality, for I was still alive. Alive
alive.' His dad rolled his eyes playfully. 'Linus knew this
would happen and explained to me beforehand that in the
aftermath of my death, he would be able to retrieve the
blade and extract my mortality from it into this Arvon.

And its been kept safe all these years for this very moment. So I can give it to you.'

David slowly plucked it out of his dad's hand. 'This means?'

'You are not dead, David. You never have been and now, you can go back.' There was a slight pause before his dad added, 'and don't you dare give it back to me!'

The two of them laughed as David held the Arvon close to his chest. 'This is perfect. So I'm still a M.G. I can still see you and be on Earth!'

'Umm, no, not quite.'

'What?'

'I'm afraid your mortality is gone David. Diego took it when he clipped you and that blade is now long gone. My mortality can send you back, but it isn't compatible with your current abilities shall we say. I wasn't a Mortal Guardian, I was just mortal and that's all I can offer.'

'Then, maybe...'

'Don't say it.' His dad scowled. 'You don't belong here. You've got so much to give. So much to live for and you need to do it at ground level.'

'But I...'

'No buts, David! You need to do this for me.'

Deep down, he knew his dad was right. Of course he was right, but how was he supposed to let him go again? How was he supposed to just give all this up? How was he supposed to move on from this? As if sensing the conflict in his head, his dad put a tight grip on his shoulder. 'David, you listen close,' he said sternly. 'You don't need to see me to know I'm still here and you don't need to be an angel to be helpful. You just need belief and a good heart.' His dad poked him in the chest. 'The world is tough. The world is cruel and it is unfair. But that doesn't mean it isn't beautiful. No matter how dark things seem. Always look for the light because it is there... and it can come from you and if our chats have taught me anything over

273

the years, I know you can thrive... and help others to thrive. To make the world a better place. And you don't need to be an M.G for that.'

David smiled. 'Okay, Dad.'

'Now let's stop all this soppy stuff.' His dad wiped his eyes laughing. 'You'd better get going.'

'I don't have to go yet do I? There's so much I want to talk to you about. I still need...'

'David. I'll still be here when you go back.' His dad smiled, putting a warm hand on his cheek. 'Besides, I think Mum would appreciate hearing it as well. I think you owe her that. I'll listen in from time to time. I don't know what rules are going to be imposed yet.'

'Okay,' David wept. 'Okay. At least I know I'll see you again.'

'I'm not going anywhere, but you need to. Now go.'

'Okay.' David cleared his throat. 'Okay, how does this work?'

'I have no idea,' his dad chuckled. 'It didn't come with instructions. Here let's have a look.' His dad took it back off him to investigate and David let him try to work it out just like any other complicated or broken thing they used to come across. 'I think you need to break it.'

'Really?'

'Yeah... I can't see... oh wait, here you go.' David took the Arvon back. 'It twists at the top. Open it and take a deep inhale.'

'Okay.' David smiled, going in for one last hug. His eyes crunching closed as he was tired of crying. 'Love you, Dad.'

'Love you, too, Son.'

David slowly stepped away. Torn in two minds whether to open it or not, but he knew he had to and not only that, he did want to. He had been away from his mum far too long.

He hooked the Arvon over his neck and in one swift movement twisted the pendant open and inhaled the cool mist which drifted out of it. A new warmth entered him like a cosy fire igniting on his heart and spread across his whole body and mind. The fence beneath him dwindled. His aura faded. His feet landing on the grass. He patted down his suit as he felt whole again and stamped his feet on the solid ground. 'I'm back! I'm home!' He smiled, looking up to his dad, but he wasn't there or rather, he just couldn't see him. 'See ya, Dad.'

Loud barking came from the front door and David ran towards it and opened it straight away. Buddy was instantly there to greet him with a wagging tail and jumped up his legs, wanting to give him a giant welcome back kiss. 'Hiya Bud! Man I missed you!'

He followed Buddy into the front room where he saw his mum sitting up on the sofa half asleep and she stared at him as if she thought he was an illusion. 'David?'

'Hi Mum.'

David approached her and fell to his knees before wrapping his arms around her body tightly. 'I'm so sorry.'

'Ssh, its okay.' His mum hugged him back. 'Everything is okay. I'm just glad you're home safe. Are you okay?'

'Yeah, I'm okay. Better now.'

'Good. Good... David...'

'Yeah?'

'What the Hell are you wearing?'

David started laughing and let go. 'I hope you're not too tired because there's something we need to talk about.'

A small smile appeared on his mum's face, lighting up her cheeks in a faint glow. 'I'm awake. I'm here.'

David took a seat beside her on the sofa. Buddy sitting between them while wanting a fuss. 'You're not going to believe half of it.'

'I don't believe half of what you tell me anyway.' His mum joked.

'True.' David raised his eyebrows. 'True, well, I'll start from the beginning...'

276

Epilogue

The bell jangled above the door as David entered the café. The sweet smell of pastries filling his nostrils the moment he entered the brightly light room. He walked up to the counter and looked out the large windows at the sunny blue sky, enriching the world in colour.

'Hi David!' Laura spoke happily. 'Where have you been?'

'Hello you.' David smiled. 'I just needed a little break from everything, you know. Did a little soul searching.'

'Oh, is everything alright? Are you alright?'

'I'm... never better.'

'Oh, I wasn't expecting that.' Laura smiled. 'Nice for you to finally be honest.' She raised her eyebrows.

'Yeah, figured it was about time.' David smirked apologetically.

'Well, what can I get you? The usual?'

'Please, and an extra tea. I'm here with my mum.'

'Ah, that's sweet, what are you two up to?' Laura asked as she began making the drinks.

'Just taking Bud for a walk. Was time they got out the house properly.'

'Awh, that's nice. I'm glad she's doing okay.'

'Thank you... Oh, and I hear a congratulations is in order.'

'Congratulations? What for?' Laura frowned.

'I saw your name on a poster at the bus stop... told you you'd get there. I've already got my ticket.'

'You haven't?' Laura blushed, pushing the drinks across to him.

'Of course I have.' David winked. 'Wouldn't want to miss your first role.' He tapped his card on the card reader and picked up the drinks. 'I'll see you Saturday, Laura.' He raised his eyebrows playfully.

'See you, then.' Laura bit her thumb. 'I'll look forward to it!'

'Me too.' David smiled. *Me too.* He left the café and handed his mum her tea. 'Here you go.'

'Thank you. She seems nice.' His mum winked peeking back into the café and nudging him. 'Is that the girl in the show you were talking about?'

David blushed. 'Yes.'

'Ooo, get you. Finally getting back out there.'

'Yes. Alright, thanks.'

The pair of them laughed as they made their way down the street with Buddy pulling them along.

Meanwhile, back in the restored D.E.I.T.Y room. Two figures stood in the centre observing the white orb floating in front of them.

'He is doing better,' a young girl spoke, wearing diamond-coloured dungarees over a light blue t-shirt. 'I would say it was a success.'

'Yes.'

'What is it, Vinicius?'

'It was too close.'

'But it worked. The mortal guardian did it. The G.A.F has been reduced in size and the Realm Guardians are already revamping their realms and enforcing the new laws.'

'Yes, that's all well and good Tylah, but Amb. Ermêl made it. She escaped and brought Idle with her... the lives of every mortal was put at risk.'

'But he did it.'

'He may have done, but not every one with a mind like his makes it through. You know that and besides, intervention was still needed. If it wasn't for Linus's dedication and Grace this would have failed. Even I had to influence him in my own way. No... we can't keep relying on these kinds of mortals to appear and keep the balance.'

'Well, what do you suggest?'

'We need to put a stop to our sister's games before things get totally out of hand. The sustainability won't work in our absence. The three of us need to get together. Put our worlds to right in order to put this world to right.'

'And what if she doesn't comply? You know she won't like that.'

'Then, at least we've still got him.'

David walked down the street with his mum at his side and Buddy, who was sniffing every patch of grass available. He had completely zoned out. Embracing the bright new world and soaked in the sun's glorious rays. He gazed up at the diamond blue sky, believing he could see something twinkling and a little smile broke out across his face.

'David... David... Hello? Anyone there?' His mum waved a hand in his face.

'Huh? Yes, sorry, I'm here. I'm still here.'